For my grandparents, Susan and Paul Zampa, and
Shirley and William Rowlands, with all my love.
And for Margie.

—J. G.

Published by
PEACHTREE PUBLISHING COMPANY INC.
1700 Chattahoochee Avenue
Atlanta, Georgia 30318-2112
www.peachtree-online.com

Text © 2020 by Jenna Guillaume
Cover image © 2021 by Steffi Walthall

First published in Australia in 2020 by Pan Macmillan Pty Ltd 1 Market Street,
Sydney, New South Wales, Australia, 2000
First United States version published in 2021 by Peachtree Publishing Company Inc.

Design and composition by Lily Steele
Cover design by Adela Pons

Printed in the United States of America in January 2021 by Lake Book Manufacturing
in Melrose Park, Illinois
10 9 8 7 6 5 4 3 2 1
First Edition
ISBN: 978-1-68263-295-6

Cataloging-in-Publication Data is available from the Library of Congress.

Content Advisory:
Please be aware that this narrative contains depictions of verbal abuse, bullying, and alcohol
use.

JENNA GUILLAUME

YOU WERE MADE FOR ME

PEACHTREE

ATLANTA

I

The day I created a boy started out like any other.

I woke up at about 6:30 AM and dragged myself out of bed. I wrote a few paragraphs for the short story I'd been working on, then I had a shower, brushed my teeth and—

This is what you're starting with? Skip to the important part!

Libby, don't interrupt. And this *is* the important part! I mean, we don't know exactly what happened that day to cause—

It definitely wasn't you brushing your teeth.

You're the one who insisted I was the best one to record what happened. Why are you questioning my methods?

I didn't think you'd start by talking about brushing your teeth. Also, the day "I" created a boy? Really, Katie? Is that what happened?

Okay, the day WE created a boy. We being Libby and me. Better?

Yes. As long as you don't talk about brushing your teeth

again. Are we going to have to go over every bowel movement you've had in the last few months, too?

LIBBY!

...Do you not think I can do this?

Don't even. Of course you're the best person for the job. But every good writer needs a good editor, right?

Well. I don't know about "good..."

I swear—

But I do know I've got a story to tell. And I can only tell it my way.

My story—*our* story—is wild...and it's completely unbelievable.

It's also absolutely 100 percent true.

Well, no truth is absolute. Everything is subjective.

Okay. It's *my* absolute truth.

All I can do is lay it out there. No matter how hard or embarrassing it might be. *Especially* when it's embarrassing or hard, because then you'll know I really am telling the truth. What you make of it from there, of course, is entirely up to you.

Now, where was I...

Right.

The day *we* created a boy. It started out like any other...

"Declan Bell Jones is the perfect guy," I said with a sigh.

(I've skipped to the interesting part, as Libby requested. Well, not the *really* interesting part—that comes a little later—but the lead-up is important, trust me.)

It was a Friday, after school, and Libby and I were dawdling by the soccer field on our way home so that I could sneak glances at Declan Bell Jones as he trained. He was in my geography class, and I'd been staring at the back of his head all year. I'd memorized every inch. The ashy blond hair. The tan skin of his neck. The little mole just below his hair line, which his collar caressed every time he moved (which was often; he was a fidgeter).

I thought a lot about what it might be like if I were the one caressing that mole.

Which might explain my marks in geography.

"I swear, if I had a dollar for every time you said that, I could afford my own car," Libby said, interrupting my thoughts about Declan Bell Jones and his mole.

"You can't even drive," I replied.

"Minor detail." She took a bite of the Fruit Roll-Up she'd wrapped and twisted around her index finger so that it resembled a weird red monster's claw. Still chewing, she said, "Anyway, what did Miss Lui say?"

I'd hung back after sixth period to talk to my art teacher about signing up to paint a mural on one of the walls around the main quad. The school had designated six areas for students to decorate. They were trying to move away from the concrete prison block look, I think.

"They just want free labor," Libby had muttered when the news was announced at assembly that morning. But she'd nagged me nonstop for the rest of the day until I agreed to speak to Miss Lui. That's the thing about Libby. She grumbles that I spend too much time daydreaming, but she's also my biggest supporter—she believes in me more than I believe in myself most of the time. I've known her for longer than I can remember (literally—we met in preschool). We have the kind of friendship where you can tell the other person anything—*anything*—and we won't take offense or judge each other.

I mean, we even fart around each other.

That's how you know it's true friendship.

"She said she thinks I'd be great," I told Libby. "'Marvelous' was the word she used, actually." I smiled to myself. Hearing my favorite teacher say that about me had unraveled the nervousness I felt about putting my art (and myself) out there.

"Maaaaaaaaaarvelous," Libby intoned, in a pretty good imitation of Miss Lui. "See, I told you."

"I still have no idea what I'd paint though," I said. "I mean, it's so much pressure! The whole school is going to see it. And it could be there for, like, generations to come.

What if it's terrible? What if I suck? What if—"

"What if it's brilliant? What if it's maaaaaarvelous? What if—"

Libby stopped abruptly, and I turned my head to see what had suddenly caused that look of horror to come over her face. We were nearing the goal area of the soccer field, and standing there was none other the devil herself, flanked by two of her demon minions.

Mikayla Fitzsimmons, Olivia Kent, and Emily McAlister. The unholy trinity.

They were giggling as they watched the boys on the field and hadn't spotted us. Yet.

"Uh, let's go back the other way and cut through the parking lot," Libby muttered.

Here's what you need to know about Mikayla Fitzsimmons: she's one of the hottest girls in our year. Tall, blonde, about 80 percent legs. Curly hair that somehow always manages to look cute and controlled, unlike my unruly mass.

Her personality, on the other hand...

She's a total feral.

Libby and I, and the rest of our friends, we're not exactly in the "cool" group at school. Although we're not at the bottom of the food chain, either (that sad distinction belongs to Tiff Richardson, who never seems to shower). But Mikayla treats basically anyone who isn't her minion—or a cute guy—like month-old garbage (the minions only get treated like day-old garbage, lucky for them).

Mum used to tell me Mikayla's insults were a sign she was jealous, but what was there to be jealous about? She never let me forget just how ugly and worthless she found me, calling me all sorts of names over the years. Pancake, thanks to my flat chest. Four-eyes, thanks to my glasses. Pinocchio, thanks to my nose. Calamari, thanks to my surname (it's Camilleri). Cousin Itt. Crater Face. Freckle Fart from Kmart.

With Libby, Mikayla had this whole thing where she pretended she didn't exist. The name-calling worked on me, I guess, because I always froze and didn't talk back, whereas Libby wouldn't hesitate to fire back a cutting remark that Mikayla would pretend she hadn't heard. It didn't seem to bother Libby. Until one day, I guess it got to be too much. Or rather, something happened that pushed Libby over the edge.

It was when we were in Year 8. Mikayla went through this spitting phase. I mean that literally—she would spit constantly. It's like she thought it made her look cool and hard or something. It was disgusting, but no one ever called her out on it.

Until Libby.

We were walking across the quad one day, on the way

to art class. Mikayla and her friends weren't far behind us, whispering and giggling. I heard that all-too-familiar *hocking* sound, and Libby suddenly came to a stop beside me. Her lip curled and her face went bright red. She slowly turned around and glared at Mikayla.

"Did you just spit on me?" she said.

Mikayla smirked and stared at the space above Libby's head. She took a step as though to keep walking, but Libby didn't budge. Mikayla was going to run right into her.

"Come on, Libby, it was probably an accident," I heard our friend Amina whisper, tugging on Libby's elbow to try and get her to move.

Mikayla took another step. And another. It seemed like everyone else was stuck in place.

And then Libby lunged forward.

She and Mikayla became a blur of limbs as they scratched and clawed at each other, screeching and yelling. Words like "disgusting" and "get off me" were soon drowned out by someone screaming "FIIIIGHT" and the noise of a stampede as the crowds that had been heading to their afternoon classes converged where we were.

I'm not sure how long it took before Mr. Green, a geography teacher, managed to elbow his way through the crowd and pull Libby and Mikayla apart. It felt like forever, but it couldn't have been more than a minute or two.

He gave them both afternoon detention for a week.

The first time in my life I ever got detention. My parents were furious.

It was worth it.

It was impressive. And it somehow got Mikayla off our backs.

Because I complained that her behaviour was part of a pattern of systemic harassment, and she got put on probation for a month. All her teachers had to fill out a sheet about her behavior every single period.

She still gave us nuclear-level death stares whenever we crossed into her line of sight, and whispered behind our backs with Emily and Olivia. But mostly they just steered clear of us.

And we *really* steered clear of them.

Which meant we were a little surprised when we saw them at the soccer field. Mikayla and Emily live a few suburbs away, and they usually catch the bus home straight after school. Olivia lives near me and Libby—we actually went to primary school with her and used to play together sometimes—but if we ever see her out of school, we all do the mature thing and look the other way. She's usually alone, so it works just fine.

That day she wasn't alone though, and I had a feeling the mutual invisibility thing wouldn't be quite as effective. Not with Mikayla the fire-breathing monster there—and with no teachers around to make her act like a human.

Without another word to each other, Libby and I frantically started to back up, trying not to draw attention to ourselves. Our eyes were on Mikayla, not the field.

Which is why I didn't see what was coming or even register the call of "Heads up!" until it was way too late.

A blur of black and white came *whooshing* at my face. For a split second I thought it was a magpie, and I screamed.

Then there was nothing but darkness and voices that sounded really far away.

My eyelids felt heavy. Slowly, I opened them.

I blinked.

Blinked again.

And thought I had died and gone to heaven.

Because looming over me, hazy but right there, was the spectacularly handsome face of Declan Bell Jones. I watched in wonder as his features rearranged themselves from concerned to relieved.

I crashed down to earth two seconds later when Libby appeared above me, shoving Declan out of the way and throwing herself on her knees next to me.

"You're alive!" she declared theatrically, cupping my face in her hands. She still had that Roll-Up wrapped around her index finger, and it was sticky against my skin.

"I think so," I said, sitting up with her help. It was

only then I took in the crowd gathered around me. Not just Declan, but all of his teammates and their coach. Plus Mikayla Fitzsimmons and her friends. Ugh.

I was contemplating the likelihood of a sinkhole opening up and swallowing me on the spot when something incredible happened.

Declan reached down to help me up.

Let me repeat that.

Declan. Reached down. To help me up.

His hands. Were gripping my arms.

His hands. Were moving to my shoulders.

His eyes. Were peering into my face.

All thoughts of Mikayla—of anyone or anything, really—instantly dissolved. I nearly fell right back on the ground.

"You alright?" Declan was saying.

I grinned and said the first thing that popped into my head. "Magpie?"

Magpie?!

"Hell, she might be concussed," I heard a deep voice say. Declan moved away from me, and his coach stepped closer. He bent forward and spoke loudly. "It wasn't a magpie, love, it was a soccer ball. Smacked you right on the head. Here, how many fingers am I holding up?"

"Huh?" I was still feeling a bit dazed, but I wasn't sure if it was from the fall or Declan's proximity.

"How. Many. Fingers. Am. I. Holding. Up?" the coach

repeated, even louder this time.

"Ummm."

"You don't need to yell, pretty sure she can still hear," Libby said. "Can't see too well without her glasses, though." She plucked them from where they'd fallen on the ground and handed them to me. I held them up to my face. The lenses were miraculously intact, but one of the arms was twisted at an angle that definitely wasn't right. I groaned. My mum was gonna kill me. I'd only had these frames for two days.

The coach dropped the hand he'd been holding up and straightened with an exasperated sigh. He turned to Declan, who was still hovering close, even though most of his teammates had started trickling back onto the field.

"We better take her to the hospital," the coach said.

"No! She's fine," Libby said. She knew how much I hate hospitals. "You're fine, aren't you, Katie?"

"Kate."

"What?"

"I told you to call me Kate," I whispered.

Through gritted teeth, Libby said, "Is this really the time, *Kate*?" Her gaze flicked toward the others. I noticed that Mikayla had moved to stand next to Declan, her hand gripping his upper arm.

"I'm fine. Just fine," I blurted out, although I was feeling anything but.

"I really have to insist on taking you to—"

"You know what, her doctor is just down the road there, I'll take her right now. No need to worry, sir," Libby was saying. She tugged on my arm.

"I think I should come with you," the coach said.

"Wait there, I'll grab my wallet. I left it in my glove box." He started jogging toward the parking lot.

There was an excruciating moment as the rest of us just stood there in silence.

Declan was the first to break it. "I'm really sorry," he said to me. "About your glasses. And your head." He laughed nervously. "Does it hurt?"

Before I could answer, Mikayla cut in. "It's not your fault, babe. They shouldn't have got in the way."

"Okay, we're done here," Libby said. "Come on, Katie."

I let her pull me away. As we rushed toward the alley-way that led to my street, I heard the coach yelling after us. It only made us giggle and speed up. I glanced over my shoulder as we rounded the corner away from the field. Without my glasses, I could just make out the blurred shape of Declan still standing there, with the smudge that was Mikayla apparently glued to his side.

"Are they going out?"

Libby snorted. "Looks like it. So much for the perfect guy."

"What do you mean?"

"I mean, how great can he be if he's interested in

Mikayla 'The Devil Incarnate' Fitzsimmons?"

I let out a huff. I still thought he was pretty perfect.

Except, of course, for the fact that he wasn't interested in me.

Not that I blamed him.

(See, I told you I'd tell you the whole truth. No matter how humiliating it is.)

It does get pretty humiliating.

II

"Are you sure you don't want to go to the doctor?" Libby was sitting on the kitchen bench at my place, swinging her legs back and forth and using a spoon to scrape any residual cookie dough from a mixing bowl so she could shovel it into her mouth.

I closed the oven and set a timer for when the cookies would be ready. "I'm fine," I said, straightening my glasses for the fiftieth time. I'd busted out the masking tape to try and repair them. They were just barely functioning and looked ridiculous, but it was all I could do for now. "I don't have a concussion. I'm not nauseous or dizzy or headache-y." We'd looked up the symptoms. Just to be safe.

"Nauseated."

"Huh?"

"You're 'not *nauseated*.' Not, 'not nauseous.' You should know that, you're the writer."

I rolled my eyes. "I'm not nauseated *or* nauseous. You might be, though, if you keep eating that raw cookie dough."

Libby shrugged and leaped down from the counter. "It's only a little bit, it won't hurt me."

"And I'm not a writer," I added.

"Oh really? So those notebooks in your room are filled with what? Math equations? And all those files on your Google Drive?" Libby bent over and let Max, my Old English Sheepdog, lick her fingers, murmuring to him about what a good boy he was.

"Libby! Chocolate is bad for dogs." I chucked a tea towel at her head.

"It's only a little bit, it won't hurt him," she said with a laugh.

I started filling the sink up to wash the dishes. "A few short stories and half-finished fanfics don't make me a writer."

"Just like all those sketches and sculptures don't make you an artist?"

"Exactly," I said. "And baking some cookies doesn't make me a pastry chef."

"Hmmm." Libby picked up the tea towel I'd thrown at her and began wiping the bowl I'd just put on the drying rack. "But it *does* make you a baker. The same way writing makes you a writer. And creating art makes you an artist."

I shook my head. "Writers have their writing published. Artists...artists have their work exhibited, like in museums and galleries and—"

"—and school quadrangles?"

I "hmphed" but didn't say anything.

"Okay, so you're not a writer or an artist. What are you then? How do you describe the great Katie—sorry *Kate*—Camilleri?" Libby asked.

I thought for a moment. How *would* I describe myself? Not "great," that's for sure.

"I'm a student," I finally said. "A work in progress." I held up a handful of soapsuds and blew some Libby's way.

"I don't know why you don't just own this stuff." Libby reached into the sink to scoop up some bubbles herself, leaning over to blow them in my face. "I mean, I'm a scientist. Just because no one is paying me to be one, it doesn't make me any less of one."

"Libby, no offense, but I don't think cutting open a dead rat in Mr. Hay's class actually makes you a scientist." I shuddered at the memory of that particularly horrific lesson. "You have to, you know, *do science*."

"Pfft, come on. I'm just demonstrating the confidence of a mediocre white man over here. Do you think Declan Bell Jones spends his time angsting over whether he's an athlete or whatever? No, he just kicks some balls around and calls himself a champion."

"Um, I think you'll find that Declan Bell Jones is anything but mediocre, thank-you-very-much."

"Mmmmm, I don't know about that. As a scientist, I

can only go off my own empirical observations, and they have led me to conclude that he is, in fact, *aggressively* mediocre."

I made a cry of mock outrage, and this time splashed not just soapsuds but also water in her direction. Libby shrieked and tried to get at the sink to splash me back. Max barked at all the excitement as though he wanted to join in.

We had to mop the floor before we were done.

When we'd finished cleaning, Libby and I sat in front of the oven, waiting for the cookies to reach their final, perfect, crispy-on-the-outside, gooey-on-the-inside form. Max curled up next to me and rested his head in my lap. It had begun to storm, and he always got extra whiny and clingy whenever he heard thunder.

"So. What do you want to do now?" I asked. The Wi-Fi had stopped working, probably because of the storm, although thankfully we still had power. Neither of us had any data on our phones.

"Watch the cookies," Libby said.

"And then what?"

"*Eat* the cookies."

"And then what?"

"And then it will probably be time for pizza." Libby grinned. My parents weren't home—Dad was on night shift, and Mum had gone out with a friend for dinner (and probably drinks afterward). She'd left me money to order pizza and given me strict instructions not to open the door for anyone except the delivery person, and to "try not to burn the house down." Even though I'm sixteen, my parents had only decided (embarrassingly) recently that it was no longer necessary for my older brother Luke to babysit—sorry, I mean "keep me company"—if they weren't home at night. Luke had taken full advantage of that fact this evening and gone on a date with his girlfriend, Mara. I also wanted to take full advantage of my newfound independence, which is why I'd invited Libby over. But the night wasn't quite shaping up how I'd hoped.

"This is boring," I said after a few more minutes of staring at the cookies.

"Hmmm. We could play silly or serious?" Libby said.

"Aren't we a little old for that game?" We'd made it up when we were younger. It was kind of like truth or dare, except without the dare bit—because we were chickens like that. You had to pick what kind of truth you were willing to admit. We usually went for silly, you know, because of the whole chicken thing.

"Come onnn." Libby nudged me.

I sighed. "Fine. Silly."

"When was the last time you picked your nose?"

I screwed up said nose. "Uh...this morning."

Libby cackled. "You're disgusting."

"You asked. Your turn."

"Silly."

I was trying to think of a decent question that didn't involve bodily fluids when I heard the back door slide open. A moment later the shaggy, wet head of my next-door neighbor, Theo, loomed above us as he leaned over the kitchen island.

"What are we watching?" He glanced at the oven. "Ah. The cookie show. Love this one."

He moved around the counter and slid down next to me. Max immediately tried to cram his whole huge body into Theo's lap, covering his face in sloppy kisses. That dog is a total traitor whenever Theo's around.

"You're dripping," I said. Theo couldn't have been in the rain for long—it was only twenty-two steps (we'd counted) from the door of his granny flat, through the broken panel in the fence, and to my back door—but somehow he got drenched.

"It's pissing down." He ran a hand through his dark hair, slicking it back from his face, and reached his hands behind his head to remove his damp hoodie. His T-shirt rode up with it, exposing his belly. I quickly looked away, knowing he was self-conscious about it since he'd put on weight last year. "Internet down for you guys too?"

"Yep," I sighed. "We were just playing Silly or Serious."

He snorted. "Thought you said you were too old for that game."

I shot Libby a look.

"Alright," Theo said. "Silly."

"You can't just butt into our game," Libby said, even though Theo had been doing exactly that for most of our lives. He was a year older than us, and at school he always hung around people in his year, but after hours were another story. He'd practically lived at my house when we were younger. Especially after his mum died. Before his dad let him move into their granny flat out back, Theo was over here all the time. Now that he had his own space, he only came around, like, half the time.

"When was the last time you slept with Mr. Fluffybutt?" I asked.

Theo grinned. "Last night."

"You're kidding."

"Gotta have something to cuddle." He nuzzled into Max as he spoke.

"Mr. Fluffybutt?" Libby asked.

"My stuffed alpaca," Theo explained. He'd had the toy since he was a baby. "Okay, KC. Silly or serious?"

"Silly," I said.

Theo glanced up, thinking. "The thing you're most embarrassed about. Go."

"The thing I'm most embarrassed about..." I paused, looking down. "Isn't that kind of serious?"

"Huh?"

"Well, you probably think it's silly. But I've never been kissed. That's the most embarrassing thing about me."

I felt Libby bristle beside me. "Please. What's so embarrassing about that?"

"Hello, I'm sixteen years old!"

"And?"

"And don't you think that's a little late?"

She rolled her eyes. "There's literally that saying 'sweet sixteen and never been kissed.'"

"Yeah, that was invented in like 1806."

"So kiss someone already," Theo cut in.

"Oh yeah, 'cause it's that easy," I said.

"Why not?"

"You kind of need someone else to be willing to kiss you."

"Yeah?" He raised his eyebrows as if to say, *What's your point?*

Boy, he could be dense sometimes. "So, I'm not exactly flooded with opportunities."

"It's really not embarrassing, Katie," Libby said again.

"Says you. You've been with Michael since you were practically in diapers."

Libby had started going out with her boyfriend in Year 6. Even though he went to the selective high school in town, while we went to the affectionately nicknamed Pleb High (short for plebeian), they'd managed to stay together, although they only saw each other a couple of times a month. She didn't really talk about him much because she didn't want to be one of "those" girls—you know, the kind whose entire personalities and lives gets overtaken by their boyfriends. Sometimes I wondered if she'd gone too far in the other direction. "Face it, I'm a freak," I added.

Her eyes flashed and she opened her mouth to say something, but Theo cut in first. "What about Sam Park? I told you he had a crush on you last year."

I scowled. "Sam Park eats his own earwax."

Theo laughed. "Mmmmm, earwax-flavored kisses."

"It can't just be anyone," I said. "I mean, after all this time, it has to be special, right? Your first kiss is something you remember for the rest of your life."

Theo snorted. "My first kiss was with Amber Jones under the skate ramp at the youth club. Cobwebs and rust. Alex timed it. Twenty-six seconds. Very special."

"Just because you'll kiss anyone, anywhere doesn't mean I have to. My first kiss...it's gotta be perfect. The perfect setting. The perfect guy..." The image of that mole on Declan Bell Jones's neck flashed before my eyes.

"You'll be waiting awhile then," Theo said. "Nobody's perfect, KC." He reached for the oven door. "Are these cookies ready or what?"

"Theo's right, you know," Libby said around a mouthful of pizza. We were sitting on the floor, the pizza box open between us, a home renovation show on in the background. Theo had gone home to practice his saxophone, which he'd picked up when he was nine. These days, if you asked him what inspired him to learn that particular instrument, he'd name-drop some super cool jazz musician, but in truth it was Lisa Simpson.

"Huh?" I said, looking at Max as he pawed at my leg, begging for some food. I'd given him a bowl of his own, but he knew mine was way more exciting. I gave him a piece of crust.

"What he said before," Libby explained. "About nobody being perfect."

"I know that." I shoved Max's face away from my plate. He was getting a little too eager.

"And you know that your first kiss, whenever it is, with whoever it is—it's not going to be perfect either, right?"

"Didn't you think yours was perfect?" I remembered her telling me Michael had kissed her while they were at putt putt in Year 7. She wouldn't give me any details. "It's personal," she'd said. I'd felt a little hurt, but at the same time it was kind of romantic.

Libby ignored my question. "Seriously, Katie. The perfect guy doesn't exist."

"I'll tell Michael you said that."

"Go ahead. He knows he's not perfect." She stared down at her last slice of pizza, picking it apart.

"Aw, come on. I mean, he's perfect for you, right?" I asked. "That's all I want. Someone who is perfect for me."

She didn't say anything for a moment, then looked up at me with a smirk. "And what would this perfect-for-you guy look like? And don't say Declan Bell Jones."

I grinned. "Alright. I'll show you."

I got up and washed my hands at the kitchen sink before heading to my room.

"What are you up to?" Libby called. She hadn't moved.

I reappeared and went over to the dining table, which we never actually used for dining. I placed what I'd been holding on it, and gestured for Libby to come over.

"Oh my god," she said. "What exactly am I looking at here?"

I laughed. "It's the perfect guy." It was a sculpture—

well, part of one, anyway. I was still working on it. Theo had given me this amazing oil-based clay he'd found at a thrift store; he was always scavenging for the retro clothes he loved, and if he stumbled upon cheap art supplies or cool old books he'd pick them up for me. I was studying human anatomy at the moment and had sculpted a pretty incredible pair of legs, if I did say so myself. They were attached to a muscular torso.

"He's missing a head," Libby said.

"Let's make him one." I sat down and started working a piece of clay in my hands.

"And a penis," Libby added.

"That comes last."

"Not from what I've heard." We both sniggered.

After a moment I said, "Do you think you and Michael will...you know?"

"I don't know what you're talking about," Libby deadpanned. She stood up and went to the kitchen.

"What are you doing?" I asked as she got out a pot and heated it on the stove.

"Science."

I figured she was actually just making herself something else to eat, and left her to it. She rifled around in the cupboards, pulling out ███████, ████████████ ████████, ████████ ████████████, ████████, and ████████ ████████████. Then she ████████ ████████ ████ ████████and ████████████. From the ████████ ████████

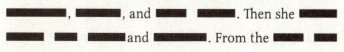

she ▬▬▬ ▬▬ ▬▬▬. She added in ▬▬▬
▬▬ ▬▬ ▬▬. And ▬▬▬ ▬▬▬ ▬▬▬ ▬▬ ▬▬
▬▬▬. ▬▬▬ ▬▬▬ ▬▬▬ ▬▬▬ ▬▬ ▬▬▬
▬▬ ▬▬ ▬▬ ▬▬▬ ▬▬▬ ▬▬.

(Libby just made me cross out all the details of what she was mixing. She says she doesn't want the formula to fall into the wrong hands. Even though I'm not entirely sure it was that which did it.)

WHAT ELSE WAS IT THEN, KATIE?

The clay.

Oh that's right, the magic clay.

If it was the potion—

Not a potion. A formula. I'm a scientist, remember?! Not a witch.

Could have fooled me.

Are you going to tell the story or argue with me?

I've been arguing with Libby. But we've calmed down now and are ready to get on with this. Aren't we, Libby?

I said...

...aren't we, Libby?

Sorry, I thought you wanted me to stop interrupting.

Sigh.

Libby was making her poti—I mean, formula—and

I was busy finishing my sculpture. We talked as we worked, outlining my perfect guy.

"He's tall," I was saying. "Like, over six foot."

"Wouldn't that make it kind of hard to kiss him, short-arse?"

"That's why heels were invented, smart-arse."

"I thought heels were invented to make it harder for women to run away from men."

"And he can bend down," I went on, ignoring her. "Or pick me up." I waggled my eyebrows.

"Alright. He's tall. What else?"

"He looks like..." I paused, thinking hard as I sculpted and trying to envision the final product. "He looks like a long-lost Hemsworth brother."

Libby snorted.

"He has floppy hair that always sits just right. And eyes like the sky on a clear summer's day." I stuck out my tongue in concentration and was silent for a few minutes. Libby hummed the tune of a classical song I was vaguely familiar with.

As I molded a mouth of clay, I said, "His lips are pink and soft. Perfect for kissing."

"And they taste like cookie dough, right?" Libby said.

"Right. And he smells like springtime. And the ocean."

"As long as he doesn't smell like the lake. Pee-yew."

(The lake near our school gets pretty stinky sometimes.)

"He has a six-pack," I went on. I'd already sculpted that. "And that hot V thing boys get at their hips." I made a mental note to work on *that* more when I was done with the head.

"And a peachy butt, I suppose," Libby said. "Huge biceps too."

"Yeah, but not too huge. He's built, but, like, lean."

"Tell me, does this lean hunk of Hemsworthy muscle have a personality?" Libby added something to the pot and—well, I better not say any more about that.

"Only the best," I said. "He's sweet."

"Of course."

"And kind."

"Same thing."

"It's not! He's kind even when he doesn't have to be. He goes out of his way to help people. And animals. He loves animals." I looked at Max, who was laying on the bed we'd bought when he was a puppy. It was too small for him now, but he still liked to sprawl across it. "He especially loves dogs. Like, with his whole soul."

"What else does he like?"

"Me, obviously," I said. "He's absolutely devoted to me. And he's romantic."

"Acts like a guy in a rom-com, I bet."

"Mmmhmmm."

Libby turned the stove off and started rifling through the kitchen drawers. "And this wonder boy who smells like the ocean and has buns of steel is sixteen, right?"

"No. He's older than me."

"What, like a teacher?" Libby mimed gagging.

"Noooo. Not *that* old." I scrunched up my nose. "Just a year older. You know, so we're on the same maturity level."

"Uh-huh." Libby walked over to me with a bowl in one hand and an eyedropper in the other.

"What's that for?"

"You made the guy a body, right? Well, I cooked him up a soul."

"Oh! How very science-y," I said.

Then—

Well, I can't tell you exactly what happened next. Libby thinks it's too risky to share it all. Even though I'm not quite sure why I'm writing this if I can't even say—

It's a record of our experience, dear Katie, but it doesn't have to reveal all our secrets.

Right. Well, let the record show that we did some things and said some things and wound up with a hunk of clay shaped like a boy and a bowl of gloop that took me twenty minutes to scrub clean.

When we were done, I said, "What, exactly, was the point of all that?"

Libby shrugged. "Nothing."

"Nothing?"

"Literally nothing. This whole perfect guy thing amounts to nothing. He doesn't exist, and you can't will him into reality, no matter how hard you try." She reached for my sculpture. "Hey, you know what we should do? Bury him."

I slapped her hand away. "It's a bit early to go burying all my hopes and dreams in the backyard just yet, don't you think?"

She laughed. "Yeah. But you're also too young to waste your life waiting around for a long-lost Hemsworth brother. Or Declan Bell Jones, for that matter."

"Oh, sure, I'll just go make out with Sam Park instead."

Libby raised her eyebrows, but whatever she was going to say next was cut off by the sound of a car beeping outside. It was her dad, come to pick her up at 10:00 PM sharp. She only lived two streets away, but her parents wouldn't let her walk it in the dark. Mine wouldn't either, for that matter.

After she'd gone, I finished tidying up and got ready for bed. Mum and Luke were still out, and Dad wouldn't be home from his shift at Target until after midnight. I placed my sculpture on the bedside table and climbed under the covers. Max stretched out on the floor next to me. He usually started out there, and then at some point during the night I typically woke up with his big body curled around my back or crushing my legs. It was annoying, but I also secretly loved it.

Except that night, I...

I...

Alright, I'll say it. That night, I went to bed yearning for someone *else* to wrap their big body around me in bed.

And I...

I...

Look, we all do weird things when we're alone, right?

Um, Katie, it's okay, you really don't have to tell the world about your masturbatory habits.

LIBBY. NO. THAT'S NOT WHAT I MEANT.

Jeeeeeeeeez.

Listen. Here's what I did.

I reached over and picked up that sculpture and... placed it next to me on the bed, okay?

...Okay.

And.

And?

And I might have kissed it goodnight.

Okaaaaaaay.

And, god, I might have shed a little tear, alright?

Aww, baby.

Can we move on now? Because we've finally reached the interesting part.

The REALLY interesting part. Yes. Let's do it.

Right. Here goes nothing.

I felt like I'd only just dozed off when I was awoken by a flash of lightning and a roaring clap of thunder. You know, the kind where it feels as though it's *right* over your head—even inside the room with you. My heart was pounding, but I took comfort from the weight of Max's body behind me. I snuggled into him, and reached my hand back to pat his belly.

My eyes shot open again when my hand found, not Max's soft, thick fur—but the smooth, warm skin of a human being.

That's when I saw Max standing by the window, and I finally registered his low growl.

And that's when I screamed liked I'd never screamed before.

III

I jumped from the bed, instinctively grabbing the closest thing to me off the bedside table to use as a weapon. I didn't pause to wield it, though. I ran from the room, my heart racing. There was something—someone— in there. *In my bed.*

I headed straight for the back door—the closest escape—groping to unlock it before running into the yard. I glanced back over my shoulder, terrified I was being followed, and immediately slammed into something hard and toppled to the ground. I was screaming again, scrambling to get up as my limbs tangled with someone else's.

"KC? KC! It's me. *Katie!*"

I stopped screaming long enough to register Theo lying beneath me on the muddy lawn, his eyes wide open, his face panicked. Rain pelted down around us.

I scrambled off him, breathing heavily. He sat up and got to his feet, and I realized he was only in his boxers and an old band T-shirt that was now plastered to his skin. I looked away, crossing my arms over my chest, conscious that my own scraggly Minnie Mouse nightie was sticking to me. A ridiculous thing to worry about in that moment, I know, but I couldn't help it. Theo seemed oblivious to what we were both wearing, though. He was reaching down to pick up a plastic bat he must have dropped when I ran into him. He straightened and stepped close to me, his hand resting on my shoulder.

"I heard you screaming. Are you okay? What happened?"

I tried to get it out between shaking breaths. "Someone. Was in. My room."

"What?! Fuck. Are you okay?"

"I'm alright," I said. "Just freaked out."

"Your parents still out? What about Luke?"

"No one's home."

His hand dropped from my shoulder, and he looked toward the house. "They still in there?"

"Huh?"

"Is there still someone in your room?"

"I don't know. I just ran."

His eyes scanned the yard. "They didn't follow you out here. They might have gone out the front—"

"Theo," I tried to cut in. I'd just come to a horrible realization.

"—Or through your window? Is that how they got in? We should—"

"Theo!"

"—probably call the cops."

"Max," I said, ignoring Theo's suggestion. "Max is still in there." And he was being very quiet.

"Max?" Theo swore and looked down at the plastic bat in his hand. He squared his shoulders. "Okay. You stay here. I'll go get him."

"No way! I'm coming with you," I said. I held up the weapon I'd grabbed in my mad dash out of my room. It was...a paintbrush. Great.

"What are you going to do, paint them to death?" Theo said.

I held up the pointy wooden end of the brush and gestured to his plastic bat. "It'll probably do more damage than that piece of junk."

Theo hesitated for a moment, then gave me a slight nod. He turned back to the house, plastic bat in one hand, the other held out in front of me in a protective gesture. I didn't try to argue with him about it. It was comforting, to be honest. I put my hand on his shoulder, and slowly we moved forward together.

We entered via the back door, both of us dripping all over the tiled floor. I started shivering, although I couldn't tell if it was from the cold or because I was absolutely losing it.

We moved through the kitchen and dining area and—

Katie, can I ask you something?

Now? Really?

Well, I was just thinking. If you thought there was some creeper in your bedroom, why didn't you stop and, you know, actually pick up a useful weapon? Like, say, all those sharp knives your dad proudly displays on the kitchen bench? I mean, that's besides the fact that calling the cops really would have been the wisest thing to do. If you were worried about Max, the chances of you being able to do anything at that point were—

Libby, you're really messing with my flow here.

Sorry, it just doesn't make a lot of sense to me. Frankly, it strains my suspension of disbelief.

Me not stopping to pick up a knife strains your suspension of disbelief? Not the whole WE CREATED A BOY thing?

I just thought you were more logical than that.

Well, when you find yourself in what you think is a life-or-death situation, please do let me know how logic works for you. Because I was running less on brain power, more on pure adrenalin at that point in time.

Hmmmmm.

Now, can I continue?

You can, and you may.

Why I oughta—

☺

Theo and I were moving as quietly as we could through my house. We paused when we reached my open bedroom door, pressing our bodies against the hallway wall.

There was silence in my room. All I could hear was the sound of mine and Theo's breathing. We exchanged a look.

"Anybody in there?" Theo called out. His voice came out about three octaves higher than usual.

"If you were a burglar or murderer, would you respond to a question like that?" I hissed.

Theo looked back at me, a finger to his lips. His eyes widened when we heard—no way...was that...a giggle?

A moment later, there it was again. Definitely a giggle.

What the hell?

Theo and I stared at each other, our faces twitching in silent communication. After a moment he shrugged as if to say, *Here goes nothing*. He rounded the corner into my room in one quick movement, swinging the plastic bat in front of him and bellowing a wordless war cry. I followed him, slamming on the light and sticking the paintbrush out in front of me like it was a fencing sword. Theo's scream died on his lips, and I let out a gasp as we both registered what we were seeing.

I don't know what Theo thought we'd find when we

entered the room. I'd had all sorts of visions flashing through my head, all of them dark and awful.

I can tell you that neither of us were expecting what we actually saw.

There, by my bed, was a bronzed, muscular guy with floppy blond hair. He was crouched down, laughing softly to himself, as he scratched at Max's sides. My oh-so-effective guard dog was absolutely smothering the guy's face in kisses, his tail wagging furiously.

Straightening up and pushing Max gently away, the guy said, "There you are, gorgeous." I instinctively looked around. Theo had a stunned expression on his face. Was this guy talking...to me?

His voice was husky. And hot. Or at least it would have been if he wasn't some rando who'd shown up in my room in the middle of the night, butt-naked.

Yeah. Did I mention he was naked? Because he was.

I tell you what, if you had've told me at the start of that day that I'd wind up with two half-naked and/or totally naked guys in my bedroom that night, I would've said you were dreaming.

For a moment, I thought I was.

Then Theo's mouth finally kicked into gear.

"Listen, perv, we've called the cops, so you better get the hell out of here right now." His words were confident, but I could hear the tremor in his voice.

The naked guy took a step forward, and Theo flicked the bat in his hand toward him in a threatening way. "Don't—don't come any closer," he said.

"Is this guy bothering you?" The naked guy said. To me.

Theo glanced my way. "You're the only one who's bothering her, mate."

The guy stood up straighter. He towered over Theo. "Me?" He made a scoffing noise. "I would never bother her."

"Leave now, and no one has to get hurt, alright."

"Kate, who is this boy? Do you want me to get rid of him for you?" This was from the naked guy.

"Uhhhh," I squeaked out. I'd been standing there with my mouth hanging open during the whole exchange, trying to take in what was happening. My brain was having a hard time processing it.

"How do you know her name?" Theo said, his voice raised. Quieter, he said to me, "Shit, is he some weirdo stalker?'"

Glasses. I needed my glasses. A suspicion had sprung up in my mind that definitely didn't seem possible. It'd been planted there by the whiff of scent I'd got when the naked guy had moved.

The smell of springtime.

And the ocean.

I dropped the paintbrush and held out my hands in a calming gesture, like the guy was some kind of wild animal.

I slowly moved around the edge of the room toward my bedside table.

"What the hell are you doing?" Theo hissed.

I didn't answer. I didn't take my eyes off the guy in front of me. Max was still at his feet, his tail wagging, like he'd found his new best friend. It was as though he hadn't even registered Theo's presence in the room, let alone mine.

I felt around on my bedside table for my glasses and slipped them on. They were still wonky, but they did their job. The room came into focus, and I got a proper look at the naked guy for the first time. He was scratching his head, his face placid, like he didn't really have a care in the world.

And why would he, when he looked like...well, like a long-lost Hemsworth brother? He moved his hand away from his head, and his hair settled smoothly into place. Just right. His eyes, which were looking at me with warmth and—was that *affection*?—were the clear blue of a summer's day. His lips, which he gently nibbled as my gaze lingered on them, were soft and pink.

Perfect for kissing.

His body...well, let's just say it was pretty damn flawless.

Except for one tiny thing.

No, not *that* thing.

I was doing my best not to look at *that* thing, thank-you-very-much.

It was something else altogether.

The guy. He didn't have a belly button.

He had a six pack to die for. That hot V thing at his hips.

But between them...nothing. Just smooth skin. No belly button.

"Oh my god," I finally said.

Theo looked at me sharply. He hadn't noticed what I had, it seemed. And I wasn't about to point it out.

The naked guy smiled and went to take a step toward me, but Theo moved quickly, pressing the plastic bat into the guy's chest. "I—I thought I told you not to move."

The guy looked down at the bat, not particularly bothered, and then glanced over at me.

"Who *is* this guy?" he and Theo said, at exactly the same time. They looked at each other, mild annoyance on the naked guy's face, fury bubbling up on Theo's.

"Oh my god," I repeated. Two sets of eyes—one pair blue, the other dark brown—looked my way.

I swallowed. No. This couldn't be.

"Did Libby put you up to this?" I asked the naked guy. There had to be some kind of logical (*cough*) explanation. His brow furrowed. "Who are you, anyway? Is this some kind of joke?" I turned to Theo. "Are you in on this too?"

Confusion clouded his face. "What?"

But I wasn't paying attention to him anymore. I was searching in my sheets, then on the floor under my bed.

"I don't think you'll find what you're looking for under there," the naked guy said in a singsong voice.

I straightened up. "How do you know what I'm looking for?"

He smiled. It was a dazzling smile. "You're looking for me. But I'm right here." He held out his arms.

Theo was glancing from me to the guy and back again, still holding the bat up between us. "KC...do you know this guy?"

"Um." It was finally sinking in. "I think so."

Slowly, Theo lowered the bat and turned to me. "You think so?"

I nodded.

"Do you maybe wanna tell me what's going on?"

I exhaled. "It's kind of a long story." *And a completely absurd one*, I thought. I couldn't quite believe I was actually entertaining the possibility that it could be true. I might not have been into science like Libby, but even I knew there was no way it was scientifically, actually conceivable that we had...that we had...

But what other explanation was there for this six-foot-who-knows-what golden god of a guy standing in my room in the middle of the night, completely naked, and calling me "gorgeous"?

It made no sense. Maybe I really was dreaming.

I pinched myself. Hard.

It hurt.

"Prank," I blurted out. "It's a prank! Libby and the girls, they, uh, they pranked me. Isn't that right?" I looked pointedly at the guy, who frowned in confusion. I rushed ahead before he could say anything. "So it's okay. You can go. Thanks for coming to check on me, though."

Theo's eyes grew wide when he realized I was talking to him.

"Huh? But—" He looked at the naked guy, who smiled at him and waggled his fingers as I moved to usher Theo out the door.

"Wait, seriously, who is this creep?" Theo whispered to me. "You sure you're okay?"

"I'm fine, really. I—I was confused at first, but now I get it. Sorry I scared you. Don't worry. This guy, um... He won't hurt me." When I said it, I had this weird sensation that it was absolutely true.

"I don't want to leave you alone with—"

"It's fine, I promise. He...he's a friend. A friend of Michael's! That I've, uh, met a few times," I said. "I just didn't recognize him in the dark. I shouldn't have freaked out like that. Really. You can go now." When Theo didn't move, I added, "Okay, bye."

Theo glanced over my shoulder and something dawned on his face. "Wait. Are you telling me—is he—are you—wait, what the f—"

"Let's talk in the morning, okay?" I said, giving him one final shove. The last thing I saw before I closed the door in Theo's face was the utter shock and dismay displayed there.

"What the fuck," I heard him say again. A moment later, the back door closed with a thud.

I leaned against my bedroom door and took a deep breath. I looked at the naked guy, took in his smiling face and his chiseled body with its conspicuous lack of a belly button and his—um, well, then I turned my gaze to the ceiling.

"Can you, uh, put some clothes on, please?" I said, my voice squeaking.

"I don't have any clothes," he said breezily.

"Of course you don't," I muttered. I cupped my hand to my face, shielding my eyes, and walked over to my wardrobe. I pulled out my fluffy pink dressing gown, which was way too big for me (because it's cozier that way), and tossed it over my shoulder.

"Are you decent?" I asked after a moment.

"I believe so," he said.

I turned back around in time to see him tying the dressing gown up at his waist. The sleeves were way too short and it didn't fully cover his torso, but at least all the important parts were hidden (ahem).

I stepped closer to him. "Are you—did you—I just—"

I couldn't help myself. I reached out and touched the smooth, golden skin of his chest. I snatched my hand back reflexively, startled by his warmth. By his rock-hard *realness*.

"No way," I whispered. He reached for my hand and began stroking it gently with his thumb. "This can't be happening."

His lips parted slightly, but he didn't say a word. His eyes—those beautiful blue summer-sky eyes—were on my lips. His other hand moved to my face, and he gently tucked a strand of hair behind my ear. It caused the broken arm of my glasses to slip. I shot my hand up to hold them in place.

"Your glasses are broken," the no-longer-naked guy said. I have to say, I've heard people's voices described as "like honey" in the past, and I never really got what that meant. Until I heard this guy speak.

"Yeah," I said, a ridiculous giggle escaping from my lips.

He reached up and plucked the glasses from my face, placing them on the bedside table.

"You have beautiful eyes," he said, turning back to me and leaning down, bringing his face level with mine. One hand cupped my chin. "It's a shame to hide them."

"Um," I said, my stomach flip-flopping at the compliment. "The thing is, I kinda like being able to see." I just couldn't keep my mouth shut.

"Oh," he breathed. I got the feeling he hadn't really heard what I'd said, anyway. His face was inching closer to mine, his eyes hooded, almost shut.

Shit. Was I about to get my first kiss? Was this really happening?

I swallowed hard. Was I losing my mind? This was all moving too fast.

I took a step back.

My legs hit the bed, and I fell onto it with a bounce.

The guy and I stared at each other for a moment. He had a thoughtful expression on his face. He opened his mouth to say something, but it was cut off by Max jumping between us, clawing at the guy, barking excitedly.

The guy laughed and said, "Were we not giving you enough attention?"

This couldn't be real.

Libby. I had to talk to Libby.

I slipped my glasses back on and picked up my phone. Libby answered after the sixth ring.

"Katie? Why are you calling me?" She sounded half-asleep and fully weirded out.

It's funny in hindsight that I thought THIS moment was weird. If only I had known what was coming...

"Libby! You will never believe what happened," I glanced at the guy, who was now sprawled on the floor, giving Max belly rubs. I turned my back from him and lowered my voice. "I—we—I—oh-my-god-I-think-we-actually-created-a-boy-and-he's-in-my-room-and-he's-petting-Max-and-he's-so—"

"Katie, what? Slow down. You're making no sense. It sounded like you said, 'we created a boy.'"

"That's exactly what I said."

"What?"

I took a deep breath and tried to speak slower this time. "A boy. I woke up and there was a boy in my bed. And he—"

"You *what*?!"

"Libby I think we actually made a boy. The perfect boy!"

"No, I'm not talking to anyone, Dad!" I heard her call. To me, she said, "Katie, this isn't funny. My parents will take away my phone if they find me on it right now."

"I'm not joking!" I said, getting shrill. "Cross my heart and hope to die."

Libby was silent. She knew the seriousness of what I was saying now. I didn't joke around about those words. I was always too paranoid the universe would strike me dead on the spot just for tempting fate. Right now it was the only way to get her to believe me.

"You must have hit your head harder than I thought," she finally said.

IV

"W e should have gone to the hospital." Libby sounded worried. "Are your parents home?"

"No! There's no one else here. Just me and the guy." I glanced over at him and was rewarded with a brilliant smile. "He's so hot," I whispered down the phone.

"Listen, I'll be right there, okay? Just stay put and don't do anything. Definitely don't fall asleep."

"Wait. You're coming over?"

"Sit tight, I'll be five minutes."

"You don't have to—" I started to say, but she'd already hung up. To be honest, I was relieved Libby was coming. I looked at the guy again. What the hell was I going to do with him?

I sat down on my bed, trying to will my heart to stop beating quite so fast. The guy got up and sat down beside me, our bodies close. Which did not help with the whole heart situation.

"So," I said, swallowing hard. "Do you—what's your name?"

"I don't have a name," he said. He frowned slightly, and there was something about his expression that sent a pang through my chest.

"How can you not have a name?" I asked, edging away from him slightly to put some space between us.

"You haven't given me one," he said simply. "You gave me this body." He held out his arms and the fluffy pink sleeves of my dressing gown floated with them. "You gave me this robe. You gave me a great many things in here." He pointed to his head. "And in here." His hand rested on his heart. "But you didn't give me a name." He reached out to touch my face.

"Well," I swallowed. "I suppose we should give you one then. I can't call you 'the guy' forever."

"Guy? Hmmm. I like that," he said. His thumb stroked my cheek, and I cringed as it landed on a pimple.

There was a loud knocking at the front door then and I jumped, startled.

"That'll be Libby," I said. "Stay here. I'll be right back."

Libby burst in as soon as I opened the door. Her hair was soaked from the rain, and her eyes were wide with worry.

"Are you okay?!" Her hands were on my face, and she was staring into my eyes. "You're conscious at least.

Should we go to the hospital?" She didn't say that last part to me. She was looking back over her shoulder—at her sister, who had just walked in behind her.

"Melissa? What are you doing here?!" I glanced down the hallway. The guy—Guy?—was still safely in my room. For now.

"Libby said you have a concussion," Melissa said. She walked straight to the kitchen table and started pulling things out of her bag. "Here, sit down."

My sister is a med student, by the way. Almost a doctor! We should probably mention that.

I was just getting to it!

Right.

Libby's sister is a medical student. Almost a doctor.

And for some reason Libby thought it was a brilliant idea to bring her around to my place at 11:30 on a Friday night.

"I didn't know what else to do," Libby said. "I woke Melissa up because I was worried you had a concussion, and we came right over but—"

"I'm really fine," I said in a rush. "You're overreacting." I tried to send telepathic messages to Guy to stay hidden. Could he receive them?

And how was that a question I was seriously asking myself?

Maybe I *had* injured my brain.

"Libby said you took quite a hit." Melissa grabbed my hand and pulled me gently toward the table. "You girls should have called me right away."

"We thought she was fine," Libby said, sitting down opposite me and chewing her lip.

"I *am* fine," I said. "Really." I tried to gesture to Libby with my eyebrows that Guy was hiding in my room, but she didn't seem to get the message.

"You rang me babbling about a guy in your bed," Libby said. Yeah, she definitely hadn't got the message. "I don't think that's fine."

Melissa froze. "Wait, you're having hallucinations?"

"What? No!" I said as Libby said, "Yes!"

"We need to go to the hospital," Melissa said, shoving the things she had just pulled from her bag back into it.

"Hospital?" a deep husky voice said from the hallway, and it was my turn to freeze. "Kate, are you unwell?"

Guy rushed to my side. Still wearing my fluffy pink dressing gown. Max was at his heels, tongue hanging out like he was having as much fun as he did chasing his giant stuffed hedgehog around the backyard during fetch.

I took in the nearly identical shocked faces of Libby and Melissa before Guy settled in front of me, his large, warm hands encircling my wrists.

"Uh, would someone mind telling me what the hell

is going on?" Melissa said, looking Guy up and down and then narrowing her eyes at me.

"Yeah, me too," Libby said, not taking her eyes off Guy.

"I *told* you, Libby," I said, looking at her pointedly. "On the phone. What happened. How he came to be...here."

"Libby?" Guy said, suddenly looking up at her. "Libby!" A smile spread across his face and he sidestepped his way over to her, leaning forward as if to give her a hug. She lurched backward, and the chair that she was sitting on tipped with her. There was a drawn-out moment where her limbs and Guy's tangled together before they both ended up on the floor, the chair somehow on top of them...and one of Guy's arse cheeks exposed.

In hindsight, it's lucky that nothing else was exposed.

In hindsight, yes. It didn't feel so lucky at the time, with your sister right there, staring at it all and demanding an explanation.

It didn't feel so lucky for me either, with some strange guy on top of me.

"Get off me!" Libby cried, and Guy extricated himself immediately, holding out his hand to help her up, which she ignored.

"Libby, can I speak to you in private?" I said.

"Nuh-uh, you're not going anywhere until you tell me what's going on," Melissa said.

"You sound just like Mum," Libby said, dusting off her butt.

"Watch your mouth," Melissa shot back.

"Guy is—he's a friend, okay?" I broke in. "It's a long story. But I'm not concussed or anything, this is all one big misunderstanding."

"You're okay?" Guy said, moving closer to me again.

"I'm okay. I—" Just then headlights flashed through the window, and I heard the sound of my mum's car pulling up in the driveway.

"*Shit*," I muttered. My stomach felt like it had dropped somewhere in the vicinity of my toes. "Quick, you have to hide." I pushed Guy back toward my bedroom. "Under my bed. Just go under there and don't come out until I say so, okay? Promise me."

"I'll do anything for you," Guy said.

"Wonderful. Just stay as silent as possible, okay?"

"Okay," he said happily. Max followed after him, wagging his tail, completely ignoring me when I tried to call him back. Oh well, that was the least of my problems right now.

I turned to Melissa. "Don't say anything to Mum. Please. You can't."

I watched her hesitate, glancing between me and Libby.

"I don't really understand what's going on, but I

know it will be good for exactly none of us if any of our parents find out. Including you, *Ate*," Libby said, invoking the Filipino term for older sister in the way she only ever did when she was either trying to make a point or get her way with Melissa.

You know me so well.

When my mum walked in a moment later, Melissa was sitting next to me, calmly shining a little flashlight in my eyes.

"What's going on?!" There was a note of panic in Mum's voice. Crap. I should have known this would set her off. But at least this would set her off less than the alternative (that is, the presence of a half-naked boy in my bedroom).

"I'm okay, Mum," I said.

"Katie got hit in the head earlier today and she's fine, but I was just worried so I brought Melissa around to check on her," Libby explained.

"What?!" Mum was not sounding any less panicked.

"It's okay, Mrs. Camilleri," Melissa said, putting her flashlight thingy away. "We're just being extra cautious. *Aren't we, Katie*?"

"Exactly."

"At this time of night?" Mum said, but she didn't wait for an answer. She was next to me now, and her hand was on my head. "Where did you get hit? Why is your hair so wet?"

"I had to get Max in from the rain," I said. "He was barking at the storm."

"Where is Max?" Mum said, apparently noticing for the first time he hadn't rushed to greet her like normal.

"I think he's sleeping," I offered up weakly. "A big night of barking took it out of him."

How did people lie all the time? This was exhausting.

Luckily my Mum seemed more concerned with me than Max at that moment in time. "So is anyone going to tell me exactly what happened?"

"The question of the hour," Melissa muttered.

"We were walking home from school," Libby began, and as Melissa continued to examine me, Libby unloaded the whole sad soccer ball story, right down to me babbling about magpies to Declan Bell Jones. By the time she was done—at which point Melissa had declared that there didn't seem to be any real concern about a concussion—everyone was laughing about what had happened. Even me, although it was more nervous laughter because I could practically feel Guy's presence emanating from my bedroom. I hoped I was the only one.

"Can I get you anything?" Mum asked Melissa as she was packing up.

"Thanks, but we better get home. Mum and Dad will be worried. We rushed out of the house without much explanation. They'll kill us if we don't get back soon." She looked at me, and there was an extra layer of meaning as she said, "You, behave yourself, okay?"

I knew we were going to have to deal with Melissa at some point, but my priority right now was actually communicating with Libby. As Mum walked Melissa out, Libby held back.

"Should I really be leaving?" she whispered to me.

"No," I hissed back. "Yes. I don't know."

"Who *is* that?"

"I told you."

"No way."

"Yes way."

"It can't be."

"It—"

"Come on, Libby," Melissa called from the veranda.

Libby hesitated before sighing and following her sister outside. "I'll talk to you later," she said, by which she meant, "I'll message you as soon as I'm in the privacy of my own room."

When Mum came back inside a moment later, I had a cup of tea ready and waiting for her. I needed as much good karma where she was concerned as I could possibly rack up.

"Oh, thanks kid," she said with a smile. "Aren't you having one?"

"I might go to bed," I said. "I'm wiped."

"Aw, come on, stay up and chat with your mum for a bit."

An image of Guy sprawled under my bed flashed through my mind. A couple more minutes would be okay, right? Just to reassure Mum that everything was normal.

"How was dinner?" I asked, and she started telling me about her friend's latest dating drama. Not that the Tinder troubles of a forty-something divorcee woman aren't thrilling to me, but with every detail of the dude's table manners Mum relayed, I could practically feel my blood pressure rising. I was painfully aware of how long this story could go on.

At the mention of the way he apparently used his thumb instead of his knife to push food on to his fork, I staged an elaborate and loud yawn, which caused my mangled glasses to slip. I groaned as I tried to adjust the masking tape.

Mum laughed. "Good thing you've been saving your money."

"Huh?"

"Those will need fixing." She sipped her tea.

"I have to pay for them myself?!" I'd started working at the pharmacy around the corner the year before, but this was *not* what I'd been saving for. Every spare cent was going toward a big trip to Europe that Libby and I wanted to take when we turned eighteen. Fixing my glasses was not in the budget.

"That'll teach you to keep your head away from soccer balls," Mum said.

"I'm going to bed," I grumbled.

"Make sure you dry that hair first," Mum said when I leaned over to kiss her on the cheek.

I rolled my eyes, but as I walked toward my bedroom I realized turning on the hair dryer would actually provide the perfect cover for to talk to Guy without Mum hearing; it's a small house, and the walls aren't exactly thick. (Yes, I have heard my parents doing it. No, I don't ever want to talk about it.)

"Are you okay under there?" Hair dryer roaring in my hand, I crouched down and glanced under the bed.

"I'm just fine," Guy said. He was folded up in a tight ball but still taking up the majority of the floor space. He did not look fine. Max was on his back beside him, only half-hidden by the bed.

"Can you stay under for a while longer?" I said to Guy over the roar of the hair dryer. "I can't risk my mum seeing you. Sorry."

"You don't need to be sorry," Guy said, and something about the way he said it made my skin prickle.

I blasted my hair for a few minutes, trying to breathe deeply to calm the nerves and tension that were zinging around my body. My curls had just about reached their peak frizziness, but I didn't have the brain space to care about that (much) right now. I shoved my mostly dry hair into a topknot, turned the light off, and slid under the covers, listening intently for the sounds of my mum moving around the kitchen. I felt like I was barely breathing.

My phone flashed. It was a message from Libby. The twelfth message from Libby, actually. She'd been having a mini meltdown, it seemed. I could relate. The last message read:

> This is definitely not a joke, right?

>> Definitely not. Where would I have pulled a guy like THAT from, anyway?

>> Thin air is the only possibility

>> I know it's ridiculous

>> I don't know how it happened

>> But we really, actually created a boy

I watched as three dots appeared, disappeared, and reappeared multiple times before Libby finally sent a string of emojis, and then:

> How is this possible????

>> You're the scientist you tell me

Folie à deux.

Bless you

Folie à deux. It's when two or more people share hallucinations.

Delusions

Like that family in Victoria a few years ago who spontaneously went on the run.

You think we're hallucinating

It's the only explanation.

But what about Melissa? And Theo???

Theo???

He saw Guy earlier.

Guy????

Oh. That's what I've started calling him.

Guy

Guy is not a real person's name.

It's totally a real person's name.

Hello, Guy of Gisborne?

Who of who?

From Robin Hood?

Some dude from 1348 being named Guy doesn't really make your case for it being a suitable name.

Anyway, technically Guy isn't a real person

He looked pretty real to me.

This is just so...

I mean...

We really...

WE CREATED LIFE?!??!

And we didn't even have to give birth

I can't believe you're joking at a time like this.

I can't believe there's a guy hiding under my bed right now

I can't believe.

Same.

My sister thinks you're some kind of sex fiend now, btw.

lmao yeah, the most virginal sex fiend in the world

…she won't say anything, will she?

Nah. But I guess I'll have to obey her every command like a good little sister, just to make sure.

I quickly slipped my phone under my pillow when I heard Mum's footsteps coming down the hallway.

"Maxie?" she whisper-called. "Maxie boy!"

My bedroom door creaked open and light from the hallway spilled in. My heart pounded in my throat.

"Just want to say goodnight to Max," Mum said

softly, not bothering to check if I was even awake. She spotted Max's feet sticking out from under my bed and moved toward them. "Maxie boy, what are you doing? Aren't you going to give—"

"Mum!" I cried, sitting up suddenly, just as she was about to bend down. She straightened up, startled. I had to say something to keep her distracted. Out came the first thing that popped into my head before I even realized what it was. "Tell me about your first kiss."

Mum's shoulder's relaxed. "I thought you were tired. Now you want to chat?" She sat down on my bed anyway and reached out to smooth a stray hair away from my face. Normally it would soothe me. Right now it was only making me tenser. But at least she'd momentarily forgotten about Max under my bed. Apparently he'd found his new fave person and he didn't want to leave his side.

"Well, let's see. I was seventeen and working at the deli..."

I knew this story. It was a long one, the way my mum told it. What had I gotten myself into? I willed Guy to stay silent and still below me.

As Mum was talking, I heard the back door sliding open. As if I wasn't stressed enough as it was. Had Theo returned? Like I needed more complications right now.

I was relieved when my dad popped his head through

my bedroom door. He was drenched. He must have ridden his bike home, despite the storm.

"Evening ladies," he said with a grin. "Didn't think you'd still be up."

Mum got up to give him a kiss and scolded him for dripping all over the floor.

Then my Dad said, "Max? Maxie? What's he found under there?" and the momentary relief I had been feeling vanished.

"Whatever it is, it must smell good. He hasn't budged," Mum said. "Probably dirty underwear."

I squeezed my eyes shut. This was a nightmare. It had to be.

Please let it be.

What do I do?

I jumped out of bed and pulled on Max's legs, dragging him out. I glimpsed Guy still curled in a ball. *Please stay like that*, I thought. I hefted Max up in my arms with a groan. He was a heavy boy. I passed him over to Dad.

"Here. Get your kisses. Can I go to sleep now?"

"Someone's in a mood," Dad replied with a sniff.

"What's gotten into you?" Mum said. She leaned over and let Max lick her face.

"I'm just tired," I said as Max, having done his kissing duties, twisted his way out of Dad's arms and scrambled back under my bed. When I heard a soft giggle I launched into my best attempt at a coughing fit.

Mum reached out and touched my topknot. "It's still damp! What did I tell you?"

I shrugged her away. "It's fine," I said through a fake cough. "I just have something in my throat." I moved toward the door, backing them out of the room. "Good night guys."

"Alright, alright we get the message." Dad kissed my cheek. "I'm gonna hop in the shower." He turned toward the bathroom.

"You're cleaning out your room tomorrow," Mum said to me. "If whatever's under that bed got Max's attention, it will probably draw the mice too." She shuddered.

"'Night Mum," I said, closing my bedroom door. I heard her sigh on the other side of it. I waited for the sounds of her moving around her own room before I crouched down as quietly as I could. Max was now curled into Guy like the little spoon.

"Are you okay?" I whispered as quietly as I possibly could. "Do you...do you reckon you can stay there until morning?" I felt totally unreasonable asking this, but I didn't know what else to do. My door was closed, and I didn't have a lock. It was too risky to let him out.

Let him out. I sounded like some kind of jailer.

"I'm quite comfortable," Guy whispered. "As long as I'm near you, I'm happy."

I shook my head. There was no getting used to this. I slid some of my spare pillows toward Guy, grateful for the first time in my life for Mum's obsession with loading every bed in the house full of decorative cushioning.

"Good night then," I said, climbing into bed for the third time that evening. Had it really only been a few hours ago that I'd been messing with clay and goop with Libby in my kitchen? And now...

"Good night." The honey whisper drifted up from below me. Quiet, but there.

I suddenly felt really, really tired. Like all the adrenaline that had been pumping through me had finally dissipated.

As my eyes fluttered shut, I felt a pang of guilt. It was Guy's first night on Earth—apparently—and this was how he was spending it.

I thought of *Frankenstein*. My nunna had lent me the book the year before. In it, the doctor, Frankenstein, was so horrified by what he had done that he abandoned his monster right after creating it.

Is that how I should feel? Horrified?

I didn't know how I felt. But it wasn't that.

And I knew one thing for sure. I might be forcing Guy to sleep on the wooden floor beneath my bed, but I would definitely never abandon him.

V

Libby was slowly circling Guy. "I still can't believe it." She reached out to poke his arm. He just smiled in response.

We were at the park down the road from Libby's place to do our official Guy handover. I had to go to work, which meant Libby was on Guy duty for the day. I felt weird about leaving him and had been tempted to call in sick, but I needed the money more than ever now that I had to pay for my glasses to be repaired. And it wasn't like I could keep him under my bed all day.

When I'd woken up and checked under there that morning, I'd half-expected to see him gone. Like the whole thing had been one long, lucid dream. But there he was, still curled in a ball as though he hadn't moved even one centimeter all night. I'd actually gotten goosebumps at the sight of him. A part of me still felt like I was dreaming, despite all evidence to the contrary.

Maybe I was in a coma? The soap opera kind, where

there's a whole narrative and you learn profound life lessons. Yeah. That seemed likely.

It had been a mission and a half to get Guy clothed (my brother's old gym clothes), fed (an apple snuck from the kitchen), and out of the house without my family noticing. Frankly I was impressed by my own achievement and was considering putting "spy" at the top of my career wishlist. Hey, it was probably more viable than "artist" or "writer."

"You should see his belly button," I said. "Or lack thereof."

"What?!" Libby paused in front of Guy, and he helpfully rubbed the smooth skin of his stomach. It was easy for him to do, since my brother was at least two sizes smaller than Guy and his jersey was practically a crop top on him.

"What *are* you?" Libby said.

"I am Guy."

"Oh, we're sticking with that are we?" Libby said, looking at me.

I shrugged. "Hey, it was either that or Frank."

"Frank?"

"Yeah. You know, like Frankenstein."

She shook her head. "Frankenstein was the *doctor,* not the monst—" She looked at Guy's smiling face and stopped short. "Not the you-know-what."

"Yeah. I know. So 'Guy' it is."

Libby turned back to him. "Where did you come from?"

"From Kate's room," he said simply.

Libby's hand went to her hip. "But what about before that?"

Something clouded his face for the briefest of moments, then he shook it off. "There was no before that. Not for me."

She narrowed her eyes. "How old are you?"

"My physical age is approximately seventeen, I believe." He ran a hand through his thick, golden hair. "But literally speaking, I am, oh"—he glanced at the sky— "about twelve hours old?"

Libby rubbed her face. "This really can't be real."

"I assure you, I'm very real," Guy said. He reached for Libby's hand and placed it against his chest, right above his heart. "See?"

She pulled her hand back. "Do you have any idea what this means?"

"That you and I are now proud co-parents to a new-born, full-grown teenager?"

She rolled her eyes. "Oh yeah, I'm sure you feel super *parental* about him."

I felt myself blushing and glanced at Guy. He didn't seem fazed. To be fair, nothing seemed to faze him. He was perpetually calm—when he wasn't completely joyful.

He took delight in the most random things. Like this morning, when I'd given him that apple to eat, he'd taken one bite and his eyes had widened and he'd said, "This is the most delicious thing I've ever eaten." Then, a beat later, "To be fair, it's the only thing I've ever eaten." And he'd laughed his glorious laugh.

"Forget about your hormones for a second," Libby said now. "This is huge. This is *history-making*. Think about it. We'll be rich! Famous!"

Alarm bells rang in my head. I looked at Guy, wanting to spare him from this talk. "Guy—have you ever swung on a swing?" I said.

He raised his eyebrows. "No, but it sounds wonderful."

"It is!" I grabbed him by the wrist and led him over to the sad little set that was the only play equipment in the park (a generous word for this patch of grass, really). A few moments later he was pumping his long, muscled legs and hooting with joy. It really didn't take much to make him happy.

I turned back to Libby, standing far enough away from Guy that I hoped he wouldn't hear us.

"Okay, we cannot tell anyone about this. You know that right?"

"But—this is so huge. How can we not?" Libby asked.

"Are you serious?"

"What do you mean?"

"I mean, no one would believe us, for starters. *You* didn't even believe it."

Libby tilted her head, reluctant agreement on her face. She pulled out a packet of cinnamon gum from her back pocket and stuck a piece in her mouth. She didn't offer me one. She knew I hated it.

"And even if they did," I continued, "you know what would happen. They'd come and take him away and chop him up into a thousand little pieces. Hell, they'd probably lock *us* up."

"You don't know that."

"Come on. Look at any TV show or movie. That's what happens every single time."

"But this isn't a movie, Katie."

"I know! It's real life, with real people and real"—I glanced at Guy—"whatever the hell he is, who could get hurt."

Libby chewed thoughtfully. "Well, what *do* we do now?" she finally said.

"I for one have got to go to work. Take good care of our baby, okay?"

She pursed her lips. "What am I going to tell my parents? I can't just bring home a giant white guy and hope they don't notice."

"So don't take him to your house."

I walked over to Guy.

"Hey, I'm heading to work," I called.

"Oh! I'll come with you," he said. "As soon as I figure out how to stop this."

"Oh you, uh—" I was about to explain how you had to basically drag your feet along the ground, but before I could even blink he'd leaped off the swing in midair and landed on his feet like some kind of Olympic gymnast. "—do that. Sure."

"You can't go with Katie, she has to work," Libby said. "You're stuck with me, buddy."

Guy looked at Libby doubtfully. "But Kate—"

"Will be back in a few hours."

"Like, five. Six, max," I said.

He stepped toward me and reached for my hand. "Do you have to go?" he said softly. Whew. I was never going to get used to him looking at me like that. Talking to me like that. Touching me like that.

Whew.

"Uhhhhh...yes?" I said, not sounding particularly convincing even to myself.

Libby cleared her throat loudly, and I broke away from Guy.

"Right, well, I'll leave you guys to it then," I said in a rush, my voice coming out rather hoarse.

"Bye, Katie," Libby said.

"I miss you already," I heard Guy call after me as I walked away.

VI

I 'm backed up worse than a priest during Lent," Mrs. Morrison was saying to me as I reached for the laxatives we kept behind the counter.

I laughed politely, even though I wasn't quite sure what she meant (other than "extremely constipated"). Mrs. Morrison was one of the pharmacy's regular customers, coming in for different medications and supplements every single week—sometimes multiple times a week. I guess that's what happens when you get old. You need a little extra help keeping your body functioning.

I was scanning the barcode and listening to her go on about her poo when I spotted who was next in line and froze. It was Declan Bell Jones. He noticed me staring and gave me a little half-wave.

I did what any normal person would do in that situation and quickly looked away.

I don't know why I was so shocked to see him there. I mean, he lived down the road, in one of the big houses by the beach. I'd seen him skateboarding past, usually with a bag from the fast food place next door tucked under one arm. But he'd never come in before. At least, not during one of my shifts.

I glanced over at Alex, my coworker, just as he was handing over change to a customer. He'd be ready to serve Declan before I was. I couldn't decide if that was a good or bad thing.

"—and then on Thursday, I ate about half a kilo of prunes, and would you believe, still not a nugget to be seen. So I went to visit my friend, Helen, because she always manages to give me the shits." Mrs. Morrison cackled at her own joke. "But then—"

My smile was becoming strained as I waited for an opportunity to inform Mrs. Morrison of the price of her purchase, while also clocking Declan sidling up to the counter out of the corner of my eye. Alex had his customer service voice on—"Hi, how's it going? Still warm outside? It's such a nice day after that hectic storm last night"—and Declan was responding politely, but I swear I could feel him watching me. I chanced looking over at him just as Mrs. Morrison said, very loudly, "Do you ever get constipated, dear?"

Declan broke eye contact immediately, his eyes darting down toward his wallet. I could tell he was trying to suppress a smile.

That's when I saw what he was buying.

Condoms.

I suddenly felt queasy.

I turned back to Mrs. Morrison, my face heating. "Uh, that's nine ninety-five," I mumbled.

"What's that, my love?" she said.

"It's NINE NINETY-FIVE," I repeated, louder this time.

"Alright, no need to yell, I'm not deaf yet." She chuckled. "Hope you don't mind some shrapnel." She began counting out coins from her heavy purse. She seemed to have an endless supply of them.

Declan had completed his purchase and was hanging back. I was trying very hard not to look his way. I hurriedly counted Mrs. Morrison's mountain of money.

"Here's hoping this clears the pipes, eh?" she said as she popped the laxatives in her bag with a flourish.

"Good luck," I said with a fake laugh that died on my lips as Declan stepped up to the counter again. Right in front of me.

"Hey," he said. "I didn't know you worked here."

"Hi," I said in a voice I didn't recognize as my own. "Um, yeah, since last year?"

"Cool."

I glanced behind Declan. There was no one waiting in line. Alex was busy serving another customer, but he shot me a curious look.

"Can I, um, help you with anything?" I said to Declan.

He rested his forearms on the counter, bringing his face close to mine.

"I just wanted to say sorry again. For yesterday."

"Oh." I swallowed. That felt like a year ago already. "Don't worry about it. It was only my head." I laughed, going for nonchalant but probably just sounding ridiculous.

"Your glasses," he said. My hand reflexively went to the broken frame. "Can I replace them for you?"

"Oh! Nah. You don't have to do that. It's no biggie." I waved my hand dismissively. I noticed an old man was now waiting to be served.

"I think I do. Or at least let me get them fixed," Declan said, looking right into my eyes.

"Um..." I seemed to have lost the ability to speak.

Declan straightened up. "Really. I insist."

Behind him, the old guy cleared his throat very loudly.

"Uh, okay, sure," I said quickly.

Declan looked gratified. "What's your number? I'll text you and we can sort out the details."

I recited my mobile number, trying not to look as astonished as I felt over the surreal turn of events. Declan Bell Jones had actually asked for my number. And I'd thought creating my dream guy out of clay would be the weirdest thing to happen to me this weekend.

Declan smiled and said, "Cool. Talk to you soon." He held up his hand in a farewell gesture. It was the hand holding the condoms he'd purchased. I felt my face turning even redder than it already was.

"I need a cream for toe warts," the old guy said.

🎨

I spent the rest of the afternoon alternating between obsessing over Declan and the fact that he had my number, avoiding thoughts of what he might be doing with those condoms he bought (and with who), questioning why Declan still had such a strong effect on me when a whole Guy existed, and feeling restless about what Libby was getting up to with Guy. I wished, not for the first time, that my boss, Phil, wasn't such a fascist about us having our phones on us during shifts. We had to keep them locked away in the staff room.

It felt bizarre to be going through the regular motions of a Saturday shift—complete with scraping chewing gum off the floor in the nail polish section—when I wanted to burst out of my skin after the events of the last 24 hours.

As we were restocking the checkout candy during a lull late in the day, Alex said in a teasing voice, "Why did Declan Bell Jones get your phone number earlier?" Alex was in the year above me at school, the same as Theo. He was actually one of Theo's best friends and had helped me get the job at the pharmacy. I wondered if

Theo had ever mentioned my crush on Declan to him.

Which reminded me, I still had to talk to Theo about the night before. I had to give him an explanation for what had happened—although I wasn't quite sure what that explanation would be.

"Have you talked to Theo today?" I asked Alex.

He looked confused at my abrupt subject change. "Briefly this morning."

"Did he say anything to you?"

"Yeah, he said things to me."

"About *me*," I said impatiently.

"What would he say about you?" Alex narrowed his eyes. "And what's this got to do with Declan Bell Jones asking for your number?"

"Nothing," I said. As I stacked Milk Duds boxes in neat formation, I explained to Alex what had happened with the soccer ball and why Declan had asked for my number. By the time I was done, he was wheezing from laughing so much.

"I wondered what'd happened to your glasses," he said. "You do get yourself into the most ridic situations."

He didn't know the half of it.

"Thanks a lot," I said, and he started cackling all over again.

From the back of the shop, where the prescriptions were dispensed, I heard Phil "harrumph" loudly. I looked back to see him watching us sternly. I turned to Alex, and we shared an oops-we're-in-trouble look, both of us trying to suppress more giggles.

When my shift was finally over, I picked up my phone with even more eagerness than usual. Libby had sent a stream of photos. Guy at the park. Guy chatting to an old man sitting on a bench ("Making friends!" Libby said). Guy doing pull-ups on the outdoor gym near the beach (I paused on that). Guy in the water (I paused on that even longer). Guy eating fries ("The best thing he's ever eaten" was the caption). Guy with one of those blood pressure test things wrapped around his arm.

Wait—what? I tapped out a frantic message.

WTF???

I convinced Melissa to do some tests. Just, you know, a standard physical.

What?!

I told her it was for a biology assignment.

Don't you think we should keep Guy away from her, you know, after last night?

It's no big deal. She just thinks he's your boyfriend. And you're a sex fiend, I told you. She was quite nice to him today, all things considered.

Just. Why?

It's not like I have my own lab. It was the closest thing I could get to running some tests.

He's not a science experiment

Okay but…he literally is? Anyway, Guy was up for it. We also did a physical down at the beach. Didn't you see those photos?

Oh I saw them

You're welcome.

Anyway, don't you want to know my highly scientific conclusion from all these tests?

…go on

The boy is fit. And healthy. In fact, he's perfect.

Yeah, we didn't need any tests to figure that out…

It's all still so weird. He's sweet though. When he's not talking about you. 😣 You should've seen at the beach. I had to stop him from stripping EVERYTHING off. People were staring.

I think we should have included "inhibitions" on your list of dream attributes.

"Declan Bell Jones already in your DMs?" Alex said.

I looked up at him. He was walking beside me, wheeling his bike next to him, on his way to Theo's. I was planning on getting changed out of my hideous polyester work uniform at home before meeting Libby and Guy at the park again. I felt giddy at the prospect.

"It's just Libby," I said, sliding my phone into my back pocket. My thoughts drifted back to the photo of Guy at the beach, his hair wet, his face grinning, looking shinier than the sun itself.

"A dollar for your thoughts?" Alex said.

I blinked. "A dollar! You're a big spender."

"Well, a penny doesn't make much sense, does it?" He scrunched up his freckled nose. "I mean, who even uses them?"

"Yeah, but you could have gone with, like, five cents."

"Alright, fine. Five cents for your thoughts." He

laughed. "It doesn't quite have the same ring to it, hey?"

"Nah," I said, returning his smile.

He nudged me with his hip. "So are you going to tell me what you were thinking that made you look like that, or do I actually have to pay you five cents?"

"What do you mean?" I asked.

He looked off into the distance, an exaggerated dreamy look on his face.

"I did *not* look like that," I said.

"You definitely did."

We walked on in silence for a minute. I thought about Guy again. About how he'd almost kissed me last night.

Would he try to kiss me again tonight?

"Hey, can I ask you something?" I said.

"Depends what it is," Alex said.

"How old were you when you had your first kiss?"

He let out a small huff of amusement. "With a guy or a girl?"

"Either."

"Well. My very first kiss was with Delilah Gadsby, in Year 7. At the soccer field after school one day." He kicked at a bit of gravel with his shoe. "I thought maybe I'd try liking girls at that point."

"And how was it?" I asked.

He gave me a wry smile. "I realized there was no point trying."

"Ah."

"My first kiss with a *guy*," he went on, affection on his face now, "was when I was fifteen. A boy I'd been talking to online. We met at the beach. Theo was convinced I was going to be murdered and insisted on coming along with me. This was when I was staying with him." Alex had lived with Theo and his dad for a while after he came out, because his own family had been pretty awful about it. They seemed to be doing better these days though. He was back at home, at least.

"And how was *that*?" I said.

Alex grinned. "The only thing that got murdered was my tonsils." He grew more serious. "It was kind of incredible, though...I guess *thrilling* would be the word for it. I felt like—like my veins had been charged with electricity. You know?"

I nodded, even though I didn't really know.

"I mean, I've had much better kisses since then," he said. "But none of them have felt quite like *that*."

"Wow," was all I could say.

He raised his eyebrow. "Why do you ask, anyway?"

"No reason," I said. My stomach fluttered nervously.

We were walking down my street by this stage, and were a couple of houses away from mine. I didn't register the footsteps behind us until a split second before I was lifted off the ground and spun around. I screamed. Then

I realized whose arms were holding me, and whose laugh was echoing in my ear.

Guy.

He put me down and placed his hands on my shoulders, steadying me on my feet. Alex was looking at us with his whole face opened wide. His eyes, his mouth—even his nostrils—looked shocked.

"I missed you," Guy was saying to me. Then he noticed Alex and nodded toward him. "Who's this guy? Is he bothering you?"

"No!" I said. "This is Alex. We work together. He's a friend of Theo's." Guy looked at me blankly. "You know, the guy you, er, met last night?"

"Ah, the short boy with the plastic bat."

"I wouldn't say short—"

"Katie, are you gonna introduce me to your...friend?" Alex had recovered slightly, but he was clearly burning with curiosity.

"Of course," I said. "Alex, meet Guy."

Guy reached out a hand for Alex to shake. "Kate's boyfriend," he added. I looked at him in surprise. We hadn't had *that* conversation.

Alex's mouth hung open again for a split second. Then he composed himself and took Guy's hand with a "nice to meet you." He turned to me, his eyes full of meaning—that meaning being, "*what the hell is happening???*"

Out loud he said, "You've been holding out on me, lady. Where've you been keeping this one?"

"Under her bed," Guy deadpanned.

A beat passed where no one seemed to know what to say.

Then I laughed. I hoped Alex wouldn't notice it was my fake customer service laugh. He apparently didn't, because he started laughing too, along with Guy.

That's when Libby reached us, out of breath.

"Sorry," she said between pants. "I told him. To wait. At the park."

I shot her a Look.

"I couldn't wait another moment," Guy said. "Every second without you was excruciating." He leaned down and kissed my forehead. I felt a blush spread to my neck and chest.

"Nice hanging out with you too," Libby said, pulling a face.

Guy laughed good-naturedly. "We had fun," he said. "I only wish Kate were there too."

I was about to suggest Libby take Guy back to the park so I could meet them there as we'd originally planned, when I heard a strangled scream from up the road.

We all turned in time to see Theo flying arse over chest through the air. He landed on the grass patch in front of his house with an "ooft," his bike lying at an odd angle in the gutter, the wheels spinning. He must have been aiming for his driveway and run into the concrete instead.

"Oh my god." I raced over to Theo, Alex close by my side. Guy and Libby trailed behind us.

Theo was gingerly lifting himself up with one arm and inspecting his other palm, which was grazed and muddy.

"Are you okay?!" I bent and reached out my hand—to touch him or help him stand, I'm not entirely sure. He shot me such a filthy look that I instinctively recoiled.

He brushed his hand against his shirt and let Alex help him up, shaking the hair out of his eyes with a toss of his head.

"I'm fine." He shrugged. "Few scrapes, no big deal." But I watched him wince as he put weight on his left foot.

He managed to stand up straighter when Guy reached us, and his face became guarded. It closed off even more when Guy slipped his arm around me and tugged me close.

"Uh—Theo, you uh, didn't properly meet Guy did you? So, um, meet Guy?"

"Kate's boyfriend," Guy added helpfully.

Theo's face was still, except for a muscle in his jaw, which was twitching wildly. His dimples were showing. They only showed when he was really happy or really annoyed. I somehow didn't think it was the former right now.

"Come on, Alex," he said. Alex threw a confused look in my direction but helped Theo turn around and limp away.

Libby reached us then, wheeling Alex's bike, which he'd dropped when Theo had crashed. I bent down to pick up Theo's own discarded bike and started pushing it toward his driveway.

"Just leave it," Theo said over his shoulder.

Now I was getting pissed off. I tossed his bike down with a little too much force and marched up to him, planting myself in front of him. I noticed Guy had started to follow me, but Libby had her hand on his arm, holding him back.

"Are we really not going to talk about this?" I said.

"I don't know what you mean." He was looking down, seeming determined not to make eye contact with me.

"I know last night was...a lot, but there's no need to act so huffy."

"I'm not huffy," he said, huffily.

I glanced at Alex, who Theo was still leaning on—although he was trying to make it seem casual, not like Alex was actually keeping him vertical. "Listen, about—about last night—Guy—"

I swallowed the rest of my sentence when Theo finally

caught my eyes with a look so sharp it (figuratively) stabbed me. "I really don't want to hear about last night and *Guy*," he said.

Now it was my turn to huff. "Well. That's great. Because I really don't need to explain myself to you." I folded my arms. The truth was I *had* wanted to explain things to Theo, but right now he was pushing every button marked "irritated" and "stubborn" with me.

His only response was another huff.

Alex cleared his throat. "Uh, guys, this seems kind of private so maybe you should, um, take this inside? I don't know what's going on but you obviously need to... talk amongst yourselves."

He untangled himself from under Theo's arm and slowly backed away to join Libby and Guy near the fence. Theo scowled and tried to move forward, but when he put weight on his left foot he winced.

"Here," I said, moving to the spot Alex had just vacated. Theo shrugged me off and tried to hobble forward again.

"Ugh, what is with you today?" I grabbed him again, slipping his arm around my shoulders and looping my own around his waist. "Since when are you such a—"

"Such a what?" he said, but he finally stopped resisting. We slowly made our way down the driveway toward his room.

"Such *a guy*."

I felt him stiffen. "Dunno if you've noticed, KC, but I've always been a guy."

I shook my head. "You're not a *guy*. You're...you're my people. At least, you usually are. Right now you're being really gross."

"What are you talking about?"

"You're being a dick to me. Because, what? You caught a boy in my room. You're basically slut-shaming me. I really thought you were more evolved than this."

"I'm not—it's not—*I am not slut-shaming you*," Theo sputtered. We had reached his door.

"But you're mad because I slept with Guy?" The thought flashed through my mind that I was being a little unfair. But right now I was too annoyed to care.

"You—" He froze with his hand midair, about to insert his key into the lock. It took him a moment to recover. He opened the door and steadied himself on the wall to shuffle inside, collapsing on his bed with a groan.

I sighed and knelt in front of him, rolling up his black work pants to examine his ankle. It was scratched up and a little swollen, but there were no bruises.

"Maybe we should take you to the hospital," I said, glancing up at him.

"No!" Theo was even less enthused about hospitals than I was. Our eyes locked, and the expression on his face—the pain there—made me pause. It wasn't about his ankle. I knew he was remembering. Like I was. All those days at the hospital. We'd go there after school to see his mum. She was too sick a lot of the time to do or say much. But we'd tell her about our day or play a game to try and distract her. To try and distract ourselves.

If it was the worst time of my life, it was at least a hundred times worse for Theo.

We didn't talk about it anymore.

About her.

"Your feet stink," I said, snapping us both out of the moment. I stood up and went into his bathroom, searching the drawers for a first aid kit. I knew there was one in here—it was one of Theo's dad's conditions of him moving into this room. He had to have everything he needed, even if the main house was locked up/on fire/flooded/ whatever other emergency might occur.

I knelt back down, dabbing iodine on his grazes. He cried out in pain.

"You're such a baby," I said. But I tried to be gentle as I applied bandages.

"You really slept with him?" Theo said quietly after a moment.

I yanked the bandage a little too tightly. "Why do you care?"

He didn't answer me straightaway. I looked at his face and saw he was chewing on his words, thinking carefully about what came out of his mouth next. "It's... I don't care, KC. Not like that. I just—I got angry because... because you made this big deal about never even kissing a guy, and then within a few hours I find—well, that you've obviously gone much further than *kissing*."

I stood up. "Right. And tell me again how this isn't slut-shaming?"

He let out a frustrated noise. "It's not coming out right." He ran a hand through his hair. "You know I'm no good with words."

The dejection in his voice relieved some of my irritation. "Try again," I said gently.

Theo sighed and looked me in the eyes. "It's not...it's not the idea of you, uh, having sex that bothers me." He swallowed. "It's the fact that you *lied* about it. It's...it's just not like you. I mean, you said it before, KC. You're my people. I thought you could tell me anything. But it turns out you're hiding this pretty freaking huge thing from me. And I'm not just talking about that guy's height." His mouth softened into a sardonic smile, and I could feel myself softening along with it.

"It's not what you think. Not even close," I said.

He shot me a questioning look.

I hesitated for a moment, weighing up how much I should tell him—*what* I should tell him—but then I thought, *he's right*. I could tell him anything.

So I did.

When I was done with the story, he just stared at me. I was sitting beside him on the bed now, and I nudged him.

"Say something. Please."

Theo was shaking his head. "You know, if you don't want to be friends anymore—"

"What? No! Why would you say that?"

"I thought you were going to tell me the truth. Instead I get some bullshit story about *creating a guy* from clay and some magic potion Libby cooked up in the kitchen?"

"It's the truth! Here, I'll prove it." I pulled out my phone and messaged Libby.

You kind of forgot about me there didn't you? Left me and Guy and Alex hanging.

I didn't mean to!

It's fine, just fine. Alex decided to head home rather than wait around for you two to sort out your drama, so I was stuck there with Guy thinking, What the hell do I do now, just hang around in this driveway waiting for Katie? *Then one of Theo's sisters—the oldest one, Sophia—arrived home and was like "Uh, why are you just hanging around in our driveway?" It wasn't awkward at all.*

Oh come on, I know for a fact she invited you in for tea. It wasn't that bad.

Sure. Keep telling yourself that.

Anyway, I messaged Libby to join us. When she appeared with Guy in tow, Theo immediately pushed himself off the bed, putting his weight on his non-injured foot. He tugged at his shirt before puffing out his chest and crossing his arms. I almost laughed—until Guy rushed over to me, basically crash-tackling me back onto the bed.

"I was getting worried," he said.

I struggled out from underneath him, pushing my broken glasses back on my face and smoothing out my hair with a nervous laugh. Guy's arm was still circled around my waist. Theo was looking down at us. He did not seem impressed.

"KC tells me she made you in a mixing bowl," he said to Guy.

"I thought you didn't want to tell anyone," Libby said, frowning.

"It's just Theo," I said.

"Who is KC?" Guy broke in.

Theo shot me a triumphant look.

"Ah, that's me," I told Guy. "That's just what Theo calls me. It's my initials, you know."

"Ah." Guy smiled, his arm moving from my waist to my shoulder, which he gave a little squeeze. "Then yes, the information you have is correct," he said to Theo.

"Although the mixing bowl was only part of it, as I understand it. I..." As Guy blabbered on, Theo stared at me, his face looking more alarmed by the second.

"Guys—what is this?" he finally said, looking around his room. "Have you got a hidden camera around here? Did you decide to start a prank channel or something?"

"Look, what's more believable?" I said. "That we created this guy, or that he's actually some random tall, blond, handsome stranger who is suddenly interested in me?"

Theo didn't say anything for a moment. He looked from Guy to me, taking us both in. Then, with a smirk, he said "Fair point."

I stuck my tongue out at him and he laughed. "Hey, you said it."

"Show him the belly button!" Libby said.

I asked Guy to stand up and show Theo the smooth skin where his belly button should be.

Theo bent over to take a closer look, then glanced up at Guy. "Can I?" He gestured to his midriff.

"Go ahead, short boy," Guy said cheerfully.

"The name's Theo," he mumbled as he reached out to touch Guy's stomach. He stood up straight, his eyes full of something approaching wonder. He tugged at his shirt again. "I can't believe this."

"But you do, right?" I said, getting excited now. "You have to."

"Yeah," Libby said. "Because we need you."

"You need me?" Theo said,

"We do?" I said.

Libby looked at both of us and then flicked her gaze from Guy to Theo's bed.

"I've just had a brilliant idea."

"Libby, you're a genius," I said as what she was suggesting dawned on me.

"I know," she said.

"Are you guys going to enlighten me anytime soon, or what?"

"Theo," Libby said, gesturing at Guy with a flourish. "Meet your new roommate."

Theo shook his head and raised his hands as if to defend himself from a physical attack. "Uh-uh. No way. Not gonna happen. Don't even. You won't talk me into it."

VII

can't believe you talked me into this," Theo muttered as I settled into the bed next to him.

I laughed. The truth was it hadn't taken much to convince Theo to let Guy crash at his place (at least until we figured out a more long-term solution). Oh, he grumbled about it, sure, but he couldn't deny the logic of the plan. With his room separated from the main house, it was the perfect hiding spot for Guy. And, if he needed to, there was a good chance he could convince his dad to let his "new school friend" Guy stay for a while because of all the trouble he was having at home. We'd concocted a story about Guy's parents kicking him out because he'd dropped out of school. It was the best we could come up with, without making Guy seem like someone you wouldn't want in your home. I'd wanted to make the cover more elaborate—there were car accidents and abusive foster parents involved—but Libby and Theo had agreed it was better to keep it as simple as possible. I just hoped it would be enough to convince Theo's dad, when it came to it...although he'd let Alex stay before without much fuss. Both the Papadopoulos men were suckers for strays.

"Dad hasn't been around much lately, anyway," Theo said.

"Oh really? How come?"

"Oh...he's just been busy with work and stuff, you know."

"Well, that's handy for us," I said. Theo gave a small shrug.

The harder task was convincing Guy.

"But I don't want to be away from you," he'd said to me, pulling me close to him, a full-on pout shaping his perfect lips. They were so pretty I got distracted for a moment, thinking about what it would actually be like to kiss them.

I was broken out of my reverie by a snort from Theo. "I know you forgot to give him a belly button, but is there anything else missing?" He was lying behind us on the bed, pressing an ice pack into his ankle. "Like, you know, some balls?"

"Actually—" Guy started to say, but I interrupted him before he could get any more out.

"Real mature, Theo."

"He does have a point, though," Libby piped up from

where she was crouched on the floor, flipping through Theo's collection of vinyl records. He was obsessed with them. He liked anything old and musty.

"What?"

"We really need to teach Guy the difference between 'co' and 'in.'"

"I know the difference," Guy said. "'Co' means joint, while 'in' means to be enclosed—"

"Uh, that's not what I meant," Libby said. "I was more thinking about what happens when you combine each of them with the word 'dependence'?"

"...co-dependence and independence?" Guy asked with a tilt of his head.

"Nailed it!" Libby said, and Guy gave her a gratified smile. "See, the thing is, adding 'co' makes dependence bad, while the 'in' turns it into something very good. Comprendé?"

"Oh, I don't speak Spanish," Guy said.

"She means you two need some space," Theo cut in, looking pointedly at where Guy's arm was still wrapped around my shoulder.

"We've had space all day," I said at the same time as Guy said, "Why would I want space from Kate?" He nuzzled into my neck as if to reinforce his point.

Theo exhaled. "Right. Rule number one. If you're gonna stay here: no PDA in my room."

"PDA?" Guy asked, not taking his eyes off me.

"Public displays of affection."

Guy finally turned to Theo, who was looking at him like he was a pitiful thing.

Theo shook his head. "It's alright, bro, just stick with me. I'll teach you everything you need to know."

I suddenly had a very bad feeling about this whole plan.

"You know," I said. "Maybe...I should stay here? Just for tonight. Just to, um, ease the transition?"

"Ugh, you're as bad as he is," Libby said, at the same time as Guy exclaimed, "Yes! Stay here. Stay with me."

I turned to Theo, giving him my most winning look. I even batted my eyelashes. Or, well, I blinked rapidly. That's what batting your eyelashes is, right? I've never quite figured it out.

Theo sighed. "Should I even bother trying to say no?"

As Libby and I left Theo's—she was heading home, while I was going to grab my pajamas (a cute paisley print shorts-and-singlet combo, rather than my scraggly old nighty this time)—she looped her arm through mine.

"What a day, huh?"

"You can say that again."

"What a day, huh?"

I shook my head at her terrible joke, but laughed anyway.

"I've been thinking, we should try again."

"What?" I said.

"You need to repeat experiments in order to verify the results. So we should—"

"What?! Libby, we're barely managing to contain our first *experiment* right now. Maybe we should cool it on the science for a little while and just, you know, try to make it through this?"

She pulled a face. "Just because all you care about is getting his tongue down your throat—"

"Hey, that's not fair." I smirked. "I want to get my tongue down his too."

Libby made a disgusted noise, then said, "But just think about the possibilities, Katie. This is perhaps the greatest discovery in human history."

"Mmmm. Perhaps. Or maybe it was just a freak accident." We stopped at my front gate and faced each other.

"Do you know how many important discoveries started out as freak accidents?" She waved her arms around as she talked. "Penicillin, microwaves...Viagra!"

"Isn't that more of an *impotent* discovery?" I cracked up laughing, but Libby was on too much of a science rant to even notice my joke.

"That's why we need to repeat the experiment! To prove it's viable."

I nudged her foot with mine to bring her focus back to me. "I just think we need to lie low for a little while, you know? Play it safe."

Libby chewed her lip but didn't respond.

"First things first," I said. "What are we gonna do with our large son in there?"

"You really need to stop talking about him like that. It's gonna get hella awkward when you finally get around to the whole tongues-down-throats situation."

"I can't help it if I simultaneously want to protect him from the world and, like, jump his bones. Don't you?"

"I definitely, absolutely, 100 percent do not want to jump his bones," she said. I felt a weird sense of relief. I guess I hadn't admitted it—even to myself—but a part of me had been wondering how she felt about Guy, and the whole situation...especially how interested he was in me. I mean, I knew Libby had Michael. But Guy... Guy was *perfect*. How could you *not* want to jump his bones?

"I do get the protective thing, though," Libby went on. "He's just so...soft. On the inside, at least."

I grabbed her hand. "We must protect him at all costs."

She sighed. "This world is gonna break him."

"Not if we can help it," I said. "So, tomorrow? Let's

work out a proper plan for him? Besides hiding him in Theo's room, I mean."

Libby pulled a face. "I'm supposed to be hanging out with Michael tomorrow. I could cancel, though."

"No, no, it'll be okay. Let's chat when you're done."

"Alright. Wonder Boy is all yours for the day. Have fun." She gave my shoulder a light punch and started walking away.

I couldn't help one last tease. "You want to create more, but you can't even be present for our firstborn!"

She spun around, walking backward for a few steps. "Have fun necking that firstborn!" She made retching noises as she turned back around.

Telling Mum I was staying at Theo's for the night wasn't as simple as I had anticipated.

"You haven't slept over there in years," she said, narrowing her eyes.

"So?"

"So why are you tonight?"

"For old time's sake?"

Apparently I didn't sound very convincing.

"You and Theo—you're not—you aren't—you and Theo aren't getting up to any hanky-panky are you?"

"*Mum!*"

"Well?"

"*It's Theo.*"

"And? He's a handsome boy, even with all that extra weight. You know, I told his dad those antidepressants were a bad idea—"

"Mum," I rubbed my face, not even knowing where to begin with all the messed up things that were coming out of her mouth. I decided to go with the most messed up. "Those antidepressants weren't a bad idea. They helped him a lot."

She opened her mouth to say something in response, but I rushed on. "And his weight has got nothing to do with anything. God. I don't know why you're making this weird. Theo's a friend. We just wanted to hang out tonight. It's not that deep."

She studied my face. "Why do I get the feeling you're lying to me?"

Probably because I was. Gulp.

I dropped the bag I'd been stuffing my things into, preparing to lay it on thick. "Look. If it's that big a deal, I'll stay here. Theo and I were just talking about how we used to make blanket forts when we were younger. You know, when we wanted to feel safe? It made us all nostalgic or whatever. But I'll message and tell him you don't want me staying over there because I've got boobs now or something."

I felt a little bit guilty when I noticed the emotional

look on Mum's face. I knew she was probably thinking about why we used to build blanket forts so often. Why we were in such desperate need of a safe space.

That year, when we weren't at the hospital visiting Theo's Mum, we spent all our spare time building blanket forts in the back room at Theo's—what was now his room, but was then just a junk-room-turned-playroom. We'd lie in those blanket forts for hours, watching movies or music videos or playing games. Sometimes talking, but mostly not. Sometimes we'd just lie there holding hands.

Our blanket forts were the opposite of the stark, overwhelming, uncomfortable world of the hospital. They were ours. Something we could control. I wondered what had made me think of them in that moment.

"No, don't be silly. Go, go!" Mum waved her hands in the air. "Just be good."

I grinned and kissed her on the cheek, grabbing my stuff to head through the door.

"And make sure the doors and windows are all locked before you go to sleep!" she called after me.

"Mum, have you seen my blue gym shorts?" I heard Luke shout as the door clashed shut behind me. Considering Luke's gym shorts were currently on Guy, it seemed I'd escaped just in time.

When I got back to Theo's, I found him teaching Guy how to play *Grand Theft Auto*.

"Don't tell me I'm going to lose my boyfriend to video games before we've even kissed," I said, flopping down on the bed. Boyfriend. It felt weird to say that out loud. I remembered how surprised I'd been before when Guy had called himself that. We still hadn't talked about it. But what else was he?

Wow. I had a boyfriend.

I looked at Guy.

I had the hottest boyfriend in the world.

I pinched myself for about the fiftieth time in the last twenty-four hours. Just to be sure.

"We could kiss now, if you like?" Guy said, raising an eyebrow.

"No, no. *I* do not like," Theo said. "Remember our discussion about PDAs? Besides, now is clearly not the right time."

"What do you mean?" Guy asked. He was looking at Theo like he was the font of all wisdom.

This was not going to work in my favor.

"Hey, eyes on the game!" Theo said, and Guy turned back to the screen. Theo glanced at me and licked his lips. "Don't you know? Katie Camilleri's first kiss has to be *perfect*. The most romantic thing to ever happen. Like something out of a rom-com. Isn't that what you're, uh, here for?" He turned back to the game.

Guy was gazing at me thoughtfully.

I felt myself blushing.

"Quick, run over that old woman!" Theo cried.

It turned out to be a really fun night. Even though I would have much preferred some alone time with Guy, it felt unfair to kick Theo out of his own room. And at least it was better than trying to sneak Guy around my tiny house without my parents noticing and risking both of our figurative (maybe) deaths. Plus, it made me feel weirdly warm inside to see Guy and Theo getting along.

Theo decided it was his duty to get Guy to talk "properly." By which he meant totally improperly.

"Leave him alone, he talks fine," I said.

"He just needs some chill, alright?"

"My temperature is at a comfortable level," Guy chimed in.

Theo looked at me as if to say, *See?!*

"Alright, first lesson," Theo said. "Proper use of the word 'mate.'"

"Ah, mate. It means friend. Or sexual partner."

I nearly choked on the popcorn I was in the process of scarfing down, which made Theo laugh so much he snorted. Which made me laugh, which made Guy laugh.

Soon we just had to catch each other's eyes to start laughing all over again. My stomach began to hurt.

Were you all high or something? It's...not that funny?

I guess you had to be there.

Wow, way to make me feel included.

That's not what I meant! You know I was kidding.

Lol relax, so was I.

Oh, okay... It's just after everything with you and—

Wait, spoilers! We're not up to that part yet.

Oh, right. So anyway, by the end of the night Guy understood the fourteen different ways you can use the word "mate," depending on the circumstances.

Ha, yeah, like there's "mate?"

And "maaaaaaate."

"Mate. Mate. Mate."

Mate.

Ooh yeah, that one is really chilling.

It was all going great until bedtime, and the extreme awkwardness of trying to figure out who was going to sleep where.

Loooooooooool.

Theo has a queen bed, and then a couple of old beanbags, and there was a lot of back and forth about who should get the bed and who would be lumped with the beanbags.

Guy was practically glitching over his desire to be

close to me (still can't quite believe that's an actual sentence I'm writing) and his selflessness in not wanting to make either me *or* Theo uncomfortable.

We went 'round and 'round in circles until we finally agreed that Theo and I would share the bed while Guy took the beanbags.

"They're actually quite comfortable," Guy said as he rested his head on one beanbag and his feet on the other. His butt was on the floor.

"Maybe you should take the bed," I said, feeling guilty that he was spending his second night on Earth not much better off than his first night.

Theo groaned. "Don't start that again. Just go to sleep." He crawled under the covers, still wearing his shorts and a T-shirt. I popped into the bathroom to change into my PJs and wash up, leaving the sink running while I went to the toilet in the hopes that Guy wouldn't hear me peeing. I would have held it in if I possibly could, but I figured it would be more embarrassing to wet the bed in the middle of the night.

By the time I emerged from the bathroom, Guy was already asleep. I could tell by the way he was breathing. I guess his first full day of being alive had really taken it out of him. I tiptoed past him and slid into bed next to Theo, who grumbled and switched off his lamp.

"Thank you," I whispered to him in the dark, putting

my glasses on the bedside table and lying back on the pillow. It smelled strongly of Theo. Like mangoes and aftershave and that distinct *boy* smell, whatever that is. Probably sweat.

"You always help me when I need it," I continued. "I know I don't say it often, but it means a lot."

Theo was silent for a moment. "You do the same for me," he said. His whisper made his voice sound hoarse.

"And I'm sorry about before. About last night. All the confusion mess and everything...it's been a pretty wild twenty-four hours. My head's kind of all over the place, you know?"

He snorted. "Yeah. I know. It's okay, KC. It's been a big day. Just get some sleep."

I turned on my side to face him, clasping my hands together, and tucking them under the pillow. "Hey, do you remember when we used to build blanket forts in here?" My conversation with Mum earlier had brought up a lot of memories.

"Yeah." I couldn't really see him, but I could hear the smile in his voice. "Remember that one we left up for, like, six weeks?"

"It was forty-seven days. I kept a tally. We were trying to break some record, which I'm pretty sure didn't even exist."

Theo chuckled softly. "And then my dad came in and

cut it down while I was at school. I didn't talk to him for days after that."

"Poor Nick," I said. After a minute, I added, "I always felt so safe and cozy in those forts...I can't remember the last time I felt that way. Why did we stop building them?"

"I dunno, KC." Theo paused. "I guess we just grew up."

I didn't say anything after that. I was trying to remember the last blanket fort we'd built. I couldn't remember if it was before or after Theo's mum had died. That time was such a blur. We stopped hanging out here so much, in the after. Theo was spending more time at my house instead. My parents were practically overdosing him with affection and food and anything he wanted. Even my brother was sweet to him. His sisters would occasionally come around too. After the funeral, Theo's dad had gone straight back to work. He said he had to make up for all the time he'd had off caring for Ella.

I think they were all just desperately trying to escape this house. The loneliness of her missing presence, even though she hadn't been there for months anyway.

I rolled on my back, stretching out my legs, and my toes grazed Theo's hairy calf. He moved it away immediately, as if my touch had burned.

"Good night," he said, and rolled to face the wall.

"Night," I replied. If Theo noticed the crack in my voice, he didn't say anything.

I glanced toward Guy. I could just make out his outline in the dim moonlight. He seemed to still be sleeping soundly. I wondered if he dreamed.

VIII

"Pwoar, KC, did you murder a small animal in the night?" Theo's voice jolted me awake.

"Wha—" It took me a moment to realize where I was—*who I was*—as I took in the vintage posters on the wall in front of me and felt Theo shift beside me.

Theo.

And then I realized what he had said. I flipped to face him. "What?!"

"I forgot how much you fart in the morning," Theo said loudly, projecting his voice as though he was on stage. "You really should get your tummy checked. It can't be healthy."

"*Shut up!*" I hissed. "It wasn't me and you know it!" I scrambled for my glasses and check to see if Guy was still sleeping. Theo was busy killing himself laughing.

I got my glasses on just in time to see Guy's grinning face as he dive-bombed onto the bed, bellowing "good morning" and landing across my legs. He rolled so he was in between Theo and me. That was enough to sober Theo up. He coughed and sat up.

"No worries mate, make yourself at home," he said.

"Are you mad?" Guy said, his face falling. "The inflection of the word 'mate' indicates you're not happy with me."

"Shouldn't have taught him that, hey?"

Theo looked down at me and maybe it was the absurdity of the whole situation—wait, no, it was *definitely* that—but I started laughing.

Theo's mouth twitched. I could see he was trying to hold in a laugh too. Next to me, Guy snuggled into my shoulder and said "I love the way you laugh."

Theo turned away then and made a move to get out of bed, but not before—

"Er, am I interrupting?"

We all turned to see Alex standing by the door, keys dangling from his hand, a bemused look on his face.

Theo scrambled out of bed while I quickly sat up. Guy didn't move, although he did wave at Alex and say a bright "good morning."

He must have got his morning cheerfulness from Libby's side of the family.

"I don't know what you're thinking, but whatever it is, it's not that," I said to Alex.

"I'll bet."

"Bro. You don't even wanna know," Theo said as he walked toward the bathroom. He closed the door before he heard Alex's answer.

"Okay, but I definitely do."

🎨

Coast is clear, I texted Theo. I was back at home, and had been practically bursting out of my skin waiting for my family to leave the house so Guy could come around. I'd left him "jamming" with Theo and Alex, which mainly involved Theo playing his saxophone and Alex playing his guitar while Guy enthusiastically clapped for both of them. Alex had been shocked when we'd told him our cover story about why Guy was staying at Theo's.

"Jeez, and I thought my parents were bad," he'd said. I was relieved he'd bought the story. Or at least he'd seemed to.

Meanwhile, I'd been killing time by texting Libby. The problem was, she wasn't writing back.

The conversation was 100 percent one-sided and looked a little like this:

> How's your date going?

> Are you too busy kissing Michael to respond?

> Do you think it's weird that Guy and I still haven't kissed yet?

> I mean, he was basically literally created to kiss me and it's been over a day and we still haven't?

> ...Is there something wrong with me?

> I really am a freak, aren't I?

> Libby can you stop kissing Michael for five minutes and help me through this crisis?

> Hello?!

Eventually I gave up and decided to stress-bake. I had my head stuck in the pantry when I heard the back door slide open. I smiled and turned, expecting to see all three guys walking through. But it was just one guy. *The* Guy.

My heart lost its rhythm as he smiled his golden smile at me.

"Hey, gorgeous," he said. I touched my broken glasses self-consciously, suddenly wishing the jeans-and-a-nice-top outfit I'd spent half an hour agonizing over was more glamorous.

Guy himself was wearing fresh clothes (finally). He

had on a pair of jeans that Theo had said he'd bought at a thrift store, intending to chop them up along with another pair of jeans that didn't fit him anymore to create a custom pair. He was always doing weird stuff like that with old clothes. He told me once he could never find what he liked that actually fit him, so he had to get creative. But I didn't quite buy that. He'd always loved playing around with his style, even when we were little kids. Like the six-month period when he wore bow ties with every outfit—including T-shirts and yes, even his pajamas. He'd go with his mum every other weekend to find new ones, and they'd get milkshakes together afterward. I suspected part of his passion for all things vintage these days was a way to feel close to her still.

So there Guy was in Theo's reject jeans, looking like he'd stepped off some kind of runway. They fit him perfectly. And I mean *perfectly*. They hugged his hips and thighs tightly...and don't even get me started on his butt. Theo had also given Guy a shirt to wear. It looked like it was from the 80s, with what my mum would call a "funky" print. It was loose on Guy, but he—or, I guess, Theo—had tucked it into his jeans, rolled up the sleeves to show off his biceps/triceps/whatever the hell else those muscles are up there, and left the buttons undone down to his chest, allowing a bit of man cleavage to peek through.

It shouldn't have looked as good as it did.

But hoo, boy, did it look good.

Thank you, Theo. If his music dreams fell through, he could definitely have a successful career as a stylist. I made a mental note to tell him so later.

For now, though, my mind was dedicated to Guy.

Who I was finally alone with.

Who was looking at me with a soft eyes and a smile playing on his lips.

I moved toward him, my heart racing in my chest. Max beat me to him, shaking and yelping with excitement, his tail wagging faster than I'd ever seen it wag before.

"Whoa, he really loves you."

"Aw, I really love *him*," Guy said in this baby voice that just about made my heart burst. Guy looked up at me over Max's furry head, and the warmth in his eyes made my heart actually stop for a moment.

Your poor old heart is getting quite the workout here. Beating out of rhythm, racing, bursting, STOPPING altogether.

What can I say? It's the Guy effect.

It's just getting a little repetitive is all.

Oh, I'm sorry. Would you like me to describe the way he was affecting other areas of my body?

On second thought…stick to your heart.

Guy and I were making cupcakes—

Oh! You've skipped ahead. Good job, you're learning.

—and it was like something out of a rom-com. Cheesier

than the cheese boards Mum puts together whenever her friends come around.

Max was safely tucked away in the corner with a KONG toy full of peanut butter. It seemed that even Guy wasn't strong enough to tempt him away from his one true love (that'd be the peanut butter).

I was showing Guy how to stir the cupcake batter when I turned the electric mixer on too fast and a cloud of flour puffed up from the bowl right into our faces.

We both broke into giggles. Guy reached up to wipe my face, and our laughter subsided as his thumb gently and slowly moved along my cheekbone. I don't know that he was actually getting any of the flour off—but in that moment, I didn't particularly care.

My breath was shallow.

My skin was on fire.

Is this it? I thought. *Oh my god, this is it.*

It was everything I'd been dreaming of. I'd been waiting for this moment my whole life. I suddenly understood that movie effect where the person is still but everything around them moves and shifts very rapidly. That's exactly how I felt. It was absolutely surreal.

I tried to ignore the nerves making my stomach bubble and fizz.

Guy leaned in. I closed my eyes.

And—

And—

And—

Come on Libby, I set that up perfectly. The one time I want you to interrupt me and you're not even paying attention.

Sorry, I couldn't focus, you lost me somewhere in that puff of flour.

Let's try again.

Guy leaned in. I closed my eyes.

And—

And—

AND I KNOCKED ON THE FRONT DOOR AND INTER-RUPTED THE WHOLE THING.

That's what you wanted me to say, right?

Because that's what happened.

YES. See, for once your interrupting fits *into* the narrative!

Glad to know I'm good for something.

You know you're good for many things.

"What are you doing here?" I said.

"Good to see you too," Libby said, pushing past me into the house and flopping down on the lounge. Guy waved at her from the kitchen with a flour-covered hand.

"I thought you had a date with Michael?" I said.

Libby didn't answer me. She had her head low as she

bent to pet Max, who'd gotten up to greet her. I returned to Guy's side, nudging him with my hip.

"Did a flour bomb explode in here or something?" Libby said a few minutes later when she joined us in the kitchen. She rubbed at her eyes.

I giggled. "Uh, no, we were just...making cupcakes." Guy and I looked at each other, and I could feel the goofy grin on my face matching the one on his own.

"Right," Libby said. She walked to the sink and splashed cold water on her face.

"Are you hot, Libby?" Guy said.

"No," she said from where she was still leaning over the sink. Her voice sounded strained.

"You got hay fever or something?" I asked her as I held up the batter-covered wooden spoon to Guy's lips. "Here, try this," I said to him with a smile.

His eyes widened as his mouth enveloped the spoon. "That," he said, licking his lips, "is the best thing I've ever eaten."

Libby cleared her throat. "Katie, could I, um, could I talk to you for a sec?"

"Yeah," I said, not looking away from Guy. From Guy's lips, in particular.

"*In private?*" Libby added.

I tore my gaze away. "Huh?"

Libby raised her eyebrows at me and turned to walk out of the kitchen.

"Guess I better see what she wants," I whispered to Guy, and he winked at me.

As soon as we were in my room, I grabbed Libby's arm. "Oh my god, we almost kissed! I think it might be finally going to happen. Today. I'm going to be kissed by the end of the day! But what if I'm terrible? Oh my god, how do you even kiss someone? I mean, I've thought about it before. A lot. I even looked up tutorials on You-Tube. But that doesn't mean I can do it. What if I suck? What if after one kiss he decides I'm not worth the effort? What do we do with him then? Should we—"

"Oh my god, shut up," Libby broke in, disrupting my word vomit. She was staring at my wall. It was covered with prints from some of my favorite artists, quotes that I loved, and a couple of sketches I'd done myself. I'd put them up mostly to remind myself of how far I had to go.

"I—what?" Libby's outburst took me by surprise; I waited for her to break the tension with a joke.

But she just shook her head. "Sometimes I really don't get you."

"What do you mean?"

"It's funny," she said, in a tone that indicated nothing was remotely funny. She brushed her fingers over a sketch of the two of us that I'd based off a photo taken when we were in Year 2. We were both eating rainbow popsicles and Libby was doing bunny ears behind my head. We were grinning, half-toothless, and happy. "You always go on about how nothing you do ever matches up to the picture you have in your head."

"Yeah," I said, not really sure where she was going with this. "It's like in my head I see Chanel, but when I try to put that on paper all I get is the ninety-nine cent store."

Libby huffed and turned to me. "What about Guy?"

"What *about* Guy?"

"We created him. *You* created him. How does he match up to the picture you had in your head?"

I paused. I hadn't really thought of it like that. "He... he's so much better, actually. He's perfect."

Libby sat down on my bed. "See. All that striving for perfection, and you did it. You actually did it."

Did I? It was still hard to believe.

"I mean, Jesus. We created a person, Katie! An *actual human being*. But all you can think about is when he's going to take your mouth virginity."

I crossed my arms, the anger in her voice raising my defences. "What are you trying to say?"

She looked down. "Forget it."

"No, tell me. Is this why you wanted to talk? To make me feel guilty about wanting Guy to kiss me? I mean...

isn't that why we created him?"

Libby snorted. "*I* created him because I was trying to prove to you that the perfect guy—perfection in general—doesn't exist. That you have to let go of this ridiculous picture in your head and make the best of the reality." She shrugged, a bitter smile on her face. "Guess that backfired on me, didn't it?" Quieter, almost like she was just talking to herself, she said, "Why does everything have to be perfect?"

"Are you...why are you mad at me?"

She made a noise of disgust. "Not everything is about you, Katie, okay? You have no idea. You just have no idea."

"You're right," I said, trying to keep my voice even. "I have no idea what you're talking about right now."

Libby looked at me then with more anger than I'd ever seen her direct my away before. "How am I supposed to tell you now?"

"Tell me what?" I said, folding my arms.

She stood up. "Just—just kiss the guy already, okay? Then maybe we can talk about something else for a change."

"What—"

"Just kiss him!" She yelled again, throwing her hands in the air and walking toward the door.

"*That's* what you wanted to tell me?" I said.

But it was to an empty room.

IX

Guy was spooning cupcake mixture into a pan when I walked back into the kitchen. I was still shaken up by the whole exchange with Libby, but the sight of Guy was a soothing balm.

"Whatcha doing?" I asked as brightly as I could muster.

He looked up at me and smiled. "Ah. I wanted to finish this for you."

"How do you know how to do that?"

"You created me with a great many innate abilities."

"Like the ability to make cupcakes?" I asked.

He raised an eyebrow. "Like the ability to read." He gestured with his head toward the open recipe book.

"Oh."

"You might have to help me with the—the oven? I don't know how to..." He looked dubiously at the buttons.

After we'd put the cupcakes in to bake, we cleaned up, and I gotta say, it was the most fun I've ever had doing the dishes in my life. I never knew it could be so...hot. And I'm not talking about the water.

Guy kept looking at me, a smile playing across his lips that I can only describe as "seductive," even though it feels all kinds of wrong to say that. I could feel my face heating up.

I was torn between just wanting to kiss him already and the fact that standing at the kitchen sink, up to my elbows in dirty dishes, while Max rolled around at our feet was not exactly the first kiss I'd been dreaming of.

I cleared my throat. "So. Guy. Tell me about yourself."

"You already know everything about me." He raised an eyebrow. I tried to remember how to swallow.

"That can't be true," I said. "We've only know each other two days."

I realized as soon as I said it how ridiculous this conversation was. Something which Guy reinforced when he said, "Well, I have only been alive two days. About forty hours, to be exact."

I laughed nervously. "Well, when you put it like that..."

"And there's still so much for me to learn," Guy went on. "About myself. About the world. About you." He said the last bit extra softly.

I dropped the sponge I'd been using in the water.

"What do you want to know?" I said.

Guy was quiet for a moment, rubbing my dad's favorite "I Like Big Mugs And I Cannot Lie" cup with the tea towel. "Everything," he finally said. "I want to see and do and hear and feel it all. As much as I can."

"Oh. Is that all?" I said.

"All?"

"Never mind."

"I want to experience everything in the world." He put down the tea towel and turned his body toward me, putting a hand on my shoulder so I swiveled to face him too. "With you."

His hand traveled down my arm, and he took hold of my hand. Which was still encased in a bright orange rubber glove. I shuddered.

"You know what," I said. "Let's get out of here." I stepped away from Guy and peeled off the gloves, replacing them with an oven mitt. I checked the cupcakes and was glad to see they were ready. "I don't know if we can manage everything in the world just yet," I said as I took the cupcakes out of the oven. "But I can take you to one of the best places in this neighborhood, at least."

Guy was grinning. "Lead the way."

"Oh no, it's not me who'll be doing the leading." I looked down at Max. "Maxie. Wanna go walkies?"

Twenty minutes later the sound of Guy's laughter was filling the dog park as every dog in the place flocked to him. It was like he was the human version of catnip, but for dogs (dognip? Is that a thing?). He was lying on the ground, having been pushed there by the sheer force of about five dogs' love. They were smothering him in kisses, tails wagging furiously. Their owners were all looking at the huddle with a mixture of bewilderment, amusement, and admiration. The latter in particular was coming from a pretty girl who looked like she was about eighteen or nineteen. I'd seen her at the park a few times before but we'd never so much as exchanged a friendly nod.

"Frodo, down," she was saying, but she was laughing. "Frodo, come on, you're going to kill him." She reached down to pull her poodle away from Guy's face.

He sat up, smiling, and looked at her with one eye shut against the glare of the sun.

"There are worse ways to die," he said. He was looking down at the dogs again, but the girl didn't take her eyes off him. Irritation bubbled in my chest. I felt like I was watching a meet-cute. She opened her mouth to say something.

"Babe," I broke in. The word felt foreign in my mouth. Guy looked up at me, and the girl turned around, an expression on her face that suggested she was surprised to see me standing right next to her. Like she hadn't even noticed me before.

"Let's take Max down to the beach," I said. "It's a little

crowded here." I looked pointedly at the girl, and her gaze shifted between me and Guy, her face screwed up as if she was doing a hard math equation.

Guy bounced up, his hair bouncing with him, catching the afternoon sun and looking more golden than ever. He really was breathtaking. I wondered what people thought when they saw him next to me. That girl had clearly not been impressed.

As we walked along the beach, Max bounding around our feet, Guy's big hand enveloping mine, a contented smile on his face, I couldn't help but catch the double takes of people as we passed.

What were they thinking? *"Wow, they look so cute?"* or *"Um, what's he doing with her?"*

I had a feeling I knew what the answer was. And I didn't like it one bit.

A splash of water hit my knees, jolting me out of my brooding. I gasped and turned to see Guy grinning at me, his tongue poking out between his teeth, a mischievous glint in his eyes.

"You—!"

It was on now. I pulled my hand from his and kicked water at him. He tossed his head back in laughter and began to chase after me as I squealed and ran away. There was water going everywhere, not helped by the fact that Max was running in and out of the waves, too, barking at all the excitement. Guy quickly caught up to me, lifting me off the ground, and swinging me around with ease. He placed me down carefully, but I still managed to lose my balance, landing firmly on my butt in the shallow water with a strangled scream. Guy bent down to help me up, and I took my shot. I lifted both of my hands through the water with as much force as I could.

"Plergh!" he cried, straightening reflexively as he was hit in the face with saltwater—and a big hunk of seaweed.

Whoops.

"Oh my god, I'm so sorry," I said, scrambling to my feet, but I was still giggling.

Guy plucked the seaweed off his head and said, "You know, if you preferred me with green hair, you could have made me that way." He dropped the seaweed and reached for me again. I shrieked and darted out of the way, running up the beach away from the water. I flopped down on the sand. I was soaked and breathing heavily. Guy lay down next to me and Max circled us a couple of times before sitting down near our feet, his face turned toward the ocean.

Guy's eyes locked on mine. We were silent for a moment, taking each other in. With the sun drying and warming my skin, the sound of the waves swirling around me, the taste of saltwater on my lips, the smell of the ocean everywhere, and Guy's summer-day eyes staring at me—I felt absolutely, completely content.

Of course I had to go on and ruin the moment by opening my mouth.

"Guy. Do you...do you really like me?" I cringed as soon as the words were out of my mouth. *Way to sound seven years old, Katie.*

"Kate." His lips twitched. "Of course I like you." He rolled on his side and propped himself up on his elbow. "I like you so much."

I could have left it there. I should have left it there.

But I didn't.

"But, like...*why* do you like me?" I played with a tassel on my top and stared up at the sky. I couldn't look at him directly.

"Why do I like you?" He laughed. "What kind of question is that? You may as well ask me why I need air to breathe. It's a part of me. A part of who I am. I exist, therefore, I like you."

It sounded romantic as hell.

So why did I feel so...disappointed?

Instead of saying "thank you" or something sweet back, the next thing that came out of my mouth, all in a rush, was, "Why haven't you kissed me yet?"

I dared a peek at his face and saw that he was moving in closer. *Oh!*

Suddenly he was over me, holding himself there with a hand on either side of my shoulders. He leaned in close, so close I could feel his breath on my face. So close that all I could see was him.

He was beautiful. *What did I look like to him?* The thought made my turn my face away.

I felt his hand under my chin. Gently, he shifted my head back toward him. He was holding himself up with one arm now.

He was so strong.

He traced his thumb along my bottom lip.

I stopped breathing.

"Do you...want me to kiss you?" he said softly. "Here? Now?"

I didn't get a chance to answer, because a large, wet tongue slobbered its way across my face, hitting me right in the eyeball.

"Eugh! Max!"

Max had shoved his head between Guy and me and was busy twisting it this way and that, licking both of us.

Guy rolled away and Max was on top of him now, not letting up on the face-licking. I sat up and tried to wipe some of the slobber on my face, but it retained that sticky licked texture. The moment was officially gone.

"Well." I sighed. "How about an ice cream?"

Five minutes later, we were sat on the brick wall in

front of the kiosk. Guy was swinging his long legs back and forth contentedly. "Now this," he said, around a mouthful of ice cream and cookie crumbs. "This is the best thing I have ever eaten."

Theo took us in with an unimpressed frown on his face. "Have fun today?"

Guy and I looked at each other and giggled. Although we'd dried off, we were both still covered in sand, our clothes all rumpled. While the effect just made Guy look softer, even his hair had that perfect beach wave thing happening—I knew I probably looked pretty scary. I reached up to smooth down my hair and winced when I felt the wiry texture.

"Nup, rinse off first," Theo said when I tried to step into his room. "Or I'll be finding sand in here for the next six years."

"What do you want us to do, hose ourselves down?" I scoffed.

"A hose-down would probably do you good," Theo said. I stuck my tongue out at him.

"Guy, you can jump in the shower I guess," Theo said, gesturing to the bathroom behind him and standing back to allow Guy to pass.

"KC, you can come back when you're sand-free. Maxie, you too. Sorry, buddy." Theo bent down to give Max a pat on the head, but Max was straining against his leash, trying to push past him to get to Guy, who had reappeared behind Theo, his shirt untucked and unbuttoned.

"You're not going, are you, Kate?"

"Yeah. She is." Theo's lips were pressed together, and his dimples were showing. "Don't worry, you'll see her again soon." He was pushing me backward.

"Wait," Guy said. He was right behind Theo now. He placed his hands on Theo's shoulders and leaned forward. Theo's head snapped toward him, his brows furrowed.

"Wh—"

"Kate," Guy said, ignoring Theo's presence even though he was literally in between us. "I want to kiss you. I really want to kiss you. But when I do, it will be when you are ready. It will be perfect. It will be everything you've dreamed of. I have it all planned out."

I let out a shaky breath. All thoughts had evacuated my brain. There was nothing I could say to that.

"I just thought you should know," Guy said.

Theo nodded. "Thank you for making me a part of this."

X

Katie.

Katie.

I have a question.

Yes?

How are we still only TWO DAYS into this story?

A lot happened in those two days, okay!

We've got to speed this thing up. Move things along.

How do you propose we do that? Should everything just be in bullet points from now on?

That's not a bad idea.

...Except it totally is.

No, try it! Think of it like a movie montage.

But this isn't a movie.

Just do iiiiiittt.

Fine. Cue the montage music! Something peppy and fun.

I've got just the thing.

Three...two...one:

Cut to: Guy hanging out in Theo's room alone all

week while we were in school with nothing but books and Theo's laptop to keep him company (Theo taught him how to use the internet).

Cut to: Guy grinning and bouncing up to greet us when we got home each afternoon, regaling us with all the things he'd learned that day. The boy was fast and smart and fascinated by everything.

Cut to: Theo and me talking Guy through the trauma of the current state of the world and trying to stave off a mini existential crisis on the day he discovered Twitter.

Cut to: Libby acting totally fine the next time I saw her after her weird freak-out in my room, causing both of us to ignore what had happened and go back to normal. Except things weren't really normal, what with the whole Guy situation. And Libby was more eye-rolly and on edge than usual. I put it down to the aforementioned Guy situation, and decided if she wasn't going to talk to me about it, that was her problem.

Cut to: Theo, Libby, and me setting up a school of our own in Theo's room, drilling Guy with the proper way to talk/behave/dress. Or sometimes the improper way, if it was Theo doing the teaching.

Cut to: daily walks with Max and Guy, featuring lots of laughs and shared ice cream and hugs and Guy waving at the old man who always hung out on the bench near the entrance like he was now his best friend. Since

Guy had kinda taken the kiss thing off the table because of his grand romantic plan, I was able to relax much more in his company. Except when I remembered that I had no idea what his grand romantic plan was or how it might unfold—which only happened, oh, every ten minutes.

Cut to: Theo, Libby, and me taking Guy shopping. We went to a few thrift stores and then walked up to Kmart to get him "his own damn clothes," to quote Theo. We made him try on a lot of ridiculous things before forking over our (MY) hard-earned cash on some T-shirts/shorts/sweaters for him.

Okay, how's THAT for a montage?

I love it. Simple. Straight to the point. We'll actually be done with this thing before middle age!

But some things happened that week that don't fit into a montage and can't be told in neat bullet-point format.

I mean, I think it's given a pretty clear impression of what the week was all about: Guy. When we weren't with him, we were talking about him. YOU were talking about him. It was Guy, Guy, Guy.

I know, but there were things that happened that need expanding on!

Like what?

Why don't you just let me tell the story and you'll see?

Honestly Libby, you have no appreciation for my creative process.

I do! I appreciate it so much I want to make it better! More efficient!

Art isn't about efficiency.

Fine. Do it your way. I'll see you in fifty-four years when you're finally finished.

One thing that happened that week, among all the montaging, was that Theo's sister, Lena, busted Guy. Apparently she'd let herself into Theo's room to do her weekly dirty dish collection (gross) and SURPRISE, there was Guy, who we had thankfully just the day before taught about the importance of lying *when the situation required it*, e.g. whenever someone asked anything about him or his life or his general existence.

"But lying is bad," he'd said.

"Not all the time," I replied, wondering if I was a morally questionable person who was maybe, definitely going to hell. "Sometimes, it's okay. If it's to protect the people you care about."

Apparently the message sunk in enough that when Lena started screaming upon discovering the presence of this random in her brother's room, Guy managed to calm her down and tell her our cover story—that he was a friend of Theo's and he'd needed a place to stay. Which, actually, wasn't technically a lie.

When Theo, Libby, and I arrived at Theo's that afternoon, we were shocked to discover Guy missing from Theo's room. I was just about to start panicking when Lena appeared at the door and said, "You guys better come inside."

We walked into the kitchen and there was Guy, happily dunking a cookie into a cup of tea. He grinned and waved at us. "Kate, come, taste this! It's the best thing I've ever eaten."

Lena nudged my wide-open jaw shut.

"I've just been getting to know your not-so-little friend." She turned to Theo. "I think you've got some explaining to do."

Theo shrugged. He looked much, much calmer than I felt. Next to me, I could feel Libby practically vibrating with nervous energy.

"I'm sure Guy here explained everything." Theo looked pointedly at Guy. "Didn't you, mate?"

Guy nodded enthusiastically. "I told her exactly what you told me to say."

Lena's eyes narrowed. Theo let out a hollow laugh. "Which is the truth, obviously."

"Mmmhmmm. That doesn't shake out at all." Lena looked at Guy. "He's not some kind of criminal, is he?"

Guy was currently licking a piece of melted cookie from where it had fallen onto his forearm. He straightened up when he noticed everyone staring at him and smiled. There was chocolate smeared on his lips.

"Come off it. He just needs a place to stay for a little while. What's the big deal?"

Lena crossed her arms. "Have you even asked Dad? I know he gave you your own space but you can't just—"

"Isn't that for Dad to worry about? Why do you care?"

Lena mimed whacking Theo on the back of the head, but she didn't actually make contact.

"Well, at least this explains your appetite suddenly doubling in size. I wondered why you were sneaking so much food out there. You're fat enough as it is."

Theo's family were always making jokes about his weight. It made me cringe, but he didn't seem to mind. I mean, he usually gave back as good as he got. But today all he said was, "Come on, let's go out the back."

"Just you wait until Dad gets home!" Lena called after us.

I was at home helping my own dad make dinner when Theo's dad, Nick, arrived home from work, so I missed the big confrontation. Except apparently it wasn't such a big confrontation, in the end. Nick was way more chill about it than Lena had been—which wasn't that surprising, really.

Theo messaged me to say his dad had just kind of shrugged, asked how long Guy was staying for, and then went off to have a shower. Which set Lena off about how Theo gets away with everything—a complaint she's made at least, oh...6,074 times in her life. I got how she felt. I mean, Luke was allowed to do way more than I was—and sure, he was older, but it always felt like it was more because he was a boy. Somehow the sexism argument never convinced Mum though.

Still, this was one time I was really glad that Theo was the baby of his family and also a boy and his dad was past the point of caring much what Theo did.

Although there was something about that which seemed a little sad too.

The second noteworthy thing that happened that week—which actually came first, whoops—was that Declan Bell Jones and I hung out after school.

Yes, you read that right.

He made good on his promise to help me with my glasses. When I saw his message on Tuesday, asking if I was free that afternoon to sort it out, it almost made the first few days of mockery I'd endured over the shabby masking-taped state of my glasses feel worth it. Almost. (Even my friends had thought it was hilarious, especially when they heard the whole story of how it had happened.

My friend, Jordan, started calling me Harry Potter. I told
her she wasn't as clever as she thought she was, but she
laughed so much she got the hiccups.)

I was in geography when I got the message.

> Hey Harry Potter, meet me by
> the bike racks after school?

> I'm no Hermione but I think
> I can still help with those
> glasses.

> This is Declan, by the way.

I stared at the back of Declan's head as a dozen
questions exploded in my brain. Like, how had Jordan's
terrible joke made it all the way to him? Or had he
come up with it all on his own? The Hermione part was
original. Had he actually read Harry Potter? Or seen the
movies? Did we actually have something in common?

And why was he messaging me in class as opposed
to, I don't know, just turning around and talking to
me?

But then, did any of that even matter, considering
Declan Bell Jones was messaging me?

At least I could answer the last question: No, no
it did not matter. All that mattered was that DECLAN
BELL JONES was messaging me.

When I messaged him back with a "Hi!" and a

"sounds good!" (totally nonchalant and chill, right?) he turned around and actually smiled at me.

I nearly screamed right there in class.

For the rest of the day, all that went through my head was *meet me by the bike racks after school meet me by the bike racks after school meet me by the bike racks after school meet me by the bike racks after school—*

"What about Guy?" Libby asked when I told her to walk home without me because I was *meeting Declan Bell Jones at the bike racks after school.*

"What *about* Guy?" I tried to sound all casual, but a pang of guilt shot through me. The truth was, I'd barely given Guy a second thought since Declan Bell Jones had messaged me. Was I a terrible person?

"You're still into Declan Bell Jones even when you've got your very own walking, talking Ken doll at home?"

"We're just going to get my glasses fixed, it's not like we're going to dry hump in the parking lot."

Libby screwed up her face. "Gross."

"And there's no rule book that says it's a crime to have a crush, even if you have a boyfriend." It still felt really strange for me to say that. "Right?"

I was hoping Libby would reassure me, but she just shook her head. "Your thirst truly knows no bounds."

"I'll take that as a compliment," I said, more breezily than I felt.

Theo and Alex appeared in the throng of people pushing to get into the cage that enclosed the bike racks. Libby waved them toward us, and they both nodded in acknowledgement. Alex had his bike unlocked first, and he wheeled it our way.

"Heeeey," he said.

"Hey. Can you double me home?" Libby got straight to the point.

"Sure. You gonna ride with Theo, Katie? Katie?"

"What?" I said. I'd only been half-listening, my eyes scanning the crowd for Declan Bell Jones.

"What's happening?" Theo said as he wheeled his bike toward us.

"The girls wanna ride with us."

"Nope, just me," Libby said. "Katie has a hot date."

Theo frowned. "But Guy told me—"

"Shut up, there he is...," I said quietly.

Declan Bell Jones was walking toward us, moving slowly through the chaos around him like he didn't have a care in the world. He adjusted the strap of his backpack with one hand—the other was clutching his skateboard—and raised his chin in greeting as he approached.

How did he look so hot while doing the absolute bare minimum?

"Ready, Harry Potter?" he said to me.

I grinned and let out a high-pitched "Yes!"

I didn't look back as I walked away from my friends with Declan Bell Jones at my side, but I could feel their eyes practically shooting holes right through me.

"Jonesy! Slumming it today?" I heard someone call out as we walked past the basketball courts. I stared at the ground in front of me, not daring to raise my head. Suddenly the exhilaration I'd been feeling a moment earlier began leaking out of me.

"Piss off, Kiwi," Declan Bell Jones called back, but there was laughter in his voice.

Kiwi said something else, but I couldn't hear it over the roar of blood in my ears. I knew my face was bright red. I hastily pulled my hair out and ran my fingers through it before shaking it out so it fell in front of my face. Then I remembered Mikayla calling me Cousin Itt and reached up to tie it back again.

Beside me, Declan Bell Jones started whistling. He was the only person I knew who whistled as much as my grandpa, but his whistling made me feel *very* different things to my grandpa's. Especially the shape his lips made as he did it.

His whistling trailed off as he looked at me out of the corner of his eye. I realized I was staring.

"Oh!" I cried out, not entirely voluntarily. Crap. *Quick, think of something to say. Be cool.* "Um, how did you get the scar on your top lip?"

Real cool, Katie.

I know. In my defense, it was a question I'd been pondering for literally years.

Thankfully, Declan Bell Jones wasn't really fazed. He traced the outline of the scar with his index finger. I had the urge to follow its path with my tongue.

Ew, Katie.

I resisted!

Such willpower.

"This?" Declan said. "Hmmm. Do you want the cool story, or the truth?"

"Um...the cool story?"

Declan chuckled. "Well I went for a surf early one morning, right? The sun was just rising above the horizon, and everything was peaceful, you know?" He gestured in the air with one hand as he spoke. "Then I noticed this dolphin coming toward me. 'Sweet,' I said to myself. 'I've always wanted to surf with dolphins.' I could just see his fin cutting through the surface of the water."

"Oh no," I said.

"Oh *yes*," Declan raised his eyebrows and nodded. He was enjoying himself. It made me smile. "I paddled closer and you'll never guess what it was—well, you can probably guess—"

"Shark!" we both yelled at the same time. Declan laughed. "That's right," he said.

"So, what did you do?" I asked, making my voice sound breathless to fit his thrilling story.

"I headbutted it, of course." He shrugged, his shoulders adding an unspoken *no big deal.*

I laughed, and Declan let out a fake sigh. "Yep. That's how I ended up with this." He shook his head in pretend dismay, raising his finger to his scar again. "You should've seen the other guy though."

"The shark?"

"Yeah. Didn't even have a fin left by the time I was through with him. 'That's the last time you ever fool me!'" Declan was shaking his fist at the air now, as if the imaginary shark was hovering right in front of him.

I was laughing so hard I almost doubled over. When I looked up at Declan, he seemed quite proud of himself.

"Alright," I said when I had calmed down a bit. "That was a cool story. But what's the truth?"

Declan cocked an eyebrow. "Ohhh, you want the truth? Okay. I stopped this guy from robbing an old lady in front of the supermarket, and he elbowed me in the face."

I gasped. "No way!"

Declan looked at me for a moment, then his face broke into a grin again. "Nah, no way."

My mouth was wide open, and I let out a noise of disbelief. Declan chuckled. "You're too easy, Harry."

He took a couple of quick steps and dropped his

skateboard on the ground, landing on it in one smooth movement and then propelling himself forward with one leg. When he was a few houses away from me he turned around, a smile on his face as he circled back and right around me.

"Now that is cool," I said with a giggle.

Unlike you in this situation.

Shhhh.

"Nah," Declan said. "*This* is cool." And he took off again, this time doing something with the skateboard that involved flipping it and riding it along the gutter before twisting it in the air.

I clapped and Declan bowed, picking up his skateboard as he did. When he straightened, his face was red. It made him even more adorable.

I felt light for the rest of the walk.

It wasn't until later I realized he never did tell me how he got that scar.

Guy enveloped me in a bear hug the moment I stepped through Theo's door.

I heard Theo cry, "Victoryyyyy!" Guy had abandoned whatever game the two of them were playing, so I guess Theo had won by default.

"I missed you so much," Guy was saying as he squeezed me tighter and tighter.

"I can tell," I squeaked out.

He loosened his hold but didn't let go except to lift one hand to smooth hair back from my face. "Did you miss me?"

"Yeah. Did you miss him?" Theo chimed in. His tone was combative.

"Of course," I said to Guy, ignoring Theo. Guilt fluttered in my chest, but I squashed it down. I hadn't done anything wrong, I told myself. I got another flutter in response. "How was your day?"

As Guy rattled off the list of things he'd read and discovered online and eaten that day, I extracted myself from his arms and plopped myself down on the bed.

"See you got your glasses fixed then," Theo said, interrupting Guy's monologue.

"Yep," I said. "Good as new."

It hadn't taken long for my glasses to be fixed. In the end, I actually kind of wished it had taken longer. While we were waiting, Declan Bell Jones and I had wandered around the store, trying on all the hideous glasses we could find. Of course, he looked good in most of them. I looked ridiculous, especially when I tried on these big round ones that did nothing to dispel the "Harry Potter" nickname I had going. But it made Declan Bell

Jones laugh—*I* made Declan Bell Jones laugh. And not in an "at" me way, either. It was with me... *He* was with me.

At one point he'd asked me if I had ever considered contacts, and I told him about this article I'd read where a woman had a whole load of lenses stuck behind her eye and how that had scared me off them for life, and instead of being grossed out, he laughed again, and he...he told me I was *cute*.

I kid you not, he actually said, "You're cute."

"And how was Declan Bell Jones?" Theo said, cutting into my thoughts.

He thinks I'm cute.

"Who's Declan Bell Jones?" Guy said.

I shot Theo a look and composed my face before turning to Guy. "He's just a guy. From school. He, uh, broke my glasses on Friday so he paid to get them fixed." I sounded casual. Like it was no big deal. Because it wasn't. Right?

Except if it was no big deal, why had hanging out with Declan Bell Jones left me feeling so exhilarated? *And why had I still wanted to kiss him so much?*

Guy stiffened. "He broke your glasses? How? Are you okay?" His hands were on my face again.

"Yeah, of course. I'm fine. It was nothing. It was kind of my fault. I got in the way of...his soccer ball."

Guy frowned. "I don't like the sound of this Declan Bell Jones."

Theo snorted. "Yeah. Me either."

"Move over," I said to him, tired of the conversation and the confused emotions it was stirring within me. "It's my turn to play."

XI

U m, why is Mikayla Fitzsimmons walking this way?"
I looked over my shoulder to where my friend, Nat,
was staring with panicked eyes. Sure enough, there was
Mikayla, flanked by Emily and Olivia, heading across
the girls' quad...straight toward where we were sitting.
I turned back to my friends, who were all fiddling with
their lunches, trying to act casual, looking at anything
or anyone other than Mikayla and her friends. It was like
when you're a little kid and you believe that if you just
squeeze your eyes shut tight enough, the monsters in the
shadows of your room won't be able to see you, and they
might even disappear.

But Mikayla wasn't disappearing. She was still
headed our way.

"What is she doing?" Jordan muttered.

"I thought we were safe here," Libby whispered
sharply. We'd claimed our seat in the girls' quad because
it was quiet and leafy and nice to sit in...and also because

the likes of Mikayla Fitzsimmons would never be caught dead in here.

You didn't sit here if you were cool. You didn't even come within a ten-yard radius of the place if you were cool.

But Mikayla Fitzsimmons was here.

Like, *here* here. She had stopped right in front of us.

I looked up at her and gulped. I'm pretty sure you could hear it.

You definitely could.

You were also shitting it, Libby.

Not gonna lie. I totally was.

"Hey guys! What's up!" This too-bright greeting came from my friend Amina, who, bless her, was always nice to everyone. Even if they were the devil incarnate.

Mikayla ignored Amina and zeroed in on me. She took a step closer so she was looming above me, blocking my vision of basically anything else.

"Listen, hag," she said. She was speaking quietly, but it was somehow twenty-two times more intimidating than it would have been if she was yelling. "Just because you're a desperado, doesn't mean you can cozy up to other people's boyfriends."

She used desperado wrong, by the way. I would have said so at the time but I was trying really hard to follow my parents' "do not engage" directive.

And *I* would have said it at the time but...

a) I was trying to process what she was even talking about, and

b) I was also trying not to get murdered right there in the girls' quad.

"What?" was the only response I could come up with.

Around me, the air felt impossibly still. Like everyone was holding their breath.

We were.

"It's so sad you'll never get a boyfriend of your own, but it's even sadder to try and take mine. I mean, it'd be funny if it wasn't so pathetic." Mikayla exchanged looks with Emily and Olivia, and they sniggered on cue.

I stared at Mikayla, trying to figure out what she was talking about. Then I realized. Of course. Declan Bell Jones. So they were actually together now? *Together* together? And I had hung out with him the day before. Oh sh—

"I didn't! I mean, I wasn't. We just—it was nothing. You have to know that, Mikayla." I was babbling, and hating myself more and more by the second. "Besides, I have a boyfriend!"

Mikayla snorted. "Yeah, right."

"It's true!" Jordan said. "She does."

In that moment, Jordan had no idea about Guy. She was lying out of her butt. I loved her for it.

"Oh yeah? Where is he then?" Mikayla said.

"He doesn't go to this school," I said. "He's...new. In town. He's new in town."

Olivia scoffed. "Let me guess, his name is George? George Glass?"

Mikayla looked at her sharply.

"You know, like from *Brady Bu*—uh, never mind," Olivia said. She looked down.

Mikayla turned back to me. I laughed nervously. "His name is Guy, actually."

"Yeah, and he's really hot." This was Jordan again. Bless her and her big mouth. She didn't know it, but she was telling the truth.

Mikayla laughed. "You guys really are tragic. Look, it's not like Declan is ever going to be interested in you anyway. It's just annoying to try and scrub the stench of loser off him after you've been near."

She reached down and picked up Nat's chocolate milk. Looking me dead in the eyes, she took three big gulps of it, finishing it off and crushing the empty carton in her hand. She had a chocolate mustache and she ran her tongue along her top lip to remove it.

"Aren't you lactose intolerant?" Emily whispered beside her.

Mikayla was still staring at me. "Yeah. I am." She dropped the carton on the ground and walked toward

the exit. Emily and Olivia looked at each other in confusion for a brief moment before composing themselves
and rushing after her. My friends and I watched them
go. As soon as they were out of sight, Jordan burst out
laughing.

"What the hell was that?"

"She thinks she's so tough."

"What was she even talking about?"

Everyone was talking at once. Except Libby, who was
quiet next to me, biting furiously at her thumbnail.

"Katie? Are you going to tell us what that was about
or what?"

"It's kind of a long story."

"Oooh," Jordan said. She leaned forward. "Spill the tea."

I told them about seeing Declan Bell Jones at work
in the aftermath of the soccer ball incident, and our little
excursion to the optometrist the afternoon before. I was
just getting to the part where he'd called me "cute" when
the bell rang.

As we picked up our bags and headed toward the F-block
building Jordan said, "You're welcome, by the way."

"Huh?"

"For backing up your boyfriend story."

"Oh. I—"

"Pfft," Nat cut in. "You made it even less believable.
'He's really hot!' Come *on*."

"Hey! Katie could have a really hot boyfriend. If she wanted to," said Amina, ever loyal.

Nat rolled her eyes. "Yeah, and I could win prom queen."

"Don't even get me started on that," Jordan said.

As my friends launched into an argument for at least the sixty-seventh time since the formal committee had announced we were having awards at our Year 10 formal—Jordan and Libby were decidedly against them, Nat and Amina thought they were fun, and I kept changing my mind—I tried not to get offended that even the people who liked me most in the world didn't buy the fact that I might have a boyfriend, let alone a hot one.

That was the third noteworthy thing to happen that week.

See, I told you there was too much for a montage.

Okay, you may have had a point.

The fourth thing was that...drumroll please...

Badum badum badum badum badum...

I was one of the students selected to paint a mural in the main quad!

And the crowd goes wild! Woooo wooo wooooooooo!

Thank you, thank you.

Of course, when Miss Lui told me the news, I promptly had a meltdown.

"I can't do this. I can't. I've got no ideas. No talent. Why did I think I could do this?"

"Because you *can*," Libby said.

"You're so talented," Amina added, reaching across the lunch table and patting my hand.

I bent over, groaning. "I'm gonna tell Miss Lui I can't do it."

"No!" At least three people said at once.

"You're doing it," Libby insisted. "You've got time to come up with something great. Don't stress."

"Didn't you have an idea when you put yourself forward for it?" Nat asked.

I shook my head, groaning again. "I guess I didn't really think I'd be selected anyway."

"Look, it's not like it's the Sistine Chapel or anything," Jordan added. "This place is a shithole. It's not like you can make it look worse."

"Was that meant to make her feel better?" Libby said.

I just groaned some more.

Later, when we were in the Year 10 girls' toilets, Libby brought it up again.

I could tell by the way your skin had turned a pale shade of green that you were still freaking out about it.

"Why don't you just put it out of your mind for a bit?" she said from the cubicle next to me. "The best ideas come when you're not looking for them, right?"

"I guess," I said, staring into the toilet bowl and feeling like I might vomit.

"Remember: you created Guy." She flushed the toilet. "You are more than capable of making something good. And perfection is boring."

Could I really take credit for Guy, though? For his beauty? I mean...I know I'd sculpted him. But what I had created wasn't anywhere near as beautiful as Guy himself. He was so aesthetically pleasing. I'd tried sketching him a few times this week, as he sat there chatting to Theo or playing games or napping on the beach beside me, Max curled up next to him. But everything I did felt so...inadequate. So small.

"Wait," I said, suddenly struck with an idea. I opened the cubicle door. "Libby, you're a genius!"

"I know." She looked at me through the mirror. "Wait, why am I a genius?"

"I'll paint Guy!"

"Huh?"

"For the mural. I'll paint Guy."

Libby raised an eyebrow. "What, like one of your French girls?"

"I should never have forced you to watch *Titanic*."

"I still think Jack could have fit on that door."

"Think about it," I said, getting back to the point. "Guy is perfect. In every way." I smiled at myself in the mirror. "Seeing his face every day sure would make school more bearable."

"Okay, but it's a mural, right? What are you gonna do, paint his face a hundred times?" Libby balled up the paper towel she was drying her hands with and threw it toward the bin like a basketball. It missed.

"That's not a bad idea," I said, trying to smooth down the frizzy flyaways in my hair with wet hands. "But what if it's, like, the day in the life of a student? A blend of different scenes..." I leaned closer to the mirror to squeeze the giant pimple that had sprouted on my chin.

Libby leaned against the sink, nodding thoughtfully. "Hmm. It could be cool. There's just one problem."

"What's that?"

"Guy doesn't go to this school."

I shrugged, switching to using my knuckles to squeeze the zit, which was a stubborn sucker. "I can just say he's a product of my imagination. The perfect student, brought to life by me. I mean, it's basically the truth, right?"

I straightened up and turned to at Libby, but froze when I spotted Mikayla Fitzsimmons over her shoulder, standing in the doorway. She was smiling a smile that reminded me of a Disney villain right before they lure their princess into a trap.

"I knew you were making that shit up."

I opened my mouth to say something but Mikayla had already spun around and left. Olivia, who had entered behind her, stepped aside and watched her go with confusion. She looked my way warily before following after her queen.

Suddenly the feeling that I might vomit was back.

☺

"You've been spending a lot of time at Theo's lately," Mum said, uncapping her favorite red lipstick and swiping it across her lips. Her friend's love life crisis had apparently escalated and a night of wine and karaoke was needed, stat. (This happened at least once every three weeks. Like they needed an excuse to drink wine and sing Shania Twain songs from the 90s.)

I stretched out on Mum's bed, using Max's big body as a pillow.

"No more than usual," I said.

Mum raised an eyebrow. "Yes, more than usual. You've been there every day this week."

"How would you know? You've been at work."

She shrugged. "I have my ways."

I narrowed my eyes. "Are you spying on me?"

"Yes. Mother is *always* watching. That's why you've gotta behave." She laughed—or cackled, I should say— but I tensed up. I somehow didn't think it was far from the truth. If there was a way to get intel on me, my mother would do it.

It was honestly a miracle we'd managed to conceal Guy from her for a whole week.

Unless—no, we would know if she knew.

I relaxed a little more at the thought of that. She was just bluffing.

"You sure there's nothing going on between you two?" She started applying mascara, her mouth wide open, because it was apparently physically impossible for her to keep it shut in the process.

"*Mum*. No." I rolled my eyes.

"Your eyes are gonna freeze that way." She was using a cotton swab to fix up a splotch of mascara she'd gotten on her cheek. "Remember you're not allowed to have a boyfriend until you're thirty-five."

I decided not to bother trying to argue the unfairness of that particular rule right now. I mean, she wasn't serious...much. The thirty-five part was definitely an exaggeration, but I still wasn't supposed to have a boyfriend yet.

This is despite the fact that Luke was fifteen when *he* started dating. Mum's attitude when I talked about the unfairness of it all was "Tough!" and "It's different for boys," and worst of all, "It's not *my* daughter coming home pregnant."

It was weird, my mum was so progressive in some ways but still living in the 1860s in others. Like she still wouldn't let me wear makeup to school even though basically *everyone* did these days and she loved wearing it herself.

I watched as she examined her now finished face in the mirror before getting up from her vanity. "Don't pout," she said. I didn't realize I had been. She sat down next to me on the bed, smoothing hair away from my face. "You know, when you and Theo were kids, you used to say you would marry each other one day. Don't you remember?"

I scrunched up my nose. Vague memories were stirring. "I remember playing house and telling Theo he had to do all the cleaning and forcing him to go through every room with that toy vacuum that had the colorful balls in it."

Mum laughed. "You were *so* bossy with him. And you said you were going to grow up and live together in a pink house with a black picket fence."

"I don't remember that at all."

"Well, you would've only been about four, I suppose." Her voice was soft now. "Ella and I used to talk about being grandmothers together. It was only a joke, but somehow I always thought..." Mum trailed off. She was looking away from me now. She cleared her throat. I felt my own get tight thinking of Theo's mom. "Anyway, I best be off before I ruin my makeup and have to start all over again." She stood up, shaking her shoulders like she was throwing off the emotions she'd just been feeling.

"Right, I'm not sure what time I'll be home. Dad's working late again, and Luke is studying at the library so you're on your own. *Behave.*" She looked at me sternly. "There's some *pastizzis* in the freezer, just put them in the oven for thirty minutes and—"

"Don't burn the house down, I know."

"Smart-arse. Don't open the door for anyone either."

"Yes, Mum."

She gave me a kiss on the forehead, then wiped where she'd no doubt left a lipstick mark.

"You're a good girl. Did I mention I'm proud of you?"

"You might have, once or twice." It'd been more like twelve times when I'd told her about the mural earlier.

"Text me when you've turned the oven off," she called as she walked out the door.

Oh my god. I just realized what happened next. You were right. It's too much for a montage.

I told you. Now, settle in.

XII

C an't get enough of us?" Theo said when I walked into his room for the second time that afternoon.

Guy leaped up from the beanbag he was on and enveloped me in a hug. He smelled so good. It sharpened the nervousness bubbling in my tummy.

"Wanna play?" Guy said, gesturing to the screen where they'd paused a basketball video game.

"Um, actually..." I looked at Theo, feeling awkward.

"What? You wanna watch a movie or something?" He messed with the controller in his hand, closing the game screen and opening Netflix.

"No. Actually, I was thinking I'd...take Guy off your hands tonight."

Theo's eyebrows shot up.

Guy said, "But we already took Max for a walk today."

"I know," I said. "But...no one is home. At my house. And they won't be all night. So. I was thinking..."

"Oh," Guy said softly.

I could feel my face heating up. I didn't dare look at Theo.

"I mean—um, see, there's this mural thing I'm doing at school? And I was—I was thinking of painting, um, you? If you don't mind? So I need to sketch you and—"

Guy had hold of my hands, and he pulled me up to his chest. "You want to paint *me*?" His voice was shining with delight.

"Yes?"

"I'm confused," Theo said. "Haven't you *been* sketching him?"

I looked at him sharply. "Yes. But that was just messing around. This is important. I need to focus."

"Ah, I see. You need to *focus*." He smirked. "Well, at least I'll finally get some peace and quiet then."

I pulled a face. "Oh yeah. Which you'll immediately destroy with your saxophone."

"I'll be the bigger person and choose not take offense to that comment."

"I enjoy your saxophone playing," Guy said to Theo.

"Thanks, mate," Theo said. He got up and picked up the instrument. "Don't worry. So does Katie. She's just being a jerk."

"Kate would never—"

"Yeah, yeah, she's perfect." He looked at us. "You better get going. Don't want to waste any precious sketch time."

I responded with my middle finger.

"You know," Guy said as I ducked through the broken fence and he followed after me. "He really does like you."

I tilted my head, amused. "I know."

Guy grinned. "Oh, good. I was just making sure. Sometimes I worry that you two don't get along. But actually, when you're not around, he's really rather sweet."

Max came bounding toward us then, flopping on his back for belly rubs at Guy's feet.

"What do you mean?" I told Guy as Max groaned from his petting.

"Oh, well, he says such nice things about you when it's just me and him." He stood up, straightening his shirt. I was momentarily distracted by the way it brushed against his chest. "Like last night. He was telling me about when his mother died. And how you were there for him. He said he couldn't have got through it without you."

"He talked about all that?" I headed inside, trying to keep my voice even.

Guy followed after me, Max right by his side. "Yeah. It must've been really hard on you too."

I felt tears in my eyes. I blinked rapidly. "It was. But it was worse for Theo. I mean, obviously." I laughed nervously. "Um, do you want something to eat?"

"Always," Guy said with a small smile.

"You know," he said a little later as he blew on a *pastizzi* to cool it down, the way I'd shown him. "I'm a really good listener."

"I'll keep that in mind," I said, picking apart a *pastizzi* and watching the contents ooze out onto my plate. "Can I ask you a question?"

"You can ask me anything."

"Does it really seem like Theo and I...don't get along?"

Guy frowned. "Well. You seem to argue a lot."

"Yeah, but not seriously. We're just old friends, you know. It comes with the territory."

Guy licked his lips and nodded. "I see. I'm glad. I want you to be good friends. Then the three of us can always be together. Well, the four of us, with Libby too. Oh! And Max. That's five of us."

I laughed. "You like us that much, huh?"

"I love you," he said. He was pushing pastry flakes around his plate, all casual and chill. Like he hadn't just dropped an L-bomb.

"You love...us?"

He looked up at me then, and something in my face made his own go serious. The effect was tainted by a bit of pastry that was stuck to his lip.

"I love you all," he said. He took my hands. "But...it's you I'm in love with."

Have you ever had that feeling where it's like, you're

thinking and feeling everything at once, and so you end up thinking and feeling nothing at all?

Like the definition of that meme, *No thoughts, head empty.*

That was me in that moment.

Something exploded inside of me. A feelings bomb.

Joy. Excitement. Fear. Uncertainty.

I was overwhelmed.

I didn't know what to say.

I stared at him. Stared at that pastry flake on his lip.

And for once in my life, I acted on instinct.

I stood on my tiptoes, closed my eyes, and I kissed that pastry flake right off his lips.

It was a gentle kiss, closemouthed but warm.

It took about three seconds before my brain finally kicked in.

What the hell am I doing—what is happening—oh god am I doing this right—oh my god I'm actually kissing him— oh my god his hand is on my waist—oh wow his lips are so soft—oh wow he actually tastes like cookie dough—oh shit what does my breath taste like—am I doing this right—am I—

I pulled away.

Guy slowly opened his eyes. He had a smile on his lips. The lips I had just been kissing.

"Hi," he said.

"Hi," I whispered.

"That was a surprise."

"Was that okay?"

Guy chuckled and affectionately touched my nose. "More than okay. I just...had a plan, that's all."

"You...you had a plan?"

"I know. I'm sorry." I was suddenly overcome with the feeling that I'd made a huge mistake.

"Don't be sorry. I wanted your first kiss to be perfect. Romantic. Like you wanted." He bit his lip and leaned in closer. His hand was on my hip now and he gave it a gentle squeeze. "And you know what? I think we nailed it anyway."

He closed the distance between our faces and this time, he kissed me. I opened my mouth automatically—I think in shock—and he slipped his tongue in.

Alright. That's it. I'm gonna stop you there.

Oh come on. The whole story has been building to this.

Katie, literally no one needs to read about tongues. In any context.

Just because *you* don't want to...

Why don't you focus on how you were feeling instead of, you know...the mechanics of it all?

How I was feeling? Overwhelmed. And clueless.

After an I-don't-know-how-long-it-actually-was period of time of our tongues fumbling together (well, it was mainly mine doing the fumbling—sorry Libby, but I don't know how to talk about this without SOME tongues involved), I pulled away again. Guy rested his forehead against mine. All I could see was him.

"So," I panted. "That's a kiss."

He laughed. "That is a kiss."

At our feet, Max barked. He'd been barking intermittently the whole time. Not exactly the soundtrack I'd had in mind for my first kiss. Guy crouched down and finally gave him the attention he was craving.

"Was I—am I... never mind." I stepped away and cleared my throat. "Should we get to that sketch?"

"Kate," he said as he followed me out of the room. "It was perfect."

I looked over my shoulder and smiled at him.

But something in my gut twisted.

Because I couldn't shake the niggling feeling that it hadn't been perfect.

Guy was an excellent kisser, of course—even with my extremely limited experience, I could tell that much. And it had felt nice. Really nice.

But there was something about it that also hadn't felt quite right.

I tried to ignore the feeling. I was just overthinking the whole situation, as usual.

Apparently my brain could never just let me have nice things.

🎨

Guy reclined on the lounge while I set myself up. This was the room with the best light in the house. I was kind of glad we weren't in my bedroom, especially after what had just happened. It would have been too distracting.

Max curled up at Guy's feet and groaned contentedly.

"So. Should I be naked for this?" Guy said, propping himself up on his elbow.

I nearly dropped my pencil. "*What?*"

He raised an eyebrow. "Is that not how artists work?"

I stared at the blank page in front of me. "That's life drawing. Um. It's okay. You won't be naked in the mural." I could feel my face burning up. When I dared to glance at Guy I noticed his lips were twitching, like he was trying not to smile. I narrowed my eyes. "On second thought, lose the shirt."

He burst out laughing but sat up, unbuttoning his shirt and shrugging it off. I almost told him to stop. Almost.

He looked me in the eye as he dropped the shirt to the ground and, I swear, he flexed his pecs. "And the shorts?"

"Hmmmm?" I was barely listening to what he was saying. The sight of his naked chest was...absorbing.

"Should I lose them too?"

I shook my head, trying to focus. "Um, no. Keep them on. Definitely keep them on."

Not that I hadn't seen it all before. My face heated up again at the memory. "Let's get started, shall we?" I mumbled.

As I sketched a rough outline, I felt Guy staring at me in a hot and intense way. My skin prickled.

"When did you get into art?" he asked.

"When I was really young. Mum says I was drawn to it before I could even talk." I chuckled. "One time I got up before everyone was out of bed and drew squiggles all over the house in permanent marker."

"Your parents allowed that?"

"Ah, no. They did not. I don't remember it, actually, but I don't think they were too happy about it."

Guy laughed. I began to relax.

"I *do* remember a masterpiece I drew on the underside of my grandparents' coffee table, though. I actually started it when I was...like, five? I think? I drew a house. Then a few years later I remembered it and went back to add to it. I turned it into this abstract drawing of a girl."

"Did your grandparents like it?"

I snorted. "They didn't discover it until they were rearranging furniture years later. I was about twelve. Mum got a phone call one day and all I can hear is the sound of my grandpa yelling through the phone, and Mum just looked at me with horror. And I knew then they had found it. I'd actually forgotten all about it until then." I was laughing now. "Mum tried to be mad, but I know she thought it was pretty funny. 'Guess we need to get you some bigger canvases,' she said."

"And now you'll be doing this painting on your school?"

I sighed. "Yeah."

Guy cocked his head. "You don't sound too happy about it?"

I paused, biting my lip. "I'm just so nervous about it."

"Why?"

I shrugged. "I don't usually show my work to that many people. I mean, I started an Instagram account, right? For my art. I follow all these artist accounts and they're just SO talented and incredible...in the end I couldn't bring myself to upload any of my stuff."

"Well, maybe you should."

"Ha. You want to know the most ridiculous part? One of the reasons I have never posted anything was because I was scared people from school would find it. And now I'm doing a painting that everyone is going to see."

The specter of Mikayla Fitzsimmons floated through my head. Even if I painted a masterpiece, I knew she was going to be nasty about it.

"You said your teacher chose you to do it, correct? I'm sure there was a reason."

I nodded. "You're right. She believes in me." I felt a bit of weight lift off my chest.

"So what are you worried about?"

I finished sketching the curve of his lips—those lips I had just been *kissing*—before answering him. "Failing. Being judged. I mean, what if it's terrible?"

"Impossible."

I shook my head. "Very possible. Believe me."

"I've seen your work. In your room. It's wonderful."

"You have to say that."

"What do you mean?"

"Never mind. I'm gonna put on some music, okay? What kind do you like?"

Guy stood up and stretched. "I like what Theo plays."

"Too much old stuff. What about something from this century?"

"I don't know. I'll like whatever you put on."

I hit play on my "the zone" playlist, which mostly contained ballads and soft, gentle songs that faded into the background while I was working.

Our conversation halted after that, but Guy didn't seem to mind. He stared at me intently as I drew. My heart was pounding and my body was tense, but not because of him. Well, not in the way it had been before. It was because of what I was doing. Creating.

I was officially in the zone. My art daze.

Something happens when I create. When I truly focus, I mean. It's like I can feel my brain switching on, becoming more alive than it is at any other time. I've never been high, but it's kind of what I imagine that feels like.

I think that's the dopamine.

Dopamine? Like dope?

YOU'RE a dope.

Whatever it is, it's good. Addictive.

Easy to get lost in.

Which is why, I guess, I didn't hear the car pulling up into the driveway.

Oh my god.

Or the keys in the front door.

Loooooooool.

Or Max stirring and jumping down from the lounge.

Hahahahhahahahahhaha.

I was dimly registering Guy sitting up when—

"What the fu—"

Hahahaaahahahhaahaahahhahahahahaaaaa.

I jumped up at the sound of my brother's voice and turned to see his shocked face in the doorway.

"What's going on here?!"

"Luke! You're home early."

He made a noise of disbelief. "Interrupting, am I?"

Guy had stood up by this stage. "Hello. I'm Guy." He held

out his hand for Luke to shake. My brother just stared at it.

"Guy is, uh," I said. "Helping me with my mural." I grabbed Guy's shirt and shoved it at him, indicating he should put it on. "You know, I'm painting one in the school quad?"

"Is that what you kids are calling it these days?" Luke said, looking from Guy to me and back again.

"Don't be gross. I was just sketching him. See?" I bent down to pick up my pad.

"You're Kate's brother? Luke?" Guy smoothed his hair down, not that he needed to. It fell naturally into the perfect place. "I'm so happy to finally meet you.'"

Luke had the look on his face he gets when he's trying to solve one of his Rubik's cubes. A mixture of confusion and frustration. He looked down to my sketch pad, and Guy followed his gaze.

"Kate, that's wonderful!" he said.

Luke head shot up and his eyes narrowed. "How exactly do you know my sister again?"

"Through Theo," I said at the same time Guy said, "Kate created me."

"What?"

"Sketched him! He means I sketched him."

Luke grabbed the sketch pad, chucked it down onto the coffee table, and crossed his arms. "So what exactly are your intentions toward my sister?"

"Don't be gross," I said, but Guy cheerfully answered.

"Intentions?" he said. "Well, to love her and take care of her and kiss her and—"

"We get the picture," I cut in, cringing.

"Is this guy for real?" Luke was staring. Guy reached out and pinched him. "Ow!"

"Oh, sorry," Guy said. "I noticed Kate does that when she's trying to prove something is real."

Luke was staring again.

"Is he..." He glanced at me. "Is he, er..."

"I'm Kate's boyfriend.'"

If Luke had been drinking something right then, he would have done a spit take. "Boyfriend?" He looked at me. "Really?"

"Um, yes?" I said. It sounded unconvincing even to me.

"Well, then." Luke's face was half astonishment, half horror. "Does Mum know about this?"

I shook my head rapidly. "And you can't say anything, Luke, please. If you love me at all, you won't say anything. Please, please, please."

My brother had never been one to be swayed by my begging.

***

I'd never seen my mum speechless before.

The silence hung heavy in the room.

I ducked my head, trying to look repentant. I was sitting on the lounge and Mum was standing over me. Luke was behind her, his arms crossed, a smug look on his face. Guy was safely back at Theo's. I'd sent him off before Mum got home. There was no point in both of us dying tonight.

Luke, on the other hand—if I was going down, he was coming down with me. I didn't know how. I didn't know when. But I was going to kill him. Wait, I'd torture him first. Then I'd finish him for good.

I stared at the floor, thinking of all the creative ways I could do the job.

"Is this true, Katherine?" Mum said, finally.

"Which part?" I mumbled and regretted it instantly when I glanced at Mum and her eyes narrowed.

"The part where you have a boyfriend." Mum's voice was eerily calm.

"Yeah." I ducked my head again.

"What about the part where he was here when no one else was home?"

"Yeah." I didn't think my head could get any lower, but it did.

"And the part where he was *half-naked*?!" Mum's voice had started to rise now.

My head snapped up. "I can explain. It's not like Luke is making out—"

"I'm not the one who was making out," my brother said sarcastically.

"Neither was I! I told you, it was for an art thing—"

"Oh yeah, as if that wasn't—"

"Enough!" Mum cut in.

The screen door banged open and my dad walked in, kicking off his work shoes as he entered. His tired face took on a stunned expression when he saw the scene in front of him.

"What's going on?"

Mum sighed. "Katherine, would you care to fill your father in?"

I winced. I opened my mouth, but my brother beat me to it. "Katie's got a boyfriend!"

I was really going to murder Luke. Then I was going to resurrect him from the dead just so I could kill him all over again.

"Wait, what?!" Dad was saying.

"I can explain. I swear," I said.

"Well. Go on then," Mum said. She crossed her arms.

"What?" I said.

"Let's hear it. Your explanation. Then we'll decide what to do with you."

I gulped. "Well, see, the thing is, you know how I got chosen to paint a mural in the quad at school?" I turned to my dad, who had sat down next to me. He still had a baffled look on his face, but he gave me a small smile of encouragement. When I looked at Mum, I noticed the corners of her mouth turning white. I pressed on. "It's really special, right? I mean, not many people were chosen. And I thought long and hard about what I was going to paint. And I decided to do a day in the life of a student..."

"Is the point coming, I've got an essay to write," Luke said.

"Go write it then," Mum snapped. My brother managed to look sheepish.

"Anyway, so I decided to use Guy—that's my, er, boyfriend?—as my model, and so I needed to sketch him. So that's why he was here today. So I could sketch him. For my school project. It was...it was all for school." The last bit came out barely above a whisper.

Mum rubbed the space between her eyebrows. Oh no. She had a headache. This was not going to be good for me.

"It was for school?" she said.

"Yep! Totally."

"So why was he half-naked?"

I exchanged looks with Dad, but he just raised his eyebrows, waiting for me to answer.

"Um, for Art? Also, he only had his shirt off."

"Oh, is that all?" Mum said.

"We weren't doing anything," I said. "I promise. Cross my heart hope to die. Cross my heart hope to be *grounded for life.*" I gave Mum my best, most innocent smile.

She stared at me a moment. "You wouldn't lie to me, would you Katie?"

I shook my head aggressively, trying to ignore the guilty knot in my stomach. Mum had always said, "If it's something you can't tell your mother about, you know you shouldn't be doing it." I'd been doing a lot of what I probably shouldn't be doing lately.

"We've always said you're too young to date," Mum said quietly. She looked at Dad. I don't know what she saw in his face, but I did *not* expect what she said next. "But...I suppose that's not entirely true anymore."

"What?" I said.

"*What?!*" Luke echoed.

"You're sixteen now. Perhaps the time has come."

I stood up, not knowing what to do with myself, not quite believing that this was the turn the conversation had taken.

"But there *will* be some ground rules."

"Of course!" I said, bouncing on my feet.

"Is that it?!" Luke cried.

"Oh, go do your essay. I'll deal with you later."

He looked between Mum and me, disbelief on his face. I stuck my tongue out at him and he shook his head, muttering under his breath as he headed to his room.

As for the ground rules, they were:

1. Guy wasn't allowed in the house without adult supervision.
2. If we were in my room, the door had to be open at all times.
3. Same rules applied at his house (I didn't tell Mum he didn't actually have a house. I figured she'd had enough shocks for one day).
4. The relationship couldn't interfere with my school-work (lol).
5. My parents wanted to meet him ASAP.

I hastily agreed to the rules, despite the fact that I couldn't remember so many restrictions when my brother first started dating Mara. But then, considering the way Guy and I had been busted, I felt like I'd gotten out of the situation relatively lightly.

At least until Mum said, "Why don't you invite Guy to *ravjul* night tomorrow?"

"Oh no."

"Oh *yes*."

"Don't you think that's a bit much, all at once?"

Every few months, my dad's family got together to make *ravjul* (which is like ravioli, but bigger and there-fore better, obviously) and drink wine and catch up. They took turns hosting it, and this time it was at our place. Mum was suggesting Guy meet literally my whole family in one go. So much for getting out of this lightly.

"I don't know, Katie, don't you think it was a bit much for me to learn all at once that my daughter is not only dating but has had her boyfriend in my house, under my roof, without a shirt on, without my permission—"

"Okay, okay, I'll bring him to *ravjul* night."

"Good," Mum said. "And just in case the rules haven't made it clear: you're still not allowed to have sex until you're thirty-five."

"*Mum*," I said.

"It's for your own good," Dad said, nudging me. He'd been quiet this whole time. When he said what he did next, I wish he'd stayed that way. "Honestly, most blokes don't know what they're doing before then anyway. It's not even worth the cost of the condoms."

XIII

Oh god, I can't take this. My whole body is overcome with secondhand embarrassment.

Don't lie. You love this.

You're right. I love this.

Especially because of what's coming next.

Ugggh.

The dinner.

It was—what's the word for it—oh yeah, excruciating.

When I brought Guy over, dressed in his very best Kmart duds (yes, he somehow made a $9 T-shirt look good), most of my family were there already. They practically fell over themselves to get a closer look at him. Mum had regaled them all with every humiliating detail of the sketch incident. She was, of course, right at the front of the line to meet Guy. I couldn't help but notice her eyes widen when she took him in. In fact, everyone in my family was wearing pretty identical stunned expressions. My dad was the first one to compose himself, smiling and offering his hand to Guy.

The actual introductions went something like this:

Dad: "How ya going, mate?"

Mum: "It's nice to *finally* meet you."

Luke: "Yeah, with your shirt on."

Mara: "Luke! Don't worry, Guy, they're actually a lovely family."

Uncle Pete: "Which family is she talking about?"

Uncle Dylan: "Not this one, that's for sure."

Auntie Roxy: "Christ, he's handsome."

Auntie Tina: "Wow. You really are handsome."

Uncle Frank: "You're brave, meeting all of us at once."

My cousin Andrea: "Don't pay any attention to them."

My cousin Eddie: "Run while you still can."

Nunna: "Woo-hoo-hoo, he's a bit sexy, Katie."

Me: *yearning to drop down dead*

Guy, for his part, took it all in stride. He smiled, he laughed, he charmed the pants off literally everyone in the room. Figuratively speaking, of course. Although my nunna wasn't far from throwing her bra at him, I think.

The first hiccup we ran into was about ten minutes later. We had made our way into the kitchen, where my dad and his sister, Auntie Roxy, were just about finished with their *ravjul* prep. Guy offered to help. Because he was perfect.

"That's fine, mate," Dad said, but Auntie Roxy chimed in with, "You can make the salad."

"I'd love to make the salad," Guy said. He stepped forward and paused. "If you could just tell me how to do that?"

Auntie Roxy looked at him, a puzzled expression on her face.

"Haha, Guy—such a joker," I said. I opened the fridge and got out the salad ingredients, placing them on the bench. "I'll help you," I said to Guy.

I could feel Auntie Roxy watching us carefully as I showed Guy how to use the vegetable peeler and the right way to cut the carrots.

"Don't do much cooking at home, then, Guy?"

Dad was watching now too. I knew this was going to be a mark in the bad books.

"Well, I don't really, I mean—" He looked at me, clearly unsure of what to say. The whole lying thing apparently went against his very nature.

"Guy's staying at Theo's, actually," I said, taking a great deal of interest in the tomato I was chopping, too scared to look anyone in the eye as I made this revelation.

"*Theo's*?!" Mum choked on the word from where she was sat at the dining table. The room suddenly got quieter. I heard a chair scraping against the tiles and felt Mum's presence at my side. I kept focused on that tomato.

"So that's why you've been there all the time lately?" Her voice was sharp.

"Maybe now's not the time to get into this, hmm?" Dad said.

"Why are you staying at Theo's?" Auntie Roxy, who had never met an inappropriate question she didn't like, asked.

"Kate thought her room was a bit cramped," Guy said before I could stop him from answering.

I swear I *heard* every head in the room snap my way. "Joking! He's joking! Haha, Guy, what have I *told* you about comments like that?" I gritted my teeth his way in a tight smile. "Guy's at Theo's because he doesn't have anywhere else to stay, alright everyone? Have you had enough of digging into his private life?"

"What about your parents?" Nunna asked, because apparently the answer to my question was an emphatic "no."

"I don't have any parents," Guy said. All casual, as was his way. "Unless you count Kate and Libby." He smiled at me, but then he noticed I was panicking. "Oh! I wasn't meant to say that."

"Huh?" This came from my cousin Andrea.

"What he means is, his parents, they disowned them. Isn't that right, Guy?" I looked at him pointedly, and he nodded obediently.

"Why would they do such a thing?" Mum said, a look of horror on her face. Whether it was over the thought of parents disowning their child or what Guy might have done to deserve being disowned, I couldn't decide.

"They had a fundamental disagreement over Guy's education," I offered. "Do we have to talk about it now? It's a bit of a sensitive subject, you know."

Mum was about to say something, but Uncle Dylan—bless him—stood up, holding up a wine bottle. "Who needs some wine?" he asked cheerfully. I shot him a grateful look, and he winked. I knew he was my favorite uncle for a reason.

"Oh, I'd like to try some," Guy said. Because, of course, he was actually a giant toddler who wanted to put everything in his mouth.

Everyone was staring at him again.

"Joking!" I cried. "He's joking!"

Guy looked at me uncertainly, his smile faltering.

This was going to be a long night.

We managed to make it halfway through dinner without any more major mishaps.

Just some minor ones.

Like when the subject of school came up, Guy admitted he didn't go.

I could practically see my parents' black book of bad things getting thicker and thicker.

"So you're working then?" Uncle Frank said.

"Ah, no. I don't work."

My parents exchanged glances. I felt the brownie points Guy had earned when he described the *ravjul* as the best thing he'd ever eaten disintegrating into nothing.

"Guys, come on," I said. "What is this, an inquisition? Give him a break."

"Ah, it's all part of the fun," Uncle Frank said.

"This isn't fun," Andrea said. I made a mental note to hug her later.

"Oh, you know what's fun?" Luke said. "Did I tell you guys how we found out Katie had a boyfriend?"

Mara elbowed him.

"Yes, Luke, we're all well aware you came home to find Katie with a half-naked Guy, thanks very much," Uncle Pete said, and half the table laughed.

"It was for Kate's mural," Guy offered. "She's a great artist."

"That she is," Uncle Dylan said.

"So," Auntie Roxy said, fixing a look at Guy as she broke apart a piece of garlic bread and stuffed some in her mouth. "Are you guys having sex yet?"

I nearly choked on my lettuce. Guy rubbed my back and said, "No. Not yet."

I think his "not yet" nearly caused Mum to choke too. "Katie *has* explained our rules to you, hasn't she, Guy?"

She looked at me. "Think we might be adding some about going to Theo's too."

I started to protest but was interrupted by Guy reciting the rules back to Mum.

When he was done, Auntie Roxy turned to Mum. "Jeez, Fi, they're teenagers. What do you expect? Wouldn't you rather them be safe at home instead of parked in some random side street or down a dark alleyway?"

That just set Mum off. What followed was an argument about where and when I should be having sex. Involving half my family. It was pretty wild, especially when you considered the fact that I had been kissed exactly one (1) time.

Well, technically twice. Although the first time I kissed *him* so—

You're getting off track. Bring it back to the dinner of doom, please.

Right. So after what felt like an eternal argument about my sex life, in which I pleaded in vain for a subject change and Guy looked from one of my family members to another with an expression of complete confusion—the most rattled I'd ever seen him, actually—my dad finally spoke up. "Alright, alright, enough." He looked at his sister. "Roxy, when you have kids of your own you can do what you want with them, but for now, respect our rules. Just like Katie and Guy will. Isn't that right, kids?"

"Of course," Guy and I said in unison. I reached for his hand under the table and gave it a squeeze. He squeezed it back, twice. I felt my insides untwist a (very) little.

Auntie Roxy, meanwhile, downed the rest of her wine in one gulp. I think she was hurt by what Dad had said (the no kids thing was a sore subject), and I began to feel bad for her. Then I remembered she'd kicked off the whole thing in the first place.

The conversation finally, mercifully, shifted away from Guy when Auntie Tina started telling the story of weirdest patient she had ever treated in the emergency room (it involved a rectum, I will say no more); basically, it was business as usual for my family.

I got up to make cups of tea for everyone and Guy followed after me to help.

"I'm so sorry about all of this," I whispered to him.

"Sorry for what? Your family is wonderful. Loud, a bit overwhelming...but wonderful." He looked back at the dining table. "It must be nice."

"What must be nice?" I said, standing on my tiptoes to get some mugs off the top shelf. "Complete humiliation?"

He stood behind me and easily plucked them down. "Having a family," he said.

I didn't know what to say to that. I stood there staring for a moment, while Guy gave me a smile that wasn't like any of the others I'd seen from him.

This one seemed...a bit sad.

"You two aren't smooching over here are you?" Nunna interrupted.

"Nunna! We're making tea."

"The water's boiled. Where's the tea?" She reached up—and I mean *reached*, my nunna is really short—to touch Guy's bicep, giving it a gentle rub. "Of course, I wouldn't blame you if you *were* smooching." She waggled her eyebrows.

"Nunna, stop objectifying my boyfriend," I said.

"Oh, poo. You don't mind, do you?" She punctuated her question with another squeeze of Guy's arm.

"Not at all," he said with a grin. He leaned down and gave her a kiss on the cheek.

She giggled (she actually *giggled*) and playfully swatted at his face. "You make an old woman blush."

"*Nunnaaaaaa.*"

"Alright, alright," she said, shrugging and picking up a couple of mugs to take back to the dinner table.

The rest of the evening was, thankfully, relatively uneventful. Guy and I escaped with my cousins and Luke and Mara outside while the adults kept drinking inside. We played Monopoly. Guy didn't know how, which admittedly seemed weird, but not so weird it was a problem. He picked it up pretty quickly.

As he was saying goodbye to me at the front door

later, he leaned down to kiss me. I felt the eyes of Mum on me from the living room, and I turned my head so his kiss landed on my cheek.

"Good night, Guy!" Mum called. "Tell Theo I'll be over tomorrow to discuss the rules!"

"It was lovely to meet you," he called back with a wave. With one last squeeze of my hand, he walked away into the night.

(And around the fence to next door.)

XIV

Our third kiss took place at the movies.

It was a Sunday afternoon session. Theo, Alex, Libby, Guy, and I went to see the latest Marvel movie. I had originally intended for it to be a double date with Libby and Michael, but Libby said Michael was too busy, and Alex said he wanted to see the movie, and we somehow ended up going in a group.

Mum was pleased with the development. She'd made good on her promise and gone 'round to Theo's that morning. His dad wasn't home, but she had stern words with Sophia, Theo's oldest sister, about the rules and how I Wasn't Allowed Alone With Guy. Sophia smiled and nodded and said, "Of course, of course." I was glad it was her and not Lena who was getting this lecture, because out of the two of them Sophia was actually the more laid-back.

"Never thought you'd have restrictions on coming over, hey," Theo said, lying back on his bed and cuddling Mr. Fluffybutt to his chest.

"Sorry about Mum," I said. Guy squeezed my shoulder.

"At least she counts my sisters as adult supervision. If she was relying on my dad you'd literally never be allowed over these days." I detected a note of bitterness in his voice, but before I could pursue it he changed the subject. "So what's the plan for today, then?"

After much discussion we wound up at the movies. Guy, unsurprisingly, was absolutely delighted by the whole process. Theo borrowed his sister's car and drove us to the theater, and as we headed down Alex's street to pick him up, Guy rolled down the window and stuck his head out like an actual golden retriever.

"This is my first time in a car!" He giggled with delight.

Every time I started to get used to his presence, he said and did stuff like that, which reminded me just how bizarre the whole scenario was. Not that I ever truly got used to him, anyway.

"It's a shame Michael couldn't come," I said to Libby as we lined up at the concessions counter. "I haven't seen him in ages."

She nodded but didn't say anything. After a moment, she said, "Wanna hang out later, just the two of us? It's been awhile and—"

"Kate! What is that?" Guy was pointing at the frozen Coke machines, where two boys were filling giant cups with every flavor they could.

"That," I said, smiling up at him, "is about to be the best thing you've ever eaten."

I was so caught up in him I didn't really notice Libby sighing behind me.

As for the movie: if you asked me what it was about, I still couldn't tell you to this day.

Guy was...distracting.

At first he was just excited to be there. The 3D glasses in particular were a revelation to him. "Whoa!" he cried as he reached out his hand at one particularly explosive moment. He quieted down after a while though. It happened around the time we interlocked hands.

His thumb started tracing slow circles on my skin and suddenly that was all I could focus on. All I could feel.

My heartbeat sped up and my breathing slowed down. After a few minutes, I let my own thumb move along the surface of his skin.

The noise of the movie faded into the background. All I could see, hear, feel was Guy and the connection fizzing between us. I shifted closer to him and soon we were pressed together, side by side. When I turned my head, he was looking down at me, a soft smile playing on his lips. He leaned forward and closed the remaining space between us, bringing our lips together. His tongue flicked across mine and—

NO TONGUES. NO TONGUES! PLEASE, I BEG.

Seriously, this was awkward enough to sit through the first time.

Yes, folks, what Katie has conveniently left out here is that I was sitting right next to her. Theo and Alex were on the other side of Guy. I exchanged looks with Theo around Katie and Guy's interlocked faces. I think we were both suddenly done with our popcorn.

Yeah, sorry about that.

No you're not.

I mean, I am, kinda? I dunno, at the time, I was just having a lot of fun.

I enjoyed this kiss a lot more than the first one.

Maybe it was something about the darkness of the movie theater. The seclusion and intimacy of it all. Maybe it was just that it wasn't the first time anymore, and there wasn't so much pressure on it.

Whatever it was, my brain kind of left the party and let my body do its thing.

You can say that again.

TL;DR they made out for basically the WHOLE MOVIE. Right up to the credits!! I don't know how you still managed to get oxygen into your system.

Hey. Maybe that explains my brain exiting stage right.

Our fourth kiss happened in Theo's room.

Wait. We're not going to have to go through every kiss, will we? Because...that will take a while.

No, not EVERY kiss.

I mean, seriously. Don't make me endure it all again.

Okay, okay, just let me finish this bit, alright?

As long as there's no mention of tongue.

"So, you and Guy seem to be, er, getting on?" Theo said to me. He bit into the piece of thread he was using to sew a button onto a shirt, snapping it off.

"Use scissors for that!" I scolded him. "It's bad for your teeth."

He playfully bit the air in my direction in response.

"And yeah." I went on, glancing at the bathroom door. Guy was on the other side of it, doing, you know, human things. "Things are going well. I mean, Mum is a bit of a nightmare with all her rules and third-degree questioning every time I get home, but other than that... things are pretty good."

Theo cleared his throat. "About that," he said. He held up the shirt, examining his handiwork closely. "I know you probably, uh, want alone time? So I can, like...make myself scarce. If you want." He glanced at me and quickly looked away.

This was so awkward.

"Oh! Um, thanks? But this is your room, I'd feel bad—"

Our conversation was cut off by Guy emerging from the bathroom.

He sat down on the beanbag next to me and reached for my hand.

Theo stood up. "Um, I'm going to go...see if Sophia needs help with dinner."

I was going to tell him he didn't have to leave. But the truth was I *did* want some alone time with Guy.

Theo paused before he went through the door. "Oh! Before I forget." He bent down and took something out of his backpack. "Here. Found these at the thrift store." He handed me a book. It was a memoir about writing from one of my favorite authors.

I gasped. "Oh my god, thank you! I've wanted this for ages!"

Theo nodded and turned away again. "Um. I'll be back," he said over his shoulder. "But not for, like, half an hour. At least. Okay? Okay." With that, he made a beeline out of the room.

"How would you feel if I got a job?" Guy's words pulled me out of my thoughts. I blinked and looked up from the book in my hand.

"Huh?"

Guy was chewing on his lip. "I've been thinking, you know. It'd be nice to work."

"Oh?" I was surprised by this sudden interest. "Are you...bored or something?"

He cocked his head. "I don't know that 'bored' is the right word for it. I love spending time with you. With Theo and Alex and Libby. Max. Even Sophia and Lena." He paused. "But when you are all away, at school or at work, it does get...what's the word for it?" He took a deep breath. "Lonely, I suppose."

I swallowed. "I had no idea you felt this way."

"That's why I'm telling you." He gave my hand a squeeze. "I did think perhaps I could go to school, but when I mentioned it to Theo, he said it would be too hard. He thought a job might do better. Also, it would mean I would have my own money. Because that seems important." He smiled. "Then I could be the one buying you gifts. What do you think?"

I glanced down at the book. "You know you don't have to buy me gifts, right?"

"I know. But I want to. Also, wouldn't work be fun?"

He had so much hope and optimism in his eyes. I didn't want to tell him that work was just about the complete opposite of fun.

"What kind of job do you want?"

He bounced a little on the spot. "I could get one with

Theo! He said the supermarket is looking for someone to push carts. Doesn't that sound awesome? And Theo said if I worked there, we'd hopefully get shifts at the same time and he could 'help me adjust.' And also, it's all cash-in-hand. I'm not quite sure what that means, but Theo seemed to think it was good. Off the books, he said, so there would be no questions."

I narrowed my eyes. "You guys have already figured this all out, huh?" I felt weird that something in Guy's life had basically been decided without me. But then, he was his own person, after all.

Wasn't he?

"We were just talking about it last night," he said.

"Well," I said. "If it's what you really want..."

Guy let out a gleeful cry and hug-tackled me into the beanbag. "Yes, thank you!" He pulled away a little to look into my face, his body still pressed against me. His eyes danced as he leaned back down and brought his cookie-dough lips to mine.

The fifth time we kissed—

Seriously? We're doing this AGAIN?

Last time, I swear.

(For now.)

Hmph.

It's because I wanted to talk about the formal...

"Formal?" Guy asked.

"Yeah, it's like a prom?" I said.

"Ugh, it *shouldn't* be like a prom," Libby said. We were in Theo's backyard, playing handball on the concrete slab near his room. We hadn't done this in years. I felt eight all over again.

"I mean, how else would you describe it?" I bounced the ball in her direction. She dove for it but missed.

"I don't know, I mean I guess it's like a prom," she said, jogging across the yard to retrieve the ball. "But it's ridiculous how cliché they're going about it."

"So it's an occasion where you dress up and dance with your partner?" Guy said, expertly hitting the ball in Theo's direction.

"Oh no," Libby said. The ball came her way again, and this time she didn't even try to dive for it. She looked at me in horror. "You're going to go *with him*, aren't you?"

This was something that had been playing on my mind. Months ago Libby and I—and the rest of the girls— had agreed to go together as a group. No dates. I mean, Libby was the only one of us who was in a relationship anyway so really it was her agreeing to go sans Michael. Which I thought was very generous of her.

"We'll have more fun this way, anyway," she'd said.

I felt really good about the whole thing, but there was a small part of me—okay, a not-so-small part—that yearned for the proper prom (sorry, I mean *formal*) experience. That wanted to be special enough to be asked out and danced with and even given a corsage. I knew it would never happen, so I was grateful to Libby for pushing the whole "friend formal" thing.

And then...Guy happened. And I didn't know how to bring it up with her, because I felt shitty about the fact that I wanted to cancel on her plans when she was the one who was sacrificing a night with *her* boyfriend to start with.

But just because I felt shitty about it, it didn't stop me from wanting it.

I dodged the ball as it bounced too high, narrowly missing my head, before answering her. "No. We're all going as friends, right?"

Theo laughed. "Come off it, KC, I know you have a whole formal fantasy sequence already playing out in your head."

I retrieved the ball and whacked it toward him. "That doesn't matter," I said. "We already talked about this."

"But I'd love to take you," Guy broke in. My heart skipped a beat. I caught the ball when it came my way again and held onto it.

"What if you invited Michael?" I said to Libby. "We

could finally actually do the double-date thing!" I may have sounded a bit too excited at the prospect.

You definitely did.

Libby's reaction was decidedly less excited. The look on her face was the same one you get when you tread in dog poo. Twice.

That's about how I felt, yeah.

"What about the other girls?" she said.

"They won't mind," I said. "And we'll all still hang out as a group. Come on, it'll be fun!"

"It'd be great to meet Michael," Guy said.

"Are we playing or what?" Theo complained.

I ignored him, clutching the ball beneath my chin as I gave Libby my best persuasive puppy dog look. "What do you think?"

It's not that persuasive, by the way. Your puppy dog look.

It managed to persuade you! (She said yes, obviously).

I didn't though, did I? What I actually said was—

"Ugh, fine, whatever. Go with golden boy."

There was a definite grumbling happening. But in that moment, it was enough for me. I dropped the ball and bounced right over to Guy myself.

"Looks like we're going to the formal together," I said with a grin. Guy picked me up, swung me around, and planted a sweet, soft kiss on my lips.

"Looks like the game's over," Theo said.

🎨

Let me save you some time before you start trying to get into sixth and seventh and twentieth and fiftieth times you kissed.

We'll just say from here on out you guys were practically glued at the lips.

Even when there were other people around.

It was like you were addicted.

Think of it this way. You know when you hear a song you really love for the first time, and it's like a tiny revelation? It makes you feel alive and all you want to do is keep listening to it? So you put it on repeat and listen to it over and over and over and over and over and over and over again because you just can't get enough of it?

Okay. I do know that feeling. It usually ends with me getting so sick of the song I can actually never listen to it again.

Well this was the stage where it was still at the top of my playlist.

(And by 'it' I'm talking about kissing Guy, obviously.)

Obviously.

XV

I'd just like to go on the record and say I wasn't kissing Guy *all* the time.

Sometimes, I was at school.

Miss Lui was excited about my idea for the mural. I showed her a rough sketch I had done and she declared it, "Marvelous!!!" (The three exclamation points were invisible, but no less present in her speech). I felt a bit of excited bubble up in among all the nerves.

Mikayla Fitzsimmons, meanwhile, sat in the corner of the art room with Emily, and snorted and mumbled something about being too old for imaginary boyfriends.

It was annoying, but not unexpected from her. I could handle it.

I was naïve to think it wouldn't get any worse.

It was my own fault really.

That's blaming the victim, and we don't do that here.

Okay, true. The thing is, what I did made things worse. Or, at least, it painted a bigger target on my back.

Mmmm still very victim-blamey.

Look to be clear: IT WASN'T MY FAULT. But. What happened was I posted this photo on Instagram. Of me and Guy.

I basically never post on my Instagram. *Especially* not photos of myself. Like I said before, I'd started it for my art but the actual account had, like, four posts. They were all photos of Max, except for one, which was a shot of my pencils (oh so original and artistic).

But after nearly a week of Mikayla whispering behind my back at school, I wanted to prove her wrong.

And why not show off my totally hot boyfriend?

I posted a photo. It was a close-up of Guy and me, our faces pressed together, both of us smiling. To be honest, looking at myself next to Guy was not exactly a thrilling experience. I spent three hours editing the photo.

After I'd gotten close enough to the aesthetic I wanted (nothing ever matched up to the picture I had in my head), I deliberated on a caption before finally settling on one that I thought was cute and a good in-joke for the three people who would get it: You were made for me 🫶

I hit post.

I refreshed the page.

Refreshed it again.

I got two likes. One from Alex and one from Theo.

Another like. Amina. And a comment. "Omg, you guys are so cute!"

Jordan posted a comment. "GET IT."

Nat posted three fire emojis. 🔥🔥🔥

They'd all been shocked when I'd told them earlier in the week that yes, I really had a boyfriend and yes, he really was hot. It felt a bit insulting, really.

At least they were being supportive now.

I put my phone down. Three minutes later, I picked it up again. And nearly dropped it immediately.

There was a like from Declan Bell Jones.

Did he even follow me?!

I checked my notifications again. He was following me now.

We hadn't really spoken much since the visit to the optometrist, although he had been smiling and nodding my way in geography, and occasionally in the quad, if Mikayala Fitzsimmons wasn't looking.

Mikayla Fitzsimmons. She would see that he'd liked this, right? She would see it? And she'd shut up about the whole thing?

Surely.

Surely.

I put my phone down feeling a weird mixture of smugness and bubbling nerves.

We were in the library for geography the next day,

supposedly to work on an assignment. Everyone was quiet, but there was this kind of buzz in the air, a restlessness where you just know nothing is getting done. Mr. Green, our teacher, was busy flirting with the librarian Mr. Moretti anyway, so it wasn't likely he cared.

I was staring into space, thinking about Guy, when I got an invitation to join a Google doc.

It was from Declan Bell Jones.

I looked around the room and saw him hunched down, staring at his screen.

I accepted the invite and entered the blank doc.

"*Hey Harry,*" he typed.

"*Hey!*" I was vibrating with curiosity, but tried to keep my cool. Maybe the exclamation point was too much? Too late now. He'd already seen it.

"*So.*"

I waited for him to keep typing.

"*That guy you posted a photo with.*"

My breath hitched.

"*Is he your boyfriend?*"

Whew.

"*Yes.*" I typed. After a second, I added a smiley face.

I waited for his response. And waited. I looked his way, and saw him staring at his screen, his brow furrowed. I watched as he typed something, and turned back to see what it was.

"You're full of surprises."

"I know. Everyone is shocked I have a boyfriend." I cringed and added a *"lol."* It made me cringe even more.

"I just," he typed. Seconds that felt like minutes passed before he finished his sentence. *"Thought you liked someone else."* He added a winky face.

What. The. Hell.

What did that mean?

Did...did Declan Bell Jones know I liked him?

And...did he *like* that?

How did I respond to that?

"Haha. Well I have a lot of 'like' in my heart."

I typed the words before I thought too much about them...and instantly regretted it.

I looked over at Declan Bell Jones before snapping my head away.

Because he had been looking at me.

And he had been smiling.

"What the hell, Katie?" Libby exclaimed. We were on our way home and I'd just told her and Alex about the geography incident. Theo had stayed back at school to work on a something for his textiles and design class, so Alex was walking with us, wheeling his bike.

"What?" I said.

"You're seriously still into Declan Bell Jones when you've got Guy?" I was surprised at the level of anger in her voice. "I mean, Guy is all you can think about or talk about. You ignore *everything* else. But Declan Bell Jones says 'jump' and suddenly it's 'Guy who?'"

"That's not true," I said. I turned to Alex. "Is it?"

He cocked his head. "You *have* been pretty into Guy. Not that I blame you."

"See," Libby said. "So you can't go saying stuff like that to Declan."

Guilt rippled through me. "What do you think?" I asked Alex. "Did I say the wrong thing?"

He puffed out his cheeks and exhaled. "On the one hand, I'd say a bit of flirting never hurt anyone."

"You think I was flirting?"

"You definitely were," Libby said. "Even I can tell."

"On the other hand," Alex continued, "I think a bit of flirting *could* hurt Guy."

"What do you mean?"

"He's so..." Alex looked at the sky. "Golden. Pure. And you're his whole world, Katie. Honestly, I think he'd be devastated if you liked someone else."

I kicked at the gravel on the road.

Golden. That was the right word for Guy. He needed to be protected. And I wanted to protect him. I really cared about him. I liked spending time with him...and I really, really liked kissing him.

Still, at the back of my brain, there was this small voice. A whisper. I couldn't quite catch what it was saying. But it was there.

A little seed of doubt.

"So you do still like Declan Bell Jones?" Alex interrupted my thoughts.

"No. Yes. I don't know? I mean, I never really stopped liking him. I've liked him so long. But then Guy came alone out of nowhere and took over everything and—it's not like I turned off my crush on Declan just because I turned one on for Guy."

Libby was shaking her head. "Yeah, but that doesn't mean you *say that* to Declan."

"I didn't!"

She shot me a look. "Whatever."

"Well what should I do?" I looked to Alex.

"I think, just forget about it," he said. "Who knows what game Declan is playing, but you should just focus on Guy."

I nodded. But what *was* Declan doing messaging me like that?

I didn't have much time to dwell on it. I was helping Dad make dinner when I got a DM from Jordan. *"You should see this,"* she said, with a link to an Instagram post. I clicked through and let out a small shriek.

It was a new profile. The screen name said Liars Exposed 2528.

There was only one post.

It was the photo of me and Guy, with numbers drawn all over it. The caption said "Katie Camilleri and her fictional boyfriend. She's even photoshopped some poor random into a photo!" It then went on to point out all the "proof" the photo was fake, such as the lighting supposedly being all wrong. The post also went into how my "fake boyfriend" had no social media and there was no proof of his existence.

"What's wrong? Did they cancel *The Great Bake Off*?" Dad joked. It was our favorite show to watch together.

"Huh?" I looked up from my phone. "Um, no, just some homework I forgot about. Do you mind if I head to my room to, uh, do it?"

"Katie Camilleri volunteering to do homework? Are you feeling alright?"

I gave him a weak smile. "Thanks, Dad."

In my room, I started frantically messaging my friends. Jordan was the first to reply to the group chat.

Jordan

It's got to be Mikayla right?

Nat

It has to be

Amina

Would she really do this
though?

Jordan

She absolutely would

Why does she even care

Libby

She doesn't. Not really. She
just has nothing better to do.

What should I do???

Libby

Report it, block it, forget it.

Nat

Def report it

Jordan

I wish we could find a way
to take her down. In a totally
nonviolent way, of course

Amina

Is there anything we can do,
Katie? x

I felt a little better after talking to my friends,
although my guts were still churning. I was so sick of
Mikayla Fitzsimmons and her demonic minions.

"Whatcha doing?" My brother appeared in my door.

I was lying on my bed staring at my ceiling. "What
does it look like?"

"Looks like you're brooding."

I didn't respond.

"Wouldn't have anything to do with a certain Insta-gram post, would it?"

I sat up. "How do you know about that?"

"Someone sent it to Mara's sister who sent it to Mara who sent it to me."

If I wasn't already feeling sick before, I definitely was now. "Just how many people have seen this?" I picked up my phone and stared at the post again. I'd reported it and so had my friends, but it was still there. I couldn't see how many likes it had, but there were about twenty comments. A mix of emojis (laughing, the detective, the thinking face), some along the lines of "*knew it*" or "*nice catch*" or simply "*lmao.*" There was just one that said "*this is mean.*" It was from Amina.

"It's not that big a deal, right?" Luke said. "I mean, it's not like they're right." He took my phone out of my hand and looked at the post. "You probably should have gone easy on the filters, hey."

I groaned.

"Listen," he said. He poked my shoulder. "Do you need me to beat anyone up for you?"

I gazed at his face. He was smirking, but there was sympathy in his eyes.

"Why are you being so nice to me?"

He screwed up his nose. "Pfft. Brood on your own then."

Before he reached my door, I called his name. "I love you," I said.

"Love you too," he said without looking back at me.

When I woke up the next day, the post—actually, the whole profile—was gone.

I dreaded going to school, but it wasn't too much worse than usual. I felt like a few people were laughing at me behind my back, but Libby insisted I was being paranoid. Of course, Mikayla and her friends were *definitely* laughing behind my back, but that was nothing new.

I was relieved to have double art in the middle of the day, because even though Mikayla was in my class, I was working on my mural, which meant I wasn't stuck in the same room as her. She had totally taken art because she thought it'd be a breeze, but she had no talent or apparent interest in it. It was so annoying.

It says a lot that, despite the slow progress I was making on the mural and the giant ball of anxiety that rocketed through my body every time I looked at it or thought about it, working on it was still preferable to being anywhere near Mikayla.

By last period, I thought the worst of it was over.

I thought wrong.

I couldn't help but panic when I got a notification on my phone. I looked at it under my desk, trying to hide it from my English teacher, Mr. Mosely, at the front of the class. It was a Facebook notification—I'd been invited to an event.

I heard sniggering from the back of the room, and the hairs on my neck stood on end. I had a bad feeling about this.

And I was right to.

BIRTHDAY PARTY FOR KATIE CAMILLERI'S
IMAGINARY BOYFRIEND.
Poor desperado Calamari is making up boys because she can't get a real one of her own. Let's support her in her time of need and celebrate the closest thing to real love she'll ever get.

The time was set for 3:00 PM that afternoon. Seventeen people had clicked "attending."

Shit.

"What do you think she's got planned?" Jordan was asking as we walked out of class.

"I'm sure it's nothing. Just a silly Facebook thing," Amina said.

"Oh yeah, just some light cyberbullying." Jordan pulled a face.

"Ugggh, I'm freaking out," I said.

"Why don't we hang back a bit?" Libby suggested. "Until after three. You know, just to be safe."

I nodded, feeling grateful.

Libby and I sat on a low brick wall near the girls' quad in silence. The others had gone home after I'd assured them I'd be okay.

I was not, in fact, okay.

My leg jiggled with nerves.

"How did Guy's interview go, by the way?"

"Hmmm? Oh, good! Theo said there were a couple of awkward moments but his boss liked Guy. He's starting tomorrow."

"Wait—he got the job?"

"Yeah! Didn't I tell you? I thought I did."

"No. You didn't." She went quiet.

"Katie—" Libby started a few minutes later, just as I was saying, "Should we get this over with?"

Libby glanced toward the main quad, which was now deserted. She sighed and picked up her backpack. "Let's do it."

As we got closer to the school hall, I began to hear the murmur of voices. When we rounded the corner of the building, we were confronted by over a dozen people gathered at the back gate.

"Should we...go out the front?" Libby whispered.

I backed up a step, ready to turn around, when the crowd shifted a little and my eyes locked with Mikayla Fitzsimmons. The triumph I saw there sent shivers down my spine. Then I saw something that made me feel about ten thousand times worse. Declan Bell Jones, standing beside her.

I squared my shoulders and grabbed Libby's arm. "No," I said. "This is the quickest way home. Come on."

I started to walk forward, but Libby resisted. "Katie... are you sure? I don't know..."

"I'm not going to let her win like this," I said quietly. "It'll be fine."

Libby peered into my face, and whatever she saw there made her nod and lift her chin high. We linked our arms and pushed forward together.

As we got closer, people started singing "Happy Birthday." When they got to the part where you're supposed to sing someone's name, it was a jumble of words, but I heard "Katie's fake boyfriend" in among the noise.

"Here they are, the couple of the hour," Mikayla said as we reached her. "Calamari and her totally hot boyfriend." She gestured to the space beside me. "Happy birthday, big guy."

There were giggles around us. I looked at Declan Bell Jones. His brows were furrowed and his eyes looked... regretful? Concerned? Pitying?

"Mikayla...," he started to say. She shot him a look. She'd produced a cupcake, presumably handed to her by Emily, who was standing behind her. It was the kind the school canteen lady made, with pieces of cake cut out to look like butterfly wings, and whipped cream and jam all around them.

"Here." She stepped forward so she was right in my face. I swallowed hard, grateful not for the first time that day that I wasn't a crier. "We got him a cake to celebrate."

I knew what was going to happen next. I knew if I ran it would just make things worse. So I braced myself to have the cupcake smashed in my face. I squeezed my eyes shut tight. I felt Libby tug at my arm, but I didn't move.

I waited. And waited. And...it didn't come. Confused murmurs rumbled around me, and I slowly opened one eye to peek through. Mikayla was looking to the right, her face twisted in surprise. And anger.

I opened my other eye and took in the scene in front of me properly. For a split second, I thought maybe Declan Bell Jones had intervened. But the guy holding Mikayla's wrist with one hand and the cupcake in the other was actually...Theo.

What was he doing here? He was meant to be at band practice. Alex was by his side, a worried look on his face. It was a stark contrast to the totally chill one on Theo's.

"Thanks, I needed a snack," Theo said. He released

Mikayla's wrist and took a bite out of the cupcake. She sneered at him but didn't say anything. He gave her his most winning, dimpled grin. He had whipped cream on his face. He left it there, raising an eyebrow as if he was daring Mikayla—anyone—to say anything about it.

"You would come running when there's food involved," Mikayla said, but her voice came out small and shaky.

People around her gasped.

Theo licked his lips. "Mmmm. It's a shame I got here now the party's over."

At that moment Declan Bell Jones stepped forward, glancing between me and Mikayla. "Right. Uh. Come on, babe," he said. He slung an arm around her, steering her toward the front gate. She resisted for a moment and then gave in.

As they passed by me, she shot a killer death stare, while Declan glanced over her head and pulled a face that seemed to say "I'm sorry." People began to disperse, some of them sneaking furtive glances at me. I felt like throwing up. I let out a shaky breath, relieved but also heavy with the feeling that this definitely wasn't over.

"You alright?" Alex said to me.

"Wanna bite?" Theo said before I could answer. He held the remains of the cupcake out to me.

"Why did you do that?" I said, irritation bubbling up in my chest. I headed through the back gate.

"What?"

"Katie—" Libby started to talk, but I cut her off.

"You should have let me handle it," I said over my shoulder. "You've just made everything worse."

Theo, Alex, and Libby followed after me.

"Are you serious right now?" Theo called.

"I suppose you would you have preferred cake smashed in your face?" Alex said.

"I would have, actually. You think Mikayla will just let this go? You embarrassed her. In front of everyone. Who do you think she'll take that out on?"

Theo's dimples were showing. But when he spoke, he sounded calmer than before. "I'm not gonna apologize for helping you, KC."

"What were you even doing there?" I cried.

"We were in the music room," Alex said. "I saw what was happening on Snapchat, and we raced down."

"I thought she was going to bash you or something. When I saw the cake—I was actually relieved. I don't know, I just acted on impulse."

I walked on in silence.

"I'd do it again," Theo said. His tone was belligerent.

Libby nudged me. "It *was* pretty cool."

I groaned and crouched down, covering my face. "Why is this happening to me?" No one said anything. "Why can't I just have a normal boyfriend who comes to school and holds my hand and makes all these bitches sorry they ever said anything bad about me."

"Guess you forgot to add that to the recipe," Theo said.

"Huh?" Alex said.

"Let's get out of here," Libby said, tugging me up. "Your not-normal boyfriend will be waiting for you."

XVI

Guy was pretty distressed when I told him about what had happened at school.

"But why would she do that to you?" he kept asking.

"She's a bitch and a bully," I said.

"But why?"

I shrugged. "She was born that way I guess."

He frowned. "I don't think people are born bitches. Everyone is innocent when they're born. Right?"

I rubbed my eyes, tired of the whole conversation. The whole day. "I don't know."

Theo chose that moment to enter the room. He froze when he saw me sitting on his bed. We looked at each other, neither of us saying anything. Finally he said, "I'm gonna have a shower."

Guy, who had been watching us carefully, turned to me once Theo shut the bathroom door. "Are you and Theo fighting?"

"No!" I said. Then, "Yes."

"Why?" Guy moved closer to me, rubbing my shoulder soothingly. Only I didn't feel soothed.

"I just...it's complicated," I offered weakly. I knew I was being unfair. Theo had only wanted to help me, but I was taking all my frustration and anger at Mikayla out on him.

Because I could.

Because he'd let me.

Because he'd still be there to listen to me and pick me up and offer me support in a way that no one else would.

Because you do that with the people you really love.

"I better get going," I said.

Guy pouted. "But you just got here."

"What time do you start work tomorrow again?" I asked, ignoring his protest.

He brightened at the mention of work. He was so excited about it. Reason 1,067: he was actually a total weirdo.

"Ten AM sharp," he said. "Theo said I have to be there at nine-fifty, which he thinks is a rip-off, but 'you have to play by the rules.'"

I nodded. "I start at nine. Sorry I can't be there. I might try to come over and see you during my lunch break though, okay? I should be able to make it if I literally run."

Guy squeezed my hand. "That sounds wonderful, but don't tire yourself."

"It's okay, I'm not a snowflake who's gonna melt from a bit of exertion," I said. I stood up. "I'll see you then, okay?" I gave him a peck on the lips and left the room just as I heard the water stop running in the bathroom.

I didn't sleep very well that night.

I was sweating by the time I reached the shopping center where Guy was spending his first full day as a real live, actually employed human being. I looked around for him as I crossed the packed parking lot. I didn't spot him until I was inside. He was standing near the shopping carts, leaning casually on the handle of one.

How did he still look good in that hideous fluorescent orange vest?

I stopped as I realized he was chatting to someone.

It was a girl. She was in a bakery uniform. She was handing him something. Some kind of cake.

He smiled broadly, said something enthusiastically, and took a big bite. His eyes widened, and he said something that made the girl clap her hands together.

Without hearing him, I knew he'd proclaimed the cake "the best thing I've ever eaten."

I turned around and headed back to work.

🎨

"—and then Scott said I was the fastest buggy boy he'd ever seen, and he was so glad he'd hired me!" Guy was telling me about his day. I was doing my best to sound interested, but I had other things on my mind.

Visions of Guy talking to that girl had haunted me all day. But it was weird. It wasn't that I was jealous. More like startled. It made me realize how limited Guy's world had been until now. How he hadn't really had a chance to experience everything the way he'd wanted to. And how when he did, maybe he'd realize he didn't actually like me that much after all.

The thought upset me, but there was also a small part of me that—as much as I didn't want to admit it—felt relieved. Free.

Theo was laughing. "He was pretty impressive." The weirdness between Theo and me seemed to have settled down from the day before. Or at least, we were both doing our very best to ignore it.

"I missed you, though," Guy said, pulling me closer on the beanbag we were sharing. "You didn't come by?"

"Oh, yeah, sorry about that. Got stuck at the pharmacy. We were busy."

Alex looked up from the game stack he was sorting through and frowned. I shook my head to let him know not to say anything. His mouth twisted, but he kept quiet.

"And Kate, look!" Guy reached into his pocket and pulled out a fifty. "My first pay! Theo suggested I frame it, but I'm going to buy you something nice with it."

"Wait, you got paid already?" I looked at Theo. "Just like that?'"

He shrugged. "Cash-in-hand. Rules are flexible."

"Nonexistent, you mean."

"Yeah, well, makes things easier with Guy here, doesn't it?"

Alex sat back. "One of these days you guys are gonna explain our cult kid's background to me properly, right?" He had a theory that we were lying about Guy's background (maybe because we were). He'd jokingly decided that Guy must have grown up in some weird cult that we were covering up. Although I'm not sure exactly how much he *was* joking.

Theo and I exchanged a look. "Not likely," he said.

Later, as Guy and I were saying goodbye at the end of Theo's driveway, I asked him a question I'd asked him before. "Why do you like me?"

He stroked my hair and leaned down to kiss my forehead. When he spoke, his lips were still close to my skin. It sent a shiver down my spine. "Hmmm. Because you're Kate."

"Yeah, but *what* do you like about me?" I said.

He chuckled and pulled back to look at me. "Everything.

Everything." He brought my hands to his lips and kissed the inside of each of my wrists.

I gently pulled my hands away. "Do you...like anyone else?"

In the glow of the streetlight, I saw confusion on his face. "I like many people."

"No, but do you *like* anyone else. You know, like...are you attracted to other people?"

He shook his head immediately. "No. There's no one for me but you. You know that." He reached out to pull me closer.

I gave him a quick hug, said good night, and headed toward my house.

He was telling the truth. I knew he was.

It somehow didn't make me feel any better.

Because Guy had been made for me. He was my fantasy come to life. Which was lovely in theory, but the reality of it was...unreal.

Everything he said was like something I'd written in one of my angsty fanfics. But unlike those fanfics, Guy and I hadn't had a meet-cute where he'd been struck by my beauty and then fallen for me more and more as he got to know me.

He'd come fully formed and ready-made to love me.

And that didn't feel any more real than what I'd put on the page.

XVII

That week at school was rough. Mikayla Fitzsimmons and her minions were relentless.

"What's the word for when you catfish yourself?" Mikayla asked loudly one math class. "You know, when you *pretend* to have a boyfriend and even use fake photos but it's all just a lie?"

"There's only one word for that," Olivia said. "Pathetic."

They giggled, and the teacher shushed them. It didn't stop everyone in class from staring at me, though.

I tried to get out of class as much as possible to work on my mural. My teachers were mostly pretty good about it. I even worked on it after school. I wasn't seeing much of my friends. Or Guy.

The mural itself...well, I hated it. So far it was only outlines, no details, but I still couldn't shake the sense that nothing I did looked right. I couldn't get lost in my art daze.

I tried to do my best to just keep going, because that's what Miss Lui told me to do.

"When you're blocked, you've just got to push through it. Put one foot in front of the other, one stroke after another, and you'll find you've made something great despite yourself."

I didn't know about something great, but at least as I was making something.

The main bright spot in my week was Declan Bell Jones.

He'd been messaging me.

It had started on the weekend. He wanted to check I was okay and apologize for what happened with Mikayla.

"*I know she can be nasty sometimes,*" he said. "*It's her way of dealing with her own shit. I'm sorry you got caught up in it.*"

I didn't tell him what I really thought. That no matter what shit she was dealing with, it didn't give her an excuse to be the kind of person she was. That I'd been caught up in it for years, anyway.

Instead, I wrote back, *Thank you.*

And I added a love heart emoji.

Which love heart emoji?

I think it was the pink one.

Katie.

I know. I'm judging myself too, don't worry.

Declan kept sending me cute and funny messages. Mostly Harry Potter memes.

I felt guilty.

But I couldn't resist.

I'd fantasized about Declan Bell Jones for so long. And now he was right here in my DMs.

And a few messages...they were harmless. That's what I told myself.

I couldn't explain away the giddiness I felt when receiving them, though.

Or the fact that a part of me (despite all the hate I was getting from Mikayla, and all the jokes) was secretly glad Guy wasn't at school. That he was separate from this life. We'd gone 'round and 'round about what to do about the situation.

"Just bring him in one day, like show-and-tell," Alex had said.

"Don't be ridiculous," Theo said.

"Let it blow over," Libby suggested. "Mikayla Fitzsimmons isn't worth any more of our mental, emotional, or physical energy."

"Exactly," Theo added. "Who cares? You're the one with the totally hot boyfriend. Just be happy in that knowledge."

"Mikayla Fitzsimmons has a totally hot boyfriend, too," I said, then immediately regretted it.

"What?" Guy said, sitting up straighter.

"I just mean...she thinks she's better than everyone because of who her boyfriend is. Among other reasons."

"Yeah but she's not, is she?" Libby said.

We all let the subject drop after that.

Nothing could have prepared me for what happened next.

We had the school awards assembly that Thursday. They take place every term. The whole school attends, and there are awards for academics and sports and music. There's always a guest speaker and a musical performance, usually by one of around three student bands in existence at any given time. Theo's band was performing this one. They'd done it a bunch of times before.

I had descended into the kind of half-conscious stupor that only listening to your vice principal talk about taking pride in your school for ten minutes can lull you into. I wasn't paying a lot of attention as Theo's band took the stage. And then I felt it. The ripple through the crowd. Excitement. Curiosity.

Eyes looking my way.

I sat up straighter, and that's when the person climbing on stage turned around and faced the audience.

Guy.

He was in school uniform. His golden hair was shining. His eyes were scanning the crowd. When he spotted me, he lit up and waved.

"What the..."

Even more people turned to look at me.

Libby grabbed my arm. "What's going on?" she whispered.

I shook my head. I had no idea.

Guy stood in front of the mic stand at the center of the stage.

On my other side, Amina said, "Is that...?"

I nodded, unable to take my eyes off the stage.

The band started to play. It was an old song, one I'd heard them perform before.

"What's going on?" Libby said.

Guy started singing.

And wow. I had thought his *speaking* voice was hot. His singing...was on a whole other level.

The atmosphere in the room changed when he opened his mouth. It was like everyone suddenly sat up, leaned in closer, and started paying attention.

Amina bounced in the seat next to me and squeezed my arm. "He's so cuuuute."

As he reached the chorus, Guy's eyes sought me out again. I felt people looking my way again as he belted out the familiar lyrics. Because instead of singing about a "sweet Caroline," he had replaced the name in the song with mine. And he was pointing right at me while he did it.

"Sweet Kath-er-ine," he belted out.

I nearly fell off my seat, not helped by the fact that

Amina still had a hold of my arm and was shaking me back and forth, squeeing with glee.

I looked at Libby again. Her nose was scrunched up. "This can't be happening."

I glanced up at Theo, on stage near Guy, playing his saxophone with his eyes shut.

The murmurs around me were getting louder. I turned my head, taking in the people around me. They all looked shocked. Some were smiling. Most looked very confused.

"Oh my god," Jordan said.

I turned back to the stage and let out an actual gasp when I saw Guy.

Because he wasn't on the stage anymore.

He was descending the steps.

He was walking down the aisle.

He was making his way directly toward where I was sitting with my friends.

He stopped right next to us.

"Get up," I heard Amina hiss, pushing me to stand.

People were giggling and talking excitedly, getting louder and louder. Guy sang on, and patches of the crowd even started contributing "bah-bah-bah's" in response to the chorus.

I stood in silence, wringing my hands together, completely dumbfounded, unsure of what to do. My face felt hotter than it ever had in my life. Hot enough to explode.

After one final, long, glorious note, the song came to an end and applause erupted in the hall. Guy stood there, grinning. He reached for my hand and pulled me into the aisle. I clambered over Amina and Jordan to get there. Then, as my whole entire school—*including my teachers*—watched, he tugged me closer and kissed me.

It was just like something out of a rom-com.

[insert gagging noises.]

I didn't hear gagging noises. I heard gasps and "wooooo" and some applause.

And then. "Katherine Camilleri, please come to my office."

If my soul hadn't already left my body, it definitely would have at Ms. Walker's words. I followed behind her, stunned by the absolutely surreal experience, not quite sure how to feel. Guy trailed after me.

I felt the weight of the entire student body staring at me. Everyone was quiet now, watching. Ms. Walker handed the mic, which she had yanked away from Guy, to Mr. Han on stage as we walked past. I got a glimpse of Theo. He nodded, a small smile on his face with a look that seemed more intent on gauging my emotions than expressing his own.

As we neared the exit, I dared to look back. I don't know how I spotted her in the sea of faces, but automatically my eyes went to Mikayla Fitzsimmons. Her mouth was open in utter shock. When she saw me looking, she scowled.

Finally, an emotion other than shock slipped through me.

Smugness.

Satisfaction.

Then I saw Declan Bell Jones sitting beside her, a twin look of shock on his face.

And something else twisted inside of me that I didn't really want to acknowledge.

XVIII

I thought you were gonna love it," Theo said, kicking at the gravel. We were on our way home from school after serving afternoon detention. "You don't seem as happy as I thought you'd be."

Yes, we'd both gotten afternoon detention. So had Alex and the other members of Theo's band. Apparently sneaking Guy into school, having him infiltrate assembly, and then kissing him in front of everyone posed a security threat in addition to violating the "hands off" policy. (The latter part, obviously, only applied to me, so I got an extra detention.)

It was the first detention I'd ever gotten in my life.

At least we weren't banned from the school formal, like Ms. Walker had threatened.

Theo and I were nearly home, having parted ways with Alex at the main road. Theo prodded me when I didn't respond to what he was saying. "I thought you'd be 'vibrating at a frequency that could shatter glass,'" he said, quoting a phrase he'd read in one of my stories that had made him laugh. "You finally got your big rom-com moment."

"Yeah. And then I got detention."

"But wasn't it worth it?"

I sighed. "I don't know."

Theo rubbed his face. "God, KC. You're impossible."

"What do you mean?"

"I mean...you always say you want one thing. You have all these daydreams. You won't settle for anything less. And then—and *then*—when you actually get what you want, when everything is *perfect* and right in front of your face—you still don't seem happy!"

I was taken aback by the edge in his voice. But his words stung more than his tone.

Because deep down I knew they were true.

What the hell was wrong with me?!

Why was I never happy?

"I'm sorry, okay?" I said. "I know I'm a mess. But I can't help how I feel."

Theo's face was tense as he stared at me. After a moment, it relaxed a little and he sighed. "Yeah. I guess none of us can control that."

We walked on in silence for a few minutes.

"How's your dad doing, anyway?" I asked, looking for a subject that felt safer than the one we'd been on. "I feel like I haven't seen him around much lately."

Theo huffed. "That's 'cause he hasn't been around much lately."

"He's working heaps, right?"

"Mmmmm." Theo's dimples were showing, but he wasn't smiling.

"Is something else going on?"

He bit his lip and looked around. We'd reached the park, which was empty. "You know what, can we sit? Just for a bit."

"Of course," I said, trying not sound as surprised as I felt.

We dropped our bags and each took a swing. I didn't say anything, waiting for Theo to open up. We hadn't *talk*-talked in so long. I felt really nervous for some reason.

Theo rocked back and forth gently. Finally, he said, "I'm pretty sure my dad is seeing someone."

"What?" I don't know what I'd been expecting Theo to say, but it wasn't that. "Oh my god."

Nick hadn't dated anyone since Theo's mum had died. Well, not that we knew of, anyway. I'd kind of always thought that Ella was it for him. They had been so in love. I could see that even when I was a kid. Watching Nick break down at her funeral was one of the most gut-wrenching things I'd ever experienced in my life. I'd never seen anyone cry like that, let alone an adult.

"Yeah," was all Theo said.

"What makes you think that?"

"He's been out a lot, and he says he's working. But. When he comes home, he looks so guilty."

"Maybe he feels guilty about working too much?"

"Mmmm, but um...he seems a lot happier."

"Well, that's good, isn't it?"

Theo adjusted his weight on the swing. "And when I went in his room looking for his stash of cash so I could get some groceries, I found a bag from the jewelers."

"*What?*"

"And it had earrings in it. I'd never seen them before."

"Maybe they were for Sophia or Lena?"

He shook his head. "My dad doesn't give those kinds of presents. Not to us. It was always Mum who made Christmas and birthdays a thing."

"Whoa," I said. "Are you—how do you feel? Are you okay?"

He scrunched up his nose. "I guess. It's just...weird." He stood up, leaning against the metal frame of the swings. "I don't know...I want him to be happy. Obviously. It's just. I don't know. It's weird."

I got off my swing and stood in front of him.

"Have you tried talking to your dad about it?"

Theo snorted. "Yeah. 'Cause we're so great at talking, my dad and me."

"Hey. You're not so bad at talking."

Theo looked down, kicking at the ground and pulling a face that said, *Yeah, right.*

"You talk to me," I said.

His eyes met mine. "That's because it's you."

A beat passed when neither of us said anything. I wanted to ask him what he meant, but something stopped me. Theo coughed and looked away before stooping down to pick up his stuff.

"Come on, we better get back to golden boy," he said. "He's probably having a minor meltdown over us getting detention because of him."

"Wait. Are we done here, though?" I asked.

"Yeah, KC. We're done."

I tried not to read in to the way he said those words.

Guy pounced on us as soon as we entered Theo's room. He was, as Theo had predicted, having a mini meltdown.

"Are you okay?" he said, grabbing my hands. "I'm so sorry, I thought—"

"It's okay, it's *okay*," I said. I laughed. Even though I was all kinds of mixed up over the day's events, I knew one thing: he had been trying to do something good for me. He *had* done something good for me. He was the sweetest, most precious being to exist on the planet.

I did not deserve him.

I gave him a hug. "Thank you so much, it was lovely,"

I said. I deliberately did not look Theo's way as I said this. "It made me so happy. But I've gotta get home, okay? I've gotta face the wrath of my parents. I just wanted to make sure you were okay first."

Guy pouted and apologized again. I reached up and tried to smooth the worry line that had appeared between his brows. "You're perfect. You know that, right?"

He held onto me as I walked to the door, and I had to pull myself away.

I was expecting a massive lecture from Mum when I got home.

The weirdest thing was she looked stern for about ten seconds before she burst into laughter.

"Well, there are worse things to get detention for, I suppose, than being serenaded by your boyfriend," she said.

And then she asked for all the details.

"Who are you and what have you done with my mother?" I asked.

"Please. As long as he's not interfering with your actual schoolwork—and you're NOT having sex, as we've previously discussed—it's okay to have a bit of fun. How did they even pull it off?"

The logistics of the scheme weren't actually that complicated. Since they were seniors, Theo and Alex were allowed to leave school at lunchtime. As soon as the lunch bell had rung, they'd borrowed their bandmate Spud's car and gone to pick up Guy. Theo had given him a spare uniform—too short and loose for him, but it did the job. And Guy had walked into school with them when they came back before the assembly without anyone batting an eyelid.

I could *kind of* see Ms. Walker's point about it being a security concern.

After dinner I shut the door to my room, collapsed on my bed, and reached for my phone. Mum had come up with a new rule that we weren't allowed screens at dinnertime because she thought we didn't talk to each other enough. We were even actually sitting together at the dinner table. It was meant to be quality family time, although the caliber of the quality was less than "high" for me that day since the meal had mostly consisted of all three members of my family making fun of me over getting detention that day.

I felt sick when I saw a bunch of Instagram notifications on my phone. *Not again*, I thought. I opened the app with a sinking feeling and saw a girl in the year above me had uploaded a video of Guy's performance and tagged me in it. I watched the video and was overcome once again with just how beautiful Guy was, in every way. As he moved closer to me, the camera zoomed in, giggles coming from the person filming.

My chest tightened as I took in my frozen face, haloed by my frizzy hair. My lips were pressed together, the color draining from my cheeks, making my freckles and pimples stand out even more.

The caption was: "This actually happened at my school today lol."

Okay, not so bad.

Then I scrolled through the comments. Some were from people I knew, but most weren't.

This is so cute omg.

This video reminded me I'm single.

Where can I get one of those?

Lmao is this some kind of joke?

This is a prank right? I've seen this movie. It ends with fire and pig's blood. Y'all better be careful.

Her? Seriously?

Was this a singing telegram? He's not seriously into her, right?

Tell me they're not dating.

I stopped reading and put my phone down. Twenty seconds later I picked it up again.

I refreshed to see if there were any new comments.

I refreshed again.

I kept on refreshing and refreshing and refreshing. At 10:00 PM, I finally cracked and messaged Theo.

> Do you know Vada Weber?

Yeah she's in history with me

> Have you seen her post?

I waited as the three dots floated on my screen. They stopped. And started again. And stopped.

> ???

Yeah I saw it…it's…cute?

> Did you see the comments???

Never read the comments KC

I started typing about three different things but I deleted them all. Instead I sent the Instagram post to Libby.

> Have you seen this?!

I waited. She didn't respond. She must have been in bed already. I dropped my phone in frustration before picking it up to refresh the comments all over again. But the post was gone. I refreshed Vada's profile again and again. But the video really had disappeared; she must have deleted it. I let out a deep exhalation, relieved.

But I spent another night without much sleep.

I wasn't used to getting attention. Most of the time, I was pretty invisible at school. So when I walked across the main quad the next day and felt everyone looking at me, I really *felt* it. Most people smiled at me. A few girls said things like "Oh my god, you're so lucky." But others simply whispered to their friends as I walked past. They might have been saying similar things. But I couldn't stop those comments on the Instagram post from running through my head.

Is this some kind of joke?

This is a prank right?

What's someone like him doing with someone like her?

"It was soooooo romantic," Amina said at break.

Jordan pulled a face. "Couldn't he have picked a better song though?"

"Don't be so judgy," Nat said.

"It *was* pretty cheesy," Libby said. "But we all know how much Katie loves cheese." She took a bite out of her banana, then held it toward me like a microphone. "So tell me, Katherine Camilleri, how does it feel to have all your dreams come true?"

I swatted the banana away. "I wouldn't say all my dreams have come true."

Libby rolled her eyes.

As I headed into math—my first class that day with Mikayla—I felt nervous, but also a little excited. I wanted to see that bitter expression on her face again. The one that said she knew she was wrong.

But when I saw her, she was wearing her usual smug bitch-face.

Well, at least she can't say anything about me today, I thought.

As usual, I thought wrong.

I was unpacking my backpack when I heard her say, "I don't know, I don't get it either. Maybe she's putting out. It's the only explanation."

I stiffened.

"I mean, why else would he be with her?" she said loudly. Pointedly.

I ignored her. Or at least I pretended I was ignoring her. I stared straight ahead, never once looking behind me. I could feel my face getting hotter and hotter as the period wore on. Mikayla was quieter but I could hear her and her friends whispering and giggling every now and then. I felt sick.

How was everything somehow even worse now?

When the bell rang, I shoved my things in my bag and got out of there as fast as I could. Mikayla Fitzsimmons's laughter echoed in my ears as exited the room.

As I headed to geography, I thought about what might happen next with Declan Bell Jones. I was expecting a message. Or another Google doc. A teasing comment. A cute meme. A personal question. Anything.

But I got nothing. He didn't even look my way when I entered the room; he stared at his textbook instead.

It was the most engrossed in it I'd seen him all year.

I'm not sure I'm ready to write what comes next.

Don't worry. I'm here for you.

That's a bit of a spoiler, isn't it?

It's alright. It's good to reassure people of a happy ending. We need that in this chaotic world, right?

Yeah. But first we've gotta get through all the crap first before we can reach it.

Anyway, Libby came over that afternoon. I was in desperate need of some best friend time.

It was just what I needed.

Until it wasn't.

I was unloading on her about the events of the day—

how everyone was looking at me, talking about me, judging me. How nobody thought I was good enough for Guy. How *I* wasn't good enough. How Mikayla Fitzsimmons was being a bigger bitch than ever. How Declan Bell Jones had been ignoring me.

She'd been listening for the most part, tossing my old stuffed Peter Rabbit up and down in the air as she lay on the bed next to me. Every now and then she'd make sympathetic noises, but then she sat up suddenly. "This is too much," she said.

"What?"

"I swear, it's like you *want* there to be drama in your life. Like you can't just let yourself be happy. I mean, think about it—you pined for the perfect guy. And bang! The perfect guy shows up. *In your bed.* You want him to be all romantic and stuff. And voilà! You got your perfect first kiss. He does this big grand gesture in front of the whole school. He's taking you to the formal. Meanwhile, you're all flirty with another guy. And you somehow twist all this into the idea that you're not— what? Pretty? Funny? Smart? Because you are all of those things, Katie. You *are* good enough. Your problem is you secretly don't think anyone or anything is good enough for *you*."

I sat up too, feeling hurt by the sudden outburst. Her words had struck home, echoing what Theo had already said to me—and what I'd been ruminating over myself.

I wasn't ready to admit any of that out loud, though. All I could say was, "Excuse me?"

Libby got off the bed. "You know what? I think I need a break."

"A break? From what?" When she didn't answer, I added, "From me?"

She hesitated a moment. Then she said one word that cracked a small piece of my heart, "Yeah."

"What? I don't—*what's your problem*?"

She just shook her head and turned to walk away.

"Fine! Be a weirdo then," I said.

She froze in the doorway. I took it as an opportunity to lash out and vent some of the hurt I was feeling.

"This is about Guy, isn't it?" I stood up. "Ever since he showed up, you've had something up your butt. You're jealous, aren't you?"

She turned to face me, her face redder than I'd ever seen it before.

"That's it, isn't it? You're jealous," I continued. "He likes me, and not you. We made him for me, and not you. Even though *you've* got a boyfriend. Not that you seem to really care about him. I mean, you never want to see Michael or talk about him. Why are you even with him?"

"Unbelievable," she said. "You just...have no idea, do you?"

"Well? Why are you acting like this? I mean, I just when I need you most, you're totally abandoning me."

"*I'm* abandoning you?! Wow. Wow." She shifted her weight from one foot to another, anger radiating off her. "You're the one who's basically ditched me for a guy!"

"That's not true," I said quietly.

She scoffed. "It is! You know what, *Kate*? *You're* the one with something up your butt. It's your giant head. It's so far up there, you can't see anyone else." She stepped closer. "You think I'm being a lousy friend? Ha. Alright. Tell me this. What kind of friend doesn't even notice that their so-called *best friend* has had her heart broken?"

I recoiled, trying to process what she had said. "Wh— what do you mean?"

"You want to know why I've been acting weird? It's because I'm completely and utterly fucking devastated."

"Is this because of Gu—"

"IT'S NOT BECAUSE OF GUY!" Her whole body was tense, her arms stiff at her sides and her hands balled into fists. I stared at her. Max got up from where he'd been curled up on my pillow and plodded over to lick her hand. After a moment, Libby let out a deep breath. "It's because of Michael."

"Michael?" Now I was really confused.

"We broke up."

"*What?!*'"

"Yeah."

"When? How?!"

"It was the weekend Guy showed up. Remember when I came to your house? You guys were making cupcakes."

"What?! But—why didn't you tell me?"

She looked away, over my shoulder. "You were so caught up in Guy. It's like you didn't have any brain space for me at all. You didn't even notice something was wrong."

I thought back to that day. Libby had been acting strangely. But I never thought it was something this serious. "You're the one who never wants to talk about Michael, or any of this stuff," I said. "How was I supposed to know?"

"You could have asked."

I made a noise of disbelief.

"You've just...," Libby added. "You've been a really shitty friend lately. Really shitty."

"I'm sorry, but you don't get to be angry at me for not being a mind reader."

"And *you* don't get to tell me how I can and can't feel."

"Fine then, be angry!" I flailed my arms.

"Fine, I will!"

"Good!"

"Good!"

We stared at each other a moment.

"Goodbye!" she finally said.

She walked out the door, and I slammed it after her.

Whew. I need a bit of a break after that.

Me too.

Gonna go bake some cookies.

Oh good. I'll come eat them.

XIX

Okay, but we're going," Alex said, flopping himself over Theo, who was lying on his bed scrolling through his phone. It was Saturday, and Alex and I had come straight to Theo's after work. Theo and Guy had gotten there before us, and as soon as we arrived Guy began recounting everything that had happened to him that day, including the fact he'd found five whole dollars in a cart. He'd handed it in to the store manager, despite Theo protesting that the guy would just pocket it himself.

Now I was flicking through my social media, sitting on one of Theo's beanbags next to Guy as he rubbed his foot against mine. I was checking Libby's profiles to see what she was up to. She'd posted about studying, and then there was a pic of her and Jordan getting ice cream together with the caption, "Get you a friend who will drop everything for ice cream."

"Don't," I said to Guy, moving my foot away from him. He thought I was joking, I think, because he giggled and reached for it again with his toes. I got up and moved to the bed, where Alex was trying to convince Theo to go to some party that night. Theo was grumbling about being too tired.

"Come onnnnn," Alex was saying. He poked at Theo's sides. "I've been at work all day. Tomorrow I'll be studying. Tonight, I need some fun."

"I'm not stopping you from going," Theo said, turning on his side and facing away from both of us.

"Some of the boys from Hill High will be there. I need a wingman."

Theo said nothing.

"And when was the last time you got any action?" Alex said, not relenting. "You've basically been a nun lately."

"Priest," Theo said without turning around.

"Huh?"

Theo twisted to look at Alex. "You mean priest."

"Oh, so you *have* taken a vow of celibacy?"

Theo sighed and glanced at me and Guy, who had moved to sit below me on the floor, his head resting on my knee. "No. I've just been busy."

"Right, which is why we should go tonight. You need to let off some steam." Alex nudged him. "And it'll give these two lovebirds some alone time."

Guy looked up at me, warmth in his eyes.

"Or we could go to the party?" I said.

"What?" Theo asked.

"Can we come with you?"

"No."

"Why?"

"I'm not going."

"Yes you are!" Alex said, eyeing Theo. "We all are. It'll be fun."

"I've never been to a party before," Guy said.

Me either, I thought but didn't say.

"See," Alex said. "We have to go now. Cult kid needs to experience a party for once in his life."

Theo looked between me and Alex for a moment, clearly debating in his head how he was going to win this fight. Then he threw his arm over his eyes with a groan, defeated.

Theo's sister Sophia dropped us off at a double-story house on the other side of the lake. A song I didn't recognize was blaring from it. I took a deep breath and smoothed down my hair, which I'd straightened with Mum's help. She'd also helped me do my makeup, all the while talking about how I wasn't to drink or smoke or do anything at the party I'd be ashamed to tell her about. It had taken A LOT of convincing for her to let me go in the first place, and she'd only agreed because Theo was going too and his sister was dropping us off and picking us up.

Guy had let out a "Wow, you're beautiful" when he'd seen me, and I willed myself to believe him and let go of some of the tension of the last few days.

Theo had nodded and said, "You look nice." Then he'd added, "But it's just a house party."

Alex elbowed him and said, "Ignore him, you look great."

When we entered the house and made our way to the backyard, where most of the crowd was congregated, I was glad I'd put the effort in. Most of the girls I noticed were pretty dressed up. And they were all looking me up and down—mainly because Guy had his arm around me, I think. They'd take him in, then see me. I was getting all too familiar by now with the surprise that widened their eyes and raised their eyebrows. Not even hair and makeup closed the gap between Guy and me.

I was beginning to regret begging Theo to let us come along.

Then I saw something that made me *really* regret it.

Declan Bell Jones was sitting by a fire that had been lit inside an old metal barrel. He was wearing a shirt that accentuated his shoulders. But I didn't have much time to dwell on that. Because sitting on his lap was Mikayla Fitzsimmons.

I froze and Guy looked down at me, which made me realize I was digging my fingernails into his arm.

"Sorry," I said. Theo, who had been walking in front of us, glanced back.

"Whose party is this?" I hissed.

"Fitzy's,'" Alex said.

Fitzy. As in Jayden Fitzsimmons. As in Mikayla's older brother. I had no idea Theo and Alex even talked to him.

"We need to leave, now," I said.

Theo turned to me, confused. "What's wrong?"

Just then, Rebecca Jackson, one of Theo's lunch group friends, came up behind him and held her hands over his eyes. "Guess who?"

Theo reached up to pull them away, and she rested them on his shoulders. She grinned as he turned toward her.

"I was hoping you'd be here tonight," she said softly, but not soft enough so we couldn't hear.

"Oh. Hey." He gave her a smile and glanced at me. I'd already started backing up, pulling Guy with me.

I turned as I reached the steps leading back into the house. I must have been moving too fast or something, because I slipped. Guy reached out to catch me, but the angle was awkward and I still hit the concrete, scraping my hands and knees.

"Timber!" someone yelled, and laughter erupted.

My face burned. I felt hands on me, helping me up.

I heard people asking if I was okay, but they were overshadowed by one clear, high exclamation that cut through everything else: "What is *she* doing here?"

I looked up and locked eyes with Mikayla Fitzsimmons, who had gotten off of Declan's lap and was stomping in my direction.

"We really should get out of here," I said, but it barely came out above a whisper.

"What do you think you're doing?" Mikayla said.

I tensed, wracking my brain for something to say but coming up completely empty.

"Take it easy, hey?" Theo said, appearing beside Mikayla.

She narrowed her eyes. "You again. What are you, her knight in oversized armor?"

"Mikkie, let's go get a drink," Declan Bell Jones said from behind her.

"Mikkie, is it?" Guy broke in. I looked up at him in surprise. He had a smile on his face. "I don't believe we've met. I'm Guy." He held out a hand for her to shake. She eyed him warily, but I saw a flicker of something in her face that I couldn't quite place. She reached out and took his hand. He nodded, gratified. "We're just here to enjoy the party. I assure you, we won't bother you at all."

"I just…" Mikayla opened and closed her mouth a few times, apparently struggling with a response. It seemed the full force of Guy's charm offensive had unsettled her.

"Mik, come on, chill," Declan said.

Still she hesitated, glaring at me.

"What's happening here?" I heard behind me. I turned to see Fitzy himself standing on the veranda above me.

He stepped down and greeted Theo and Alex with those part-handshake, part-high five, part-shoulder rub things boys do. Then he put his arm around Mikayla, moving into a gentle headlock and rubbing her glossy curls with his knuckles. "You're not causing trouble, are you, little sis?"

"Let me go," she screeched.

He released her and she straightened, trying to smooth out her hair. Beside her, Declan Bell Jones was chuckling, but his face dropped in less than a second when Mikayla shot a look his way.

"Do I need to send you to your room?" Fitzy said.

"Don't talk to me like that."

"What are you gonna do, tell Mum? If you're lucky maybe she'll respond to your email within the next four to six months."

Mikayla opened her mouth but didn't say anything. Instead, she turned and slunk away back to the circle around the fire. I noticed Emily and Olivia there, putting comforting hands on Mikayla's shoulders as she sat back down between them. Declan Bell Jones stood awkwardly by us for a moment. He shot me a small smile before ducking his head and following after Mikayla.

"Brat," Fitzy muttered. He turned back to us. "Where are your drinks, people? Come on, let's get this party started."

We joined the crowd under a pergola and sat around a rectangular glass table. The backyard was pretty big, so we were a decent distance away from the group by the fire, but not enough for my liking.

"Sorry," Theo said to me quietly when he caught me sneaking looks in that direction. "I totally forgot she was Fitzy's little sister." He gave my shoulder a squeeze. "Are you okay?"

I shrugged him off and didn't answer. From my other side, Guy placed a hand on my thigh, his thumb rubbing small circles on the skin there. I fought the urge to bat his hand away too.

Rebecca Jackson, who was sticking by Theo like a burr in Max's fur, said, "What did you do to her, anyway?"

I scrunched up my nose. "Exist, I guess?"

"We can go home if you want," Theo said.

"Aw, come on," Alex whined. "Don't let a bully like her ruin your night. We're here to have fun."

"You're just saying that 'cause you're horny," Theo said.

"Well? You are too." Alex raised an eyebrow. Theo shot him a warning look and glanced at Rebecca, who was smirking.

"Speaking of which." Alex nodded toward where a group of guys were setting up a game of beer pong. "There's Billy." He got up, scraping his chair against the pavement. "You guys gonna play?"

Theo groaned. "Do I have to?"

Alex rolled his eyes. "You're so boring tonight." He looked at the rest of us expectantly.

"Is it a game?" Guy said.

Alex grinned and held out his hand. "Come on, I'll show you."

"Uh, I don't think that's such a good idea," Theo said.

"It's a great idea. A rite of passage." Alex grabbed Guy's hand and started pulling him toward the game. "Come on, Katie. You too."

"I'll pass, thanks!" I called. Guy looked back at me, a question on his face, and I gave him a thumbs up and a nod.

"Are you worried about him?" Theo said to me.

Rebecca was looking between the two of us, a bemused expression on her face. "He's a big boy, isn't he?"

"Yeah," I said. "Exactly. He'll be fine." The truth, which I didn't dare express out loud, was that I was kind of relieved to have some space. As wonderful as he was, it was getting pretty exhausting being Guy's whole world. And I was becoming acutely aware of the fact that he wasn't the whole of mine.

My relief started to fade within a few minutes. Rebecca was talking to Theo in a low voice, her body turned toward his and her hand rested on his arm. They were just talking about one of their other friends from school, nothing serious, but I began to feel distinctly like a third wheel.

I looked over to Guy, who was enthusiastically downing a cup of beer while Alex slapped him on the back, cackling with laughter. A drunk Guy sure was going to be interesting.

I tried to resist turning my head toward the fire, but I couldn't stop myself. I instantly regretted it because the first thing that caught my eye was Mikayla, who was not only on Declan Bell Jones's lap again, but had her face attached to his at the lips.

I suddenly wished I wasn't so terrified of Mum and could actually have a drink myself. If there was ever a time where I felt like I needed one, it was now. Not that I knew what drinking felt like, but it was meant to help you de-stress, right? Which I definitely needed, because

I was about 89 percent stress at that point. The other 11 percent was fear of my mother, of course.

It was a potent 11 percent.

I turned my attention back to Theo and Rebecca, who were laughing about something I hadn't heard. I think they'd forgotten I'd existed. I got up.

"Where are you off to?" Theo said.

Oh, *now* he was looking at me.

"Uhhhh, just going to the bathroom?" I rushed toward the house before he said anything else. It wasn't until I reached the back door that it dawned on me I had no idea where the bathroom was.

Why did I ever think it'd be a good idea to come to this party?

A girl from my year who I'd spoken to maybe twice before—her name was Primrose—was sitting on the kitchen counter with another girl I didn't recognize. They appeared to be having a rather energetic conversation about IKEA furniture.

"Sorry, do you know where the bathroom is?" I said.

"I think it's down the end of that hall," Primrose said, gesturing, before turning back to her friend and her ode to the wonders of bookshelves.

"Thanks," I said, but neither of them were paying attention to me anymore.

It turned out there were three doors "down the end

of that hall." It felt like that scene in that horror movie where the characters have to choose between doors marked "not scary at all," "scary," and "very scary." One was partially open and clearly a bedroom. That was the "scary" one then, and I knew to avoid it. I hesitated a minute, trying to choose between the two closed doors. I leaned in and put my ear to them one at a time, trying to detect any noises, but the music coming from the back room was all I could hear.

Well, here goes, I thought, choosing the door on the right.

It took me a second or two to register that it was another bedroom. I was about to leave when something caught my eye. A framed photo of Mikayla and Declan. I looked around the room, my eyes adjusting to the dim light.

Holy shit. I was in Mikayla Fitzsimmons's bedroom.

I should have walked out and closed the door behind me right then and there.

No, five seconds before that.

I should have. But I didn't.

I glanced in the hallway. There was no one around. I stepped further into the room, unable to resist this peek into the devil's lair.

Mikayla's room was…not what I was expecting. It was pink. Very pink. She had a large double bed, four-poster, with little lace curtains surrounding it. It seemed like her mum—or she—had the same fondness for cushions as my mum did, because her bed was covered in them. There were also a bunch of teddy bears, one way more worn than others. I made a mental note to tell Theo that Mikayla Fitzsimmons had her very own version of Mr. Fluffybutt she probably slept with every night too.

Next to the photo of Mikayla and Declan on the bed-side table, there was also one of her with a really old lady. The old lady was laughing and cupping Mikayla's face in her hand, and Mikayla was looking down at her with a big joyful grin and eyes full of affection. The kind I'd never seen on there during all my years of knowing her.

I was suddenly overcome with the strangest sensa-tion. This room—it was so normal. So nice. So *human*. Concepts I did not remotely associate with Mikayla Fitzsimmons.

I was turning back toward the door when something else caught my eye. A print, hung up on the wall on the other side of the bed. I moved closer, just to make sure I really was seeing what I thought I was.

Yep. There it was. A work by Frida Kahlo, right there in Mikayla Fitzsimmons's room. The exact same print that was also pinned up in my bedroom.

I looked around, double-checking it really was her room. That was definitely her jewelry scattered on the dresser. A cardigan I'd seen her wearing at school slung over the desk chair. Her backpack below the desk.

I had to get out of here before I lost my entire concept of reality and my brain melted out of my ears. I took a step toward the door and heard voices coming down the hallway.

Shit.

I ducked down beside the bed, hidden from view from the door.

The voices...entered the room.

Shit. Shit. Shit.

"It's okay, Mikayla won't mind," I heard a girl whisper. Olivia.

There was a low chuckle from a guy.

And then...oh no. Kissing noises. Wet, sloppy kissing noises.

Shuffling sounds.

Weight shifting onto the bed.

Oh god, I had to get out of there.

Slowly—*painfully* slowly, emphasis on the pain—I inched forward, staying on all fours. I rounded the corner of the bed, trying desperately to ignore the noises coming from above me. I was promptly hit in the face with a shirt and almost squealed, but managed to swallow the sound just in time. I was closer to the door now, but about to move away from the safety of the bed, which had so far blocked me from view.

I weighed my options and decided my best was to make a crouch-run for it and hope to make it out of the room before being spotted.

You might not be surprised to learn I barely made it three steps before—

"What the—"

"Sorry! Sorry!" I straightened up but kept my eyes on the door. "I'm just—"

"*Katie?*" A male voice said.

I froze. Turned around.

"*Michael?*" I said.

He was standing up, scrambling to find his shirt and pull it over his head. His face was flushed. But it was definitely him.

Michael Hartley.

Libby's ex-boyfriend.

"Uh, hey," he was mumbling. He looked awkwardly at Olivia, who was sending daggers my way with her eyes.

My mind was really reeling, trying to put the pieces of the puzzle together. We'd all gone to primary school together. Had Olivia stayed in contact with Michael? Had she brought him here tonight?

"What—what are you doing here?" I said to him.

"I could ask *you* the same thing," Olivia said.

"I couldn't find the bathroom!" I ignored her and looked back to Michael.

"Oh, um," Michael stammered. "I came with some mates from school? They play ball with Fitzy." He kept runnning a hand through his hair.

"But..." I wanted to ask what he was doing there with Olivia, but my brain was also trying to come up with an excuse as to why I was crawling around Mikayla's bedroom.

Olivia was standing now too, her arms crossed. "Seriously. What are you doing in here?"

Shit. I was really dead.

I made a strangled noise and turned to leave the room again, but Michael reached out to grab my arm.

"Wait. You're not going to tell Libby about this, are you?"

"What?"

"I just—please don't tell her." His eyes looked desperate.

Olivia said something that sounded like a protest, but I wasn't really paying attention to her. I was thinking about what Libby had said, about having her heart broken.

"Why do you care?"

"What? Of course I care."

"Oh yeah, it seems like it," I said. "You break her heart and five minutes later you're going at it with Olivia Kent?"

"Broke *her* heart?" Michael said. "She's the one who dumped me!"

"I—what?"

Michael let go of my arm. "What did she tell you?"

Even less than I'd thought, it seemed—and that wasn't much to begin with.

"I've got to go," I said.

"Don't tell her, please?" Michael called after me. I left him there to deal with Olivia, who was looking just about the unhappiest I'd ever seen her, and that counted when she peed her pants in Year 1 and had to wear a pair of sweatpants from lost and found for the rest of the day.

When I reached the living room, I paused. So much for getting a breather, I was feeling even more over-whelmed than I had before. I could feel tears pricking at my eyes.

What the hell? I never cried.

I wasn't ready to face the chaos in the backyard again just yet.

I turned and headed out the front door. When I reached the gutter, I sat, the tears freely falling down my face now.

My first party experience was a complete and utter disaster.

"Hey," I heard from behind me. I turned around, startled, hurriedly wiping at my eyes. When I realized who it was, I felt like clawing my skin off.

"Are—are you okay?" Declan Bell Jones said. He

looked unsure, his hand half-raised in my direction, hovering in the air like he didn't know where to put it. Eventually he settled on right back at his own side.

"What are you doing out here?" I said, hoping my face wasn't currently streaked with mascara, but not liking my chances.

"I uh—I was just calling my mum." He gestured to the front veranda. "She worries, you know. And you rushed past me. And I thought, well, you seemed, like, not okay? So I wanted to see if you were. Okay, that is."

"Oh," I said. I looked down at the road in front of me.

"So are you?" Declan Bell Jones said, taking a step closer. "Okay, I mean."

"Um. Not really." My voice wavered, and I could feel the tears rearing their ugly, soggy heads again.

Declan Bell Jones sat down next to me. "Listen. Don't worry about Mikayla, okay? She's exhausting but..." He glanced back at the house and bit his lip. "Anyway. I'm sorry. For how she treats you."

"You don't have to keep apologizing for her," I said. "You're not responsible for her."

He shrugged. "It's just. I dunno. She's got issues. I try to help but..." He sighed.

I picked at the nail polish on my fingers. I'd been so hopeful when I'd applied it earlier.

"Why do you like her?" I said quietly.

"Huh?"

"Why," I repeated, taking a deep breath and looking Declan Bell Jones in the eyes, "do you like Mikayla?"

He raised his eyebrows. He seemed surprised by the question. After a moment he said, "Can I be honest with you?"

"I want you to be."

He let out a small, humorless laugh. "Sometimes I don't."

I don't know what answer I had been expecting, but it hadn't been *that*.

"So why are you with her then?" Sitting next to Declan Bell Jones, in the gutter, in the dark was making me all kinds of brave.

He sighed. "Well. I mean, she's alright, you know, when we're alone. Like, we have fun...I guess." He scrunched up his face and covered it with his hands. "You're making me think way too hard for a Saturday night."

I self-consciously rubbed my own face. "Sorry," I said, laughing nervously.

"Oh! Um." Declan Bell Jones patted his pockets before grabbing the bottom of his shirt and stretching it in my direction. I tried not to notice the strip of bare skin I could now see. "You can wipe your eyes on this." He grinned at me.

I laughed again. "No, it's okay."

"Here. Let me." He scooted closer and pulled his shirt toward my face, causing him to lean into me. He brushed at my cheeks with the rough material but I barely registered the sensation. My insides were in full-on chaos mode at just how close Declan Bell Jones was to me.

I held my breath.

He chuckled. "It's not really helping, sorry." He dropped the shirt but didn't move away. Now his thumbs were on my cheeks. I felt a jolt as his eyes met mine. I wondered if he did too. He might have, because his face grew more serious.

"The truth is, Mikayla, she's hard work," he said. His hands were still on my cheeks. "She's not like you. With you, it's so easy. You think everything I do is amazing. It's cute."

My thoughts whirred as he leaned in closer, his breath hot on my skin. I could smell some kind of alcohol on it. I wondered how much he'd had to drink. He didn't seem too out of it.

"Um." He swallowed. "I, uh..." He trailed off, but he didn't move away.

I didn't say anything. I couldn't say anything. I couldn't move. All I could do was stare at Declan Bell Jones.

And then Declan Bell Jones closed the gap between

our faces. He closed his eyes. And he brought his lips to mine.

He kissed me.

He kept kissing me.

I was still frozen for what felt like whole minutes but was probably more like three seconds. Then my brain caught up to the fact that *Declan Bell Jones* had his tongue in my mouth. It was messy, it was sloppy, and it tasted strongly of alcohol.

This is my first taste of alcohol, I thought.

Then I thought, *I hope Mum doesn't smell this on my breath.*

Then I thought, *Shit, stopping thinking about Mum.*

Then I thought, *Just stop thinking.*

Declan Bell Jones tongue was really going to town in my mouth. It was like he was shooting for my tonsils or something.

Is this why it's called tonsil hockey?

I've never been a fan of hockey.

Why am I still thinking about hockey?

Argh. Stop thinking, stop thinking.

Kissing Declan wasn't like kissing Guy.

Oh. Guy.

Oh no.

Oh no no no.

"Ahem," someone coughed behind us.

Declan and I sprang apart so quickly he fell back onto the gutter. I looked up and saw a figure silhouetted by the light coming from the house. I couldn't see his features, but I could tell by the slant of his shoulders that he was angry.

I knew the slant of those shoulders better than I knew most things in my life.

It was Theo.

XX

Declan was scrambling up, muttering a stream of swear words. He glanced at me once before rushing past Theo—nearly charging into him—and into the house.

Theo stood absolutely still. I could feel the emotion radiating off him.

I tried to catch my breath. Declan Bell Jones had quite literally taken it away, which had turned out to be much less fun that it sounded. "Theo," I said, panting. "I—"

"I'll message Sophia. Tell her to come get us early." His voice was low. To a stranger it might have sounded calm. To me it sounded anything but. I stood up, taking a step toward him.

His phone lit up his face as he typed. The expression there made me pause and my stomach dropped somewhere around my knees.

Theo was furious. *Really* furious.

He put his phone back in his pocket.

"Stay here. I'll go grab Guy and Alex."

"Theo—"

"Try not to kiss anyone else while you're waiting," he shot at me as he walked away.

I sunk back down into the gutter, and the tears that I thought were all dried up started pouring out again. It was like five years' worth of tears wanted to come bursting out all in one night.

Shit shit shit.

What had I done? What had I been thinking?

I sobbed out loud, painfully aware I needed to get myself under control. Guy should not—*could not*—see me like this.

That only made me sob harder.

I was still desperately trying to rein in my despair when I heard Guy's panicked voice calling my name, and I found myself being embraced and picked up in one smooth motion.

"Kate? What happened? Are you okay?!"

"She's fine," Theo said from somewhere at Guy's elbow. "Seriously, put her down. My sister will be here in a sec and she'll freak out." I felt his hand tug at Guy's arm. Guy somewhat reluctantly placed me back on my feet, but his hands stayed on me, traveling up to cup my face as he stared into it in the dim light. I caught a faint whiff of beer, but he didn't seem even tipsy. Maybe his worry had sobered him up.

"Why are you crying?" he said. He wiped at my tears with his soft thumbs, and I was reminded of Declan Bell Jones doing the same thing earlier. The guilty sobs hovered around the back of my throat, threatening to spill out again. I swallowed hard and wiped my nose with my fingers. A big glob of snot stuck to them.

Gross.

"I..."

I was saved from saying anything else by headlights flashing over us and Theo's sister's car pulling up to the curb.

"Come on," Theo said. His voice was sharp.

"Let's talk when we get home, okay?" I whispered to Guy, wiping my face again before climbing into the back seat and shuffling over so Guy could slide in next to me. Theo got in the front. I turned to the window, letting my hair fall in my face as much as possible so Sophia wouldn't glimpse the wreckage of my breakdown.

"You guys didn't last long," she said. "Where's Alex?"

"He met up with some other friends, so he's gonna stay."

I wondered if he was with the guy he'd come here for. Billy, was it? He must've been, if he wanted to stay.

"The party was a dud then?" Sophia persisted. She reached over and changed the song playing to an upbeat one by ABBA. Theo wasn't the only one in his family who loved old things.

"Yeah. Total dud."

"I thought it was fun," Guy said.

"You think everything's fun," Theo muttered, and Sophia snorted.

Thankfully the rest of the ride was consumed with Sophia belting out "Super Trouper," and she didn't really ask us any more questions. I gotta tell you, that's the first time in my life I've ever used the word "thankful" in connection with Sophia's singing.

We were nearly home when my phone buzzed. It was a message from Theo in the front seat.

> You better come inside and wash your face before you go home, or your mum's head will explode.

I couldn't help but smile. It was a small smile, but still. *Maybe he's not so angry after all*, I thought.

It shouldn't be a surprise that, yeah, I thought wrong.

🎨

"So are you going to tell me what's going on?" Guy asked, stroking my back. I was bent over at Theo's sink, washing my face with his mango face scrub. My makeup had been beyond fixing. I was worried Mum might question me coming home with *no* makeup on, but at least it was better than having it streaked all over my cheeks. I splashed extra cool water around my eyes to try and cool down the puffiness.

I heard Theo's door open and bang shut. When I walked out of the bathroom, he was gone. I suspected he'd headed inside to give Guy and me some privacy. I wished there was another reason we needed it right now.

What was I going to tell Guy? I'd ruined everything.

"Kate?" Guy was looking at me, his expression soft, a gentle smile on his lips. He was so lovely. Golden. Would this take some of his shine away? What would he think of me? I didn't even know what to think of myself.

Guy reached out and gave my hand a squeeze.

I couldn't do this.

Suddenly there were words coming out of my mouth that I didn't even really think about. "It's just the fight I had with Libby. It's really upsetting me, I suppose."

Well, that wasn't a total lie.

But it wasn't the total truth either.

I shifted my weight from one foot to another. "Listen, I'm tired...I'm just—I'm gonna...go." I pulled my hand out of his. "Good night."

He raised his eyebrows. "Oh. Okay. Good night. I'll see you tomorrow?"

"Yeah. Sure. Of course."

He reached out, I think to grab my hand again—probably to give it a kiss—but I was already walking to the door.

"Bye!" I called as I closed it behind me.

I stopped short when I saw Theo sitting on the back veranda of the house, his head down. He looked up when he heard me.

"That was quick," he said. He stood up. "Is Guy okay? Are—are you okay?"

"I didn't tell him," I whispered.

"What?!"

"Shhh!" I glanced back toward Theo's room and pulled him further into the yard. "I couldn't, okay? I just...I need to think."

Theo huffed. "Yeah, you really do." His voice had an edge to it again.

My voice, on the other hand, came out tiny. "Are you...mad at me?" I asked, even though I knew the answer already.

He ran a hand through his hair and looked up at the sky, groaning. When he looked back down—back at me—I couldn't see his face clearly, but I could *feel* the anger there. "I don't even know what to say to you."

"What do you mean?"

"I mean—god, Katie, of course I'm fucking angry with you!"

I flinched. He'd never yelled at me like that before.

He was only just getting started. "I mean, fuck. What were you thinking?"

I wasn't.

"You're the one who went on and on about wanting the *perfect* guy—and—and he's there, Katie! He's right there! He's perfect! And you know what else? He's *good*. He'd do absolutely anything in the world for you. And you—you go and kiss someone else!" He took a deep breath. "It's like, you have these ridiculously high standards that no one and nothing can ever meet. But look at yourself!"

I opened my mouth to speak, but he kept going.

"And I'm *not* slut-shaming you or anything like that okay, so don't even start on that. It's just—it's really not like you to just kiss some random guy at a party, let alone when you already *have* a boyfriend. I don't get it. I don't get you. I..." He paused to take a breath, coming to a stop in front of me. "I feel like I don't even know who you are right now."

That hurt more than anything else he'd said. I'd thought earlier that I couldn't possibly feel any worse, but this, *this* was worse times infinity.

I'd never felt so far away from Theo...from Libby... from the people who knew me best. Who loved me best. I didn't even recognize myself—and I definitely didn't like whoever it was that I was becoming.

Just when I thought things couldn't get any messier, a twig snapped. Theo and I both looked up.

Guy.

He was walking slowly toward us. Theo swore under his breath.

"Kate?" Guy said. His voice sounded shaky. "Is this true? Did you—did you kiss someone at the party?"

He was in front of me now, and in the moonlight I could see his face. The emotion there. The fear.

"Fuck," Theo muttered under his breath again. "I'll, uh, I'll let you guys talk…" He turned to walk away but I grabbed onto his wrist.

"Stay. Please."

Theo looked from me to Guy, his eyes wide with worry. But he didn't move away.

"Kate?!" Guy prompted me.

"I…" I swallowed. Dropped Theo's arm. Looked down. "Yes. It's true."

"It's…true?"

I didn't answer.

"But…what? Why? Who? Why? Why? Why would you do that? Why would you… I don't understand."

His voice broke with the last word. And that broke me.

"I'm sorry," I whispered. "I'm so sorry."

"Are you…are you not happy with me? Am I not good enough for you? Is that it?"

My head snapped up. "No! What are you talking about? Of course you are. You're—you're *too* good for me."

Guy was shaking his head. I could see tears shining in his eyes.

"It's true," I said. "You're...well, you're just perfect, aren't you? And then there's me."

"What?"

"Well, I'm not exactly perfect, am I?"

Guy let out a small sob. "You're perfect to me."

"That's the thing though. It's not true, is it? It's not real. You think that—you thought that...but. It's not real. *You're* not real."

And there it was. The thing that had been niggling at me ever since Guy popped up in my bed. The little buzz at the back of my mind I had been trying to ignore. The reason why I couldn't fully enjoy—or fully fall for—Guy and everything he was saying and doing.

Yes, he liked me. Loved me, even. But not because of who I was. It was purely because he had to. He had no other option—I built him that way. And I wanted someone to love me for *me*.

Not that I was conscious of this when I kissed Declan Bell Jones. And I had only barely worked it out standing there in Theo's yard.

I've had a lot of time to think about it since then. To think, and to regret.

That night, though, I was acting on pure instinct.

I could feel Theo's eyes on me, but I didn't take mine off Guy. His face—his beautiful, lovely face—had crumpled.

"If I'm not real," he began, speaking slowly, "then what are these feelings?" He brought a hand to his chest. "What is this heart?" His voice was getting louder and louder. "If I'm not real, then why does it hurt so much?!"

I didn't know what to say to that. What *could* I say?

Libby and I might have created a guy...but I was the one who had turned into a monster.

XXI

Well. That was dramatic.

Hey! It's how I felt!

I'm not complaining. You were pretty monstrous for a while there.

I know. I was. ☹

It's okay. The important thing is that you learned and grew from it.

Wait, I'm getting to that.

The rest of that weekend was, in a word, absolutely freaking miserable.

That's three words.

Yes, thank you, Libby.

Here's what I did that night after arriving home: crawled into Mum's arms and cried my heart out. Again. I hadn't needed to worry about the makeup or lack thereof after all.

I told her about the breakup with Guy (I mean, those exact words hadn't been said, but things felt pretty broken).

I didn't tell her the details. She was sympathetic (especially after she'd establish that I hadn't been drinking—yes, she sniffed my breath). She rubbed my back the way she used to do when I was little and I needed help falling asleep.

Here's what I did the next day: stayed in bed and wallowed. Tried to ignore my phone, which was pinging with messages from numbers I didn't know, calling me all sorts of names I won't bother to repeat.

Mikayla Fitzsimmons had found out what had happened, it seemed.

I didn't hear anything from Declan Bell Jones. Or Theo. Or Guy. Or Libby.

Max stayed by my side all day, except when he got up to pee or eat. It's like he sensed something was wrong. Mum came in to check on me a few times, bringing me chocolate milk and ice cream. Even Luke stuck his head in to see if I was alright, and Dad tried to cheer me up by piling art supplies and notebooks on my bed, telling me to use my pain to *create*.

"Don't you know that's how some of the greatest art is made? This is a gift, Katie!"

I promise, it was much less cold-hearted than it sounds. He was joking. Mostly. I think.

He did inspire me to pick up my sketch pad and try to draw some of those FEELINGS out. The only problem with that was the first thing I saw when I opened it were my studies of Guy. I promptly snapped the book shut. Seeing his smiling face, captured so poorly by my clumsy pencil, just reminded me of how terrible I was. At everything.

I wasn't looking forward to confronting the nearly finished mural at school tomorrow, which had his face literally all over it. I needed to finish it, but I didn't know how I was going to do it.

I needn't have worried about it, though. Mikayla Fitzsimmons took care of it for me.

That Monday had already been bad enough. Mum refused to let me have the day off—her sympathy only extended so far—but I moved so slowly in the morning I was late and missed roll call. In first period I sat with Amina, so that was okay. She was her usual cheery self, although she conspicuously didn't ask how my weekend was. Frankly I was grateful, and her calm presence began to put me at ease.

That feeling lasted a whole half a period, because in Health I sat next to Libby, who had decided that I didn't exist anymore. She didn't look at me, let alone speak to me. When I asked her if we could talk, she just stared straight ahead before turning to ask Peter Tran on the other side of her about something in the textbook.

Libby wasn't the only one ignoring me. Mikayla Fitzsimmons was too. She walked right past me in math without even flicking a glance my way. I knew better than to feel relieved. There was no way she wasn't cooking up something awful.

The rest of the day followed the same pattern. If I'd thought people were whispering about me before, it was so much worse now. I felt hideous. I hid in the library at break and lunch, too afraid to face—well, anyone.

I had art after lunch. That was when I saw it.

I made sure the quad was clear of any post-lunch stragglers before I removed the tarp that had been covering my mural over the weekend.

I braced myself, but I was wholly unprepared for the pain I felt.

It wasn't the sight of Guy's smiling face that caused it, though.

It was the complete lack of it.

His face was gone. Every version of it had been covered over with black blobs.

That wasn't even the worst part. All over the mural, words were smeared. The kind I had been getting through anonymous messages for the last thirty-six hours.

Slut.

Skank.

Fugly-ass ho-bag.

There were more, but I think you get the picture that about sums it up.

I let out a horrified shriek and stood there staring at the mess. I was shaking.

My stomach twisted when I heard a familiar high-pitched laugh behind me. I turned to see Mikayla Fitzsimmons, a wooden bathroom pass in one hand and her phone raised in the other, snapping photos of me next to the ruins of my mural.

"*You*," I said. "*You did this.*"

She smirked. "Prove it." She pocketed her phone. "I warned you to stay away from my boyfriend. He told me how you came onto him."

What? How I came on to him?

"We had a good laugh about it," she continued, walking closer as she spoke. "What, did you actually think he'd go for someone like you? I can't believe you were so desperate to actually try to kiss him. He might have been nice to you in the past because he felt sorry for you, but even he knows the truth: you're nothing but a sad, pathetic, ugly piece of gutter trash." By the time she said the last words, she was so close I could feel her breath on my face.

"I– I'm not," I muttered.

"Heard your golden boy dumped your ass too. Guess he finally woke up to what a loser you are." She glanced up at the wall, which had once held my art and was now covered in her writing. "You should be thankful. It's a massive improvement on your finger painting."

I clenched my fists, but with a flick of her hair, Mikayla was walking away. My fingernails dug in to the flesh of my palms.

"I'm not!" I yelled.

Mikayla paused and looked back at me. "What?"

"I'm not a loser." I took a deep breath. "And I'm not gutter trash. I'm not sad or pathetic or ugly." As I said the words, I felt something in me lighten.

I felt their truth.

Mikayla rolled her eyes. "Keep telling yourself that." And before I could say anything else, she was gone.

The tiny burst of exhilaration I had felt drained out of me. I turned back to the wreckage of my mural and sank down to the ground.

I don't know how long I sat there like that, but I hadn't moved when Miss Lui came out to check on me. I looked up when I heard her gasp, and the horror on her face mirrored exactly what I'd been feeling.

"What happened?" she said. "Who did this?"

I briefly considered telling her it was Mikayla Fitzsimmons, but what she'd said was true. I couldn't prove it was her. And when I thought about having to explain *why* she might have done it and where that would lead...

"I don't know," I said.

I got up and stood next to Miss Lui, who had her

hands on her hips. After a moment she nodded, like she'd just come to a decision. "It's okay. We can fix this."

"What's the point?"

"What do you mean what's the point?"

I shrugged. "It's not worth it."

"It absolutely is. It was coming along beautifully. And you know I don't just say that to everyone."

I kicked at the ground. "It doesn't matter."

Miss Lui turned to face me. "Listen to me, Katie. Listen. Setbacks happen. This is horrible, I know, and I'm absolutely *furious* at whoever did this to you. But you can't let it get in your way, okay?"

"I don't really want to do it anymore, Miss Lui. I'm sorry."

"Well I'm sorry too Katie, because you have to."

I was shaking my head. "I can't. I can't. I mean, maybe this is a sign. I've kind of...lost my inspiration."

"Oh, fuck inspiration."

"What?!" I stared at her with wide eyes. Had she really just said—

"Yeah, I said it." She looked around and leaned in closer. "Just don't tell anyone, okay? It's true though. You think being an artist is about inspiration? I've got news for you. It's about work. Hard work. Even when you're tired. Even when you don't feel like it. Even when you're *uninspired*. I mean, sure, inspiration is wonderful and all, but do you know how rare it is? If every artist waited around for the muse to show up, there'd be much less art in the world. And wouldn't that be a sad state of affairs?"

I frowned. "I guess?"

"Right. So here's what we're gonna do. We'll cover this up, okay? And then this afternoon, you and I will give it a nice new base coat and then you can start again. I'll talk to Ms. Walker about letting you out of some extra classes this week to work on it. And we'll try to get to the bottom of who did this, okay?"

"O...kay," I said, still not feeling entirely convinced, but also relieved to be given a plan of action that I didn't have to think through myself.

Of course, covering it up did absolutely nothing because by that afternoon the photo Mikayla took had spread on social media. She hadn't uploaded it herself—Emily had, and she'd tagged me in it. I reported it and within an hour it was taken down, but by that stage it had popped up in other people's stories anyway.

After messaging Luke to let him know I'd be home late, I turned off my phone.

Miss Lui and I had just started painting over Mikayla's handiwork when I heard someone say, "Need any help?"

My heart leaped. When I turned around and confirmed who was there, I could have danced on the spot with joy. Instead, I just smiled and nodded and held out my hand.

"That'd be nice," I said.

Libby stepped forward, the uncertainty on her face dissolving as she joined our hands and gave mine a squeeze.

I'm so happy we got to this part.

Whew. Me too.

You did such a good job recounting all that.

Thanks for being here.

Always.

Right back atcha.

But wait. We should probably mention that big talk we had, right?

Oh...I wasn't sure how much you wanted to...?

We promised to tell the whole truth, right?

Well, except the parts you censored.

Yeah, but those needed censoring. This part...it doesn't.

I'm not ashamed.

I'm so proud of you.

We'd been painting mostly in silence for about ten minutes when Miss Lui announced she was going to make a coffee.

"You girls want anything?" she called as she walked away. We both shook our heads.

The silence continued for another moment, then Libby and I both spoke at once.

"I'm s—"

"Are you—"

Libby smiled at me. "I'll go, okay?"

I nodded.

"Are you okay?"

I sighed. "Not exactly...but I'm feeling a little better now." I put down my brush and turned to her. "Libby, I'm sorry. I'm sorry I haven't been there...I know I've been really absorbed in my own shit."

She nodded. "You have. But I mean, so have I." She kept painting. "I tried to talk to you about it all a bunch of times, but I don't know...I just couldn't. And it wasn't only because of you. It's on me too." She looked me in the eyes. "I'm sorry too."

"Can we hug now?" I said.

She grinned and held out her arms, and I leaned right into them.

That was the part that broke the ice. Then Miss Lui came back and we all chatted about minor things, like this YouTuber Libby and Miss Lui were both obsessed with, and the merits of oat milk over almond milk. It was kind of exactly what I needed.

But what came next, I needed even more.

As Libby and I walked home, we talked and talked.

And she came to my place, and we talked and talked some more.

I spoke about everything that had gone on over the weekend—with Guy, with Declan, with Theo...and with Michael.

"I'm not surprised," she said, with hurt in her eyes. "I suppose I should tell you what happened...with us."

"Wait, let me make you some tea first," I said.

Once we both had big cups of peppermint tea, Libby and I settled on my bed, Max on his back between us.

"Things hadn't been right with us for...a while," Libby said. She pressed her lips together. "He kept...he kept saying he wanted to get more physical. And it made me really uncomfortable."

She took a sip of her tea, considering her words before she went on.

"I never told you this—but Michael and I, we never really even kissed."

"*What*?"

Libby cringed. "Yeah. It's—every time you mentioned how you felt like such a freak because you'd never been kissed, I wanted to die a little bit inside. Because, well, if that made you a freak...what did it make me?"

"Libby I—I'm so sorry."

She shrugged. "You didn't really know, and that's not your fault. Obviously, I didn't like to talk about it. But...

that didn't mean it didn't hurt. The thing is, I *could* have kissed Michael, if I'd wanted to. But I didn't want to. At all."

She looked at me then, like she was trying to read my face. I waited for her to continue.

"I really, really care about him. I love him, even. But whenever he tried to get physical, it just made me recoil." She sighed. "It was okay when we were younger. I mean, it's not like he was really trying much anyway. I told him I didn't want to kiss him, and he respected that. But in the last year, he kept bringing it up. And then he started to say that he wanted to do more. And he said he felt like I wasn't attracted to him. And he didn't know why we were even together if I didn't even want to kiss him."

"Oh, Libby," I said. I placed a hand or her arm and she looked at me with tears in her eyes.

"So I told him—I said to him, fine. Let's just break up then. And so we did."

I could feel tears in my own eyes as hers spilled down her face. I leaned over and enveloped her in a hug. It was awkward, because Max was between us, but we made it work.

"Why didn't you tell me any of this?" I said quietly.

She pulled away. "I didn't really know how. I mean— at first, I was scared. And then you were so caught up with Guy. I wasn't exaggerating when I said it felt like you'd abandoned me."

"I'm so sorry," I said for the thousandth time that day.

"I know. I get it. Mostly. But it made it really hard. And, besides, I was trying to process it all myself. Figure out what it meant. I did *a lot* of googling." She put down her cup on the floor and turned to me, her shoulders squared. "Here's the thing," she said. "I think I'm...I'm...asexual."

"Oh," I said. "Okay."

"And maybe aromantic too...I'm still kind of working through it all." She picked up her cup again, tracing her finger around the edge of it. "The romance stuff is honestly the most confusing to me. I mean, like I said before, I'm pretty sure I love Michael, but what does that even mean? What kind of love is it? I don't know." She took a sip of tea. "I do know I don't feel sexual desire. And it turns out that's actually a totally normal thing. A lot of people experience it. I didn't even realize, but then I found all these YouTube videos and—wow, it made me feel so much better. But it's been...a process. It still is."

I nodded. "Can you show me? Some of the videos, I mean? I'd like to understand more."

She smiled and let out a deep breath. "Okay. You...you don't think I'm a total weirdo?"

"Oh, I do," I said, smiling back at her. "But not because of this. Not remotely."

She laughed and pulled out her phone. We spent the rest of the afternoon, heads together, watching videos and talking and talking.

It felt like I was home again.

Okay. Now I'm crying again.

Sorry. I...hope that was okay? Everything I said?

Yes. Yes.

Katie...I'm glad we're friends.

Me too. More than anything.

<3

<3

XXII

School was easier to face now that Libby and I were friends again...but that didn't make it easy.

Declan Bell Jones ignored my existence, which just piled more scap onto the stacks and stacks of regret I was filled with. For kissing him...and for even liking him in the first place. He'd really just been using me, I'd realized. He'd enjoyed the attention, but he'd never really cared about me; he'd thrown me under the bus when things got sticky. What a gutless disappointment he'd turned out to be. I couldn't believe I'd wasted so much time and energy on him.

I'd spent so long obsessed with perfection, with this twisted idea of what I wanted and needed in my life. I'd got it all wrong. I'd messed everything up. And now I'd have to live with it.

Mikayla Fitzsimmons and her friends, meanwhile, had all come down with terrible coughs. You know, the kind that caused them to splutter *ahem* *slut* *ahem* whenever I was within two yards of them. I'd managed to block all the messages I'd been getting, although some still slipped through, and I was determinedly ignoring them in real life as well. But I can't say it didn't hurt.

Libby was cooking up all kinds of ideas for revenge, but I pointed out that making out with Mikayla's boyfriend was maybe the worst thing I could've done to her already.

"Anyway," I said. "Now she's stuck with a cheater like him who can't even kiss. I almost feel sorry for her."

Libby snorted. "I can safely say I will never feel sorry for her."

I laughed and tried to push away my worry that Mikayla would strike again. It joined my ever-present niggling guilt about Guy.

I hadn't spoken to him—or Theo—since the night of the party.

I hadn't even *seen* Guy. I thought about going around to talk to him so many times, but whenever I imagined the possible conversations we might have, they always just ended in more hurt. So I kept my distance. He was better off without me, anyway.

I'd glimpsed Theo in his yard a couple of times, and at school occasionally. He acknowledged my presence with a nod, but that was it. It was the longest we hadn't spoken to each other. Longer even than the Great Monopoly Incident when we were kids.

It made my heart ache more than just about anything else that had happened.

I threw myself into getting the mural done again. Ms. Walker had, miraculously, given me permission to do it during classes and to stay back after school so I could finish it by Friday—the day of the formal, and when the unveiling of the murals was supposed to happen. It was stressing me out, but it was also a very welcome distraction.

I'd changed the design, just to make things harder for myself. But I also weirdly felt more passionate about it. After Miss Lui's big talk on how unimportant inspiration was, I'd actually found some again. I just hoped it would turn out how I wanted. Or, at least as close to what I wanted as was physically possible. My finished works never looked quite as good as they did when they were just in my head. But I had learned that done was better than perfect.

It's not like perfection actually exists, anyway.

XXIII

I don't know about this," I said, looking in the mirror and adjusting the straps of my dress. It was a vintage one from the 90s I'd picked out on a shopping trip with Theo months and months ago. Remembering his smile when he'd convinced me to buy it sent a stabbing pain in my chest, which was already feeling tight. "It feels wrong to be going with...everything that's happened."

Libby came up next to me and fixed the corsage she'd bought me on my wrist. She was wearing a black suit and looked absolutely killer. "We've been through this already. You can't hide out in your room for the rest of your life. You'd regret not going."

It was the regret thing that had convinced me in the end. That, and the idea of doing something like this with Libby felt important. We'd agreed to go together, with the rest of our friends, just like we'd originally planned. It had been a totally weird, wild, and rough couple of months, but it felt important to celebrate our friendship tonight.

Libby and I stood side by side, looking at ourselves in the mirror hung on the back of my wardrobe door. "Let's make this formal our bitch," she said.

We were laughing as we made our way into the living room. The smile disappeared from my face when, amidst Mum's gushing and Dad snapping photos, Theo stood up, running a hand through his hair and sending me a small—but dimpled—smile.

"Hey," he said. He looked me up and down and nodded. "You look...nice."

I opened my mouth but nothing came out of it. I didn't know what to make of his presence.

"And what about me?" Libby said.

He laughed. "You look good too."

"Let's get some photos of the three of you together," Dad was saying, and Mum pulled Theo over and arranged us in front of the plant in the corner because that was the "nicest backdrop" apparently.

"I can't believe how much you've all grown," Mum said, swatting at a tear in her eye.

"Muuumm, don't start," I said.

"Oh, your parents are here," Dad said to Libby, looking out the window. Her parents were driving us to the function center where the formal was being held. Libby and my parents headed outside to meet them, and I started following after them, but Theo grabbed my hand.

"Actually, can I talk to you for a sec?"

"Oh, um, sure," I said, trying to ignore the way my heart had started thudding in my chest.

"I really liked the mural," he said softly.

I felt myself blushing. "Thank you."

The murals had been "unveiled" today at the school assembly, which was held in the quad.

I'd finished mine literally that morning, and while there was still a lot of work I would have liked to do on it, the main gist of it was there and that was all that mattered.

All that mattered. That's what the mural was. The people that mattered to me.

I'd kept the idea of showcasing the different aspects of school life. And Guy was still in there. But just once now. The other scenes were now with Libby, and Amina, and Nat, and Jordan, and Alex...and Theo.

It was far from perfect. But it was there. *I* was there.

It felt good. I'd done something no one else could. Oh, sure, other people could paint murals. But not that one. That one was all mine, complete with its flaws—and its beauty.

Just like me.

Theo reached into his pocket and pulled out a small box.

"Listen...I know it's been a weird week. Slash month.

Slash year. And I'm not gonna lie and say I'm not still mad at you. I mean, I still don't really get it all and—well, I think we've got a lot of stuff we need to talk about." I bowed my head, and he gently placed a hand underneath my chin and raised it again. "But tonight's not the time for that. Tonight...you should just have fun. You deserve it. You *do*," he said when I scrunched up my nose.

He grabbed my hand and opened the palm, placing the box he'd been holding into it. "I bought these awhile back. After you got the dress. I just thought they'd go, you know...but, uh, you don't have to wear them if you don't like them." He cleared his throat.

Inside the box was a pair of earrings, sparkly and blue, perfectly suited to the color of my dress.

"They're lovely," I said, looking up at Theo. Our eyes locked for moment before I blinked and turned away. I was slipping the earrings on, telling myself the awkwardness in the air was due to the unresolved issues we had to talk about, and not *other* unresolved feelings that I wasn't quite ready to acknowledge.

Before Theo and I could say anything else, Libby stuck her head in the door, with Melissa right behind her.

"Look at you!" Melissa cried, holding up her phone to snap some photos. "I had to see you girls all glammed up."

"Are you coming or what?" Libby said to me, talking

over her sister and earning a pointed side-eye, followed by an affectionate chuck under the chin.

"Let's get this show on the road," she said.

By the way, don't think I didn't notice the way Theo said, "have fun" to you and the way he touched your shoulder and the way you looked at him and—

As for the formal itself, where do I even begin...?

The decor was tacky as hell. The formal committee had zilch for budget so they'd used crepe paper to fashion—

No one cares about the decor.

People totally care about the decor.

You're stalling. Get to the good stuff.

Good stuff? Like when we were dancing with Nat and Jordan and then we managed to drag Amina onto the dance floor and all five of us did that silly routine we made up at Jordan's sleepover in Year 8?

That was pretty good.

Or when Mikayla Fitzsimmons and her friends were pointing at us and laughing but we were having so much fun we didn't even care?

That was even better.

Or when I was heading to the bathroom and Mikayla Fitzsimmons tried to trip me, but I managed to maintain my balance because, well, miracles do happen, I guess?

Yes. That was the best. At least until what happened next.

Ah, you mean the part where—

Yes! That part! Tell it properly.

Oh NOW you want me to go into detail.

Mikayla Fitzsimmons had tried tripping me over, like I said. But I *didn't* fall. Instead, I turned to her and said, "What is your *problem*?!"

She laughed a hollow laugh. "Isn't it obvious? You are."

She reached behind her to where Declan was standing and pulled him closer, grabbing his hands and placing them around her waist. She stuck out her chin and raised an eyebrow, daring me to react. Declan, meanwhile, apparently found a spot on the ceiling absolutely fascinating, because he was staring up at it like it was all he cared about in the world.

I sighed. "Listen, Mikayla. I'm sorry about what happened at the party. I really am. It was a mistake." I looked at Declan, who had now found something on the floor to distract himself with. "A big one. But you've been treating me like crap for years. And I don't deserve it. Neither do my friends." I looked at Libby, who had made her way to my side. She smiled and looped her hand in mine.

"Whatever."

I opened my mouth to speak, but Libby squeezed my hand and started talking instead. "Oh, Mikayla. Mikayla, Mikayla, Mikayla. You want to hear something that's really sad? This is it for you. This is your peak. Life doesn't get better than this for you. But for us? It's only the beginning."

"And we're off to a pretty good start," I said.

Together, we turned and walked away.

Mikayla called something after us, but it didn't even matter.

She had no power over us anymore.

Mic drop! Boom!

I love this part.

Of course, it helps that she's not coming back to school next year. We don't have to worry about her at all.

But we wouldn't anyway. Because we've GROWN. Unlike her. Or Declan Bell Jones, the douche.

Oh my god, Katie. That IS character growth.

Wait, sorry, I mean Kate.

It's okay. You can call me Katie.

What's this? More growth? You better watch it, soon you'll be hitting the ceiling.

Alright, that's enough.

Okay but it's really not, because we haven't even gotten to the highlight of the evening yet.

I thought that was us telling Mikayla Fitzsimmons that she was sad and pathetic.

Come on, Katie. You're the desperate romantic.

Ohhhh right. Yeah, I did love the part where you told me you were going to speak to Michael and talk through everything. Because you didn't want to leave things so messy. How did that go, by the way?

We're talking. We both got hurt. It's still messy. But…it's less messy than it was. Anyway, THAT'S NOT EVEN THE POINT.

It's not?

Do you want me to write it? Because I will. You know I will.

Hahahaha okay, okay.

Wait, let me make a cup of tea. Then I'll dive right in.

I'm shaking my head at you. Can you see me? I'm shaking it. (Make me one too, please.)

XXIV

Libby and I were dancing to a slow song, our arms on each other's shoulders, when she gasped, her fingers digging into my skin.

"Ow," I said, but she didn't respond. She was too busy staring at something over my shoulder, her chin stuck out and her eyes wide in a way that was not unlike Ginny Weasley when she comes downstairs and finds Harry Potter sitting at her breakfast table in the *Chamber of Secrets* movie.

My first thought was that Michael had shown up.

My second thought was that Mikayla Fitzsimmons was heading our way.

My third thought was—

"Guy," Libby whispered.

I held my breath, my heart pounding in my ears, almost drowning out the music, as I turned.

It felt like I was moving in slow motion.

And there he was.

He was wearing a suit with a velvet jacket that matched

the blue of my dress. His hair was pushed back from his fore-head, with a single lock dangling down and caressing his face.

He was smiling.

He was beautiful.

And he was walking toward me.

I exhaled and took a step toward him. Dimly, I regis-tered Libby pressing my hand before letting it go.

Guy reached me. We stood there, taking each other in for a moment.

"May I have this dance?" he asked.

I nodded.

His hands encircled my waist, and I reached up to place my hands on his shoulders. We swayed in time to the music and stared into each other's eyes.

A beat passed. And another.

"I never expected to see you here tonight," I said. It was so quiet I thought maybe he wouldn't hear me above the music. But he did.

"I promised to take you to the formal. I couldn't dis-appoint you."

"But I disappointed you. I...I broke your heart. I don't deserve this."

He smiled sadly. "You did break my heart. But hearts mend. Or so I've been told. And so do relationships. But that takes work. Showing up. So...here I am."

"Wait—"

"Oh, I don't mean..." He paused, looking as though he was gathering his thoughts. "I still care about you, Kate. I would like to try to be your friend."

"You want to be friends?"

He nodded. "More than anything. I don't like carrying around this pain. I've been talking about it. A lot. With Theo. And Roger."

"Roger?" I thought for a moment. "Wait—the old guy who hangs out on the park bench all the time?"

Guy chuckled. "That's the one. And...I'd like to forgive you. And heal."

"I'm so sorry, Guy. For everything. You don't know how sorry I am."

"I think I do." His hands on my back gave a gentle, reassuring press. "I know you, Katherine Camilleri. And I forgive you."

I felt tears prick my eyes. "I hate myself for hurting you."

He pulled me into a hug. "Please don't. I don't hate you." Into my ear, he said, "I did say I wanted to experience everything with you. I guess I didn't think heartbreak was on that list but...I'm happy to be alive to experience it. To experience anything."

He took a step back. "You were my world, Kate. But what I didn't realize was...that probably wasn't a good thing. Not for you...and not for me, either. I need to figure things out for myself. Learn. Grow. Find my own purpose. Become my own person." He smiled. "A real human being."

I squeezed his hand. "If I can help in *any* way..."

"I'll let you know." He reached up and tucked a strand of hair behind my ear. "Until then..." His thumb trailed a line from my temple down my cheek before coming to my lips. He leaned down one last time.

The kiss was soft. The kiss was sweet.

It tasted like cookie dough.

It also tasted like goodbye.

He pulled away first. I opened my eyes and looked into his.

We both smiled. We understood each other.

It was over.

It might not have been perfect, but it had happened. And that was what mattered.

"What now?" I said.

He grinned and spun me around. "Now I go and find my own purpose."

I laughed and pulled myself in closer to him. "That's right. And forget all about me."

He brought his forehead to mine. For that one final moment, all I could see was him.

"I could never forget about you," he whispered.

And then he disappeared into thin air!!!

It's true. After that night, I never saw him again. He just vanished into thin air. Or wherever he came from.

By the way, where DID he come from? I think we should do some more experiments and—

No. No more experiments. No more playing around with life itself. We're not gods.

Of course we're not. We're scientists. Well, I'm a scientist.

And I'm an artist. A writer, a painter, a sculptor...a creator.

Yeah, you are.

Hey, we did it! We told the story. The truth, the whole truth, and nothing but the truth.

I think you're forgetting one thing though.

This is the story of Guy. Guy's story is over.

We both know this is your story. And it's definitely not over.

Well, I'd hope not. I want to live until I'm at least 107 years old and we're both in a nursing home with no teeth and barely any memories, cackling at something ridiculous that no one else understands.

That sounds lovely. But right now let's talk about Theo.

Theo?

Theo.

XXV

Theo.

What can I say about Theo?

He's my best friend in the world (other than Libby, of course).

Of course.

And I love him. Of course I do.

I've loved him for most of my life.

But it was only this next moment that I was finally ready to admit I liked him too.

I mean *liked* him. You know.

We know. You wanted to jump his bones.

Libby!

Okay, okay. You wanted to smoosh your face against his.

I mean...yeah, basically.

Let me back up.

It was a couple of weeks after the formal, and Theo was at my place. We were playing Yahtzee at the kitchen table. We weren't talking much. There'd been a weird awkwardness between us since the whole Guy thing. I put it down to the fact that we hadn't unpacked what had happened. I was too scared to break our shaky truce to bring it up, and Theo didn't really seem mad anymore.

That was my excuse, anyway.

"Yesss," I hissed as I rolled a full house, writing down my score. I looked over at Theo. He was frowning. "You may as well give up now," I said. "There's no way you can beat me."

He didn't say anything, just took the dice and shook them in the cup before rolling them onto the table. He'd rolled a small straight, but he picked up all of the dice except one to roll again.

"What are you doing?" I said. "You had a straight!"

"Huh?" He looked at the dice in his hand. He seemed to be in a bit of a daze. "Oh. Oops."

I shook my head. In the past I would have teased him more, but it felt strange now. Because of our fight and all.

Or so I told myself.

Theo was rolling the dice around in his hand.

I couldn't help myself. "Are you going to roll or what?"

He blinked and looked at me. "What? Ah. Yeah. Sorry." He rolled the dice again. Instead of finishing his turn he turned to me. "Want to come to my place for dinner tomorrow?"

"What?" I'd been to Theo's for dinner approximately

a billion times in my life...but I couldn't remember the last time he'd actually asked me over.

He cleared his throat. "So, you remember how I thought Dad was seeing someone?"

I nodded.

"Turns out I was right."

"Oh."

Theo pressed his lips together, his dimples on display. "And he's bringing her home for dinner. Tomorrow night."

"*Oh*."

"Yeah."

"Are you—are you okay?"

He shrugged. "I dunno. I think so? But...I dunno. I'm nervous, I guess. Lena and Sophia have been arguing since Dad told us on Wednesday. Sophia says we should be happy for Dad, but Lena's having a fit. I don't even know what to think."

"Sounds tense," I said. I tentatively reached out and placed my hand on Theo's, which was resting on the table. "Is it really a good idea for me to be there?"

He looked down at our hands. "Yeah." His voice was soft. "I think I need you there? I mean. I think we all do? It'll break the tension, you know."

I gave his hand a squeeze. "Will your Dad be okay with it?"

"Of course. He loves you."

☻

"Katie! What are you doing here?" Theo's dad, Nick, was patting at his eyes with the back of his hand, which was holding a knife. He was in the middle of chopping onions.

"Um, Theo invited me over for dinner?"

Nick was squeezing his eyes open and shut. "Oh, he did, did he? Well. I suppose that's alright."

"Come over for the show, have you?" Lena said, walking into the kitchen and opening the fridge. She stared into it for a second before closing it again. "Theo's still at work." She leaned her head on the fridge and crossed her arms.

I nodded, feeling more awkward and unwelcome than I'd ever felt in this house before. "Do you need any help?" I asked Nick.

"No, no. It's fine. It's fine. We're going to have a lovely evening." He looked at Lena through narrowed eyes, although whether that was a result of the onions or more of a warning look, I'm not sure. She scowled and walked out of the kitchen.

Nick sighed.

"Um...I'll just go wait in Theo's room if that's okay?"

Nick waved the knife in my direction distractedly. "No worries."

Any other time I might have insisted on helping him with dinner. But today...I had other plans.

I don't need to tell you that the dinner was awkward as hell. Kim, Nick's girlfriend (wow, that's a weird thing to call an old person), seemed really nice. But it was still strange to see someone other than Theo's mum sitting at that dinner table. And Nick smiling and laughing with someone other than Ella.

But it was also kind of nice to see him smiling and laughing at all.

Kim was trying her best to ask questions and make conversation. Sophia put a lot of effort in, and Theo did pretty well too, although I could tell he was stressed. He kept jiggling his knee, and whenever nobody was looking—except me, I guess—his dimples would come out, and not because he was smiling.

Then there was Lena. She basically grunted at Kim whenever she tried to talk to her. It got to the point where Nick dropped his fork and said, "Lena, come on."

She just stared at him and said, "I'm done eating. Can I be excused?"

He sighed, and I could see him hesitating. He was probably trying to decide whether it was worth an argument or not. I guess he decided it was not, because he said, "Sure, go ahead."

"Us too?" Theo said quickly.

Nick looked at him, surprised, and then his face fell and he nodded.

"We'll wash up," I said.

Kim said, "No, don't be silly! I'll do that." She was smiling, but there was a tightness around her eyes. This must've been really weird for her too.

"Come on, KC," Theo said. He grabbed my hand and tugged me toward the back door.

"Thanks for dinner," I said over my shoulder.

Once we were outside, Theo took in a deep breath. He didn't drop my hand.

"How are you feeling?" I said.

He paused and glanced back toward the house. "She seems nice."

"She does."

"I'm happy for him," he said, but I could hear a tiny crack in his voice.

I stepped forward and circled my arms around his shoulders. He buried his head in my neck. We didn't say anything for a moment. We just held each other tight.

"Sorry," Theo said, pulling away. "I'm okay. Really, I am. I'm just..."

"Sad?" I said.

He nodded. "Yeah. I'm a little sad."

"I think I know exactly what you need."

He raised an eyebrow questioningly. I stepped in front

of him and opened the door to his room, pulling him in behind me. I turned so I could watch his face.

His eyes widened in surprise, and then his dimples were back, only this time it was because he was smiling so wide.

"When did you do this?" he said with a small laugh. He stepped through the gap in the blanket fort I'd snuck in and built earlier. "Whoa."

I followed in after him and admired my handiwork. I'd strung our spare Christmas lights up along one side of the fort, and placed all of Theo's favorite snacks (and some of mine) on his bedside table. On the bed, I'd placed a piece I'd been working on for a while and had called in sick at work that day to finish off. It felt like the right time to give it to Theo.

"You owe me," Alex had said when he agreed to cover my shift.

"Add it to my tab," I'd responded.

Theo picked up the painting. I'd used an old photo of him and his mum for reference, one of my favorites. Each held a cone stacked high with ice cream. Their noses were dabbed with ice cream. Their heads were tossed back in laughter, their matching smiles with their matching dimples on display.

I'd done my best to capture the love and the warmth and the happiness that emanated from that photo—not just how it looked, but how it *felt*. How I remembered it.

"Do you like it?" I said. I tried to sound casual, but my heart was in my throat. I felt more nervous about this than the mural being unveiled.

Theo didn't speak. He just nodded. I sat down on the bed and got a better view of his face. There were tears shining in his eyes.

"I just thought...I dunno. I've been working on it off and on for ages. I knew today was going to be hard, and I didn't want to make it harder. But I thought—"

"It's perfect," he said. "You're perfect."

"It's—what?"

He put the drawing down and ran his fingers through his hair, backing up a step. "Um, I mean. I love you. It! I love it. I—oh god."

I stared at him, not quite knowing how to process the direction the conversation had taken.

"I'm glad you love it," I said finally.

His shoulders slumped. "You," he said, so quietly I wasn't sure I had actually heard it.

"Huh?"

"You." His voice was louder this time. He met my eyes. "I love...you."

I inhaled sharply. "I-love-you-too?" It came out quickly, sounding like a question.

Theo sighed and took a step closer. He hesitated for

a moment then sat down on the bed next to me. "No. Not like that. Like...You know. Like *that*." He glanced at me out of the corner of his eye and then stared straight ahead, his lips pursed.

"Oh," was all I could get out.

"Yeah. So. Well. I wasn't going to tell you. Ever. It was going to be my secret. I was going to ignore it until it went away. I mean, we've been friends forever and I didn't want to wreck everything, you know. But I just like you. So much. I like how you dream. I like your ambition. I like how you cheat every time we play Monopoly but will never admit it. I like how you laugh and how you talk and how you think and how you feel and—god. I even like it when you're mad and when you annoy me and...the thing is, I'd never thought about kissing you until that night we talked about first kisses—you know, just before—well, Guy. Then it was like all of a sudden, it was all I could think about. But you were with him. And he was so...*Guy*. He was so. Perfect. What you wanted. That was what you wanted. And I realized you'd never want me. Like that. Like I...like I wanted you. And it's okay because they're my feelings, and you don't have to return them and we can still be friends—oh god please I hope we can still be friends—and I'll work through it okay, I'll—"

He stopped short when I placed my hand on his.

Suddenly I felt calm. It was like he was absorbing all the possible nervousness that could exist between us. I'd realized something as he spoke. It was like a switch had been flicked inside of me. And what had always been there came into the light. Those feelings. Saying, *"Ha! You've been ignoring us but you can't any longer!"*

Theo had always been there for me. He'd been a friend. One of my best friends.

But he was also so much more than that.

He was funny, and sweet, and thoughtful, and caring...and beautiful.

When he smiled and his dimples showed...when he talked about music and his whole being lit up...when he rocked a new outfit he was proud of...when he just lay there, chilling, doing nothing but being himself.

He was so goddamn beautiful.

And I did want him. Like *that*.

"Theo," I said. "You're rambling."

He swallowed. "I am."

"I've never heard you ramble before."

He let out a small laugh. "I don't think I ever have rambled before."

"It's cute," I said.

"It's—cute?"

"You're cute." I was grinning now.

"*I'm* cute?" He was looking at me with bewilderment.

I nodded. I leaned toward him. We looked into each other's eyes.

Are we really doing this? his eyes said.

We're really doing this, mine replied.

And then I closed them, and kissed him.

It wasn't my first kiss.

It wasn't even my second.

But that didn't matter.

Because it was Theo.

And he was made for me.

Ugh. You guys are sickening.

You asked for it!

And I loved every second of it.

Kate, are you sure this is how you want to end it? I mean, you've done a wonderful job, but it's not exactly the whole truth, is it? The part where you said I disappeared into thin air wasn't really acc—

Did you hear something, Katie?

Nope. Did you?

No. I didn't see anything either. Certainly not a six-foot-something guy who should know better.

Yeah. Because he disappeared. And is staying safe. Somewhere far, far away from here. Where no one knows about him or could possibly find him and cart him off for science experiments. Where he can be his own person.

A real human being.

But I—

THE END.

ACKNOWLEDGMENTS

If you're reading this message it means my second book has successfully been published and is a real thing that really exists, which, wow, how incredible is that? Very incredible, obviously.

Although my part in the creation of this book involves mostly being alone in a dark, cold room, hunched over a laptop and snarling at anyone who dares interrupt me like the swamp goblin I secretly am, there are actually a great many people who helped bring it to life, onto shelves and into readers' hands.

Thank you to my agent, Danielle Binks, for being the best champion and sounding board, for encouraging me to write my strange little "Untitled *Weird Sciencey* Thing," and for coming up with the perfect title that is infinitely superior to the aforementioned "Untitled *Weird Sciencey* Thing." Thank you also to Natasha Solomun for helping to take my weird little book to the world (and overseas!), and to the whole team at Jacinta di Mase management for being the best girl gang to have on my side.

Thank you to the team at Peachtree for embracing *You Were Made For Me* and giving it a home in North America. I'm especially grateful to Jonah Heller for once again wrangling with weird Australian candy and slang and helping smooth out any potential cultural confusion. Thank you to Elyse Vincenty and Media Masters for your mad publicity skills in helping my books to find an audience in America.

A great big thank you to incredible cover artist Steffi Walthall for wrapping my story in the perfect packaging.

Thank you to my Australian publishers Pan Macmillan, especially Claire Craig, Georgia Douglas, Brianne Collins, and Rebecca Hamilton, who all helped shape this book.

Thank you to Mari Diaz, Michaela Garcia, Jay Dalziel, Tobias Madden, Rachel Nacilla, and Natalia Wikana, who each gave me guidance and feedback on the authenticity of my characters, and made this book so much stronger as a result.

Thank you to Elspeth Lamorte and Sofia Casanova for helping me with the rewriting process, for always being encouraging and supportive, and most especially for K-drama watch parties. Thank you also to Melanie Mutch for being a constant source of comfort, feedback, advice, support, joy and BTS memes. I'm also grateful to

Amanda Salles, Kathleen Cusack, and Rebecca Finn for their continued friendship and cheerleading.

Thank you to my family: my husband, my parents, my brother, as well as the Zampa, Rowlands, Spiteri, and Guillaume clans. You all helped shape who I am, and who I am shaped this book. Thanks especially to my husband, Chris Guillaume, for enduring my swamp goblin behavior, making me lots of dinners and even more tea, and always being my first reader. And a big thank you to my mum, Alison Zampa, who is still my number one fan and always only a phone call away. She told me to state she's the best mum in the world, but I probably would have said that anyway.

Thank you to my dogs, who yes, deserve their own space. To Ollie and Jasper for being my constant, cuddly company. To Jed and Tilly and Sue Sue and Ralph too. Max is a bit of all of them wrapped up in one giant fluff ball.

Finally, to everyone—friends, family, colleagues, teachers, booksellers, librarians, readers, writers, strangers—who has helped me on this author journey. Who has read my writing, attended events, sent me messages, shared my book, and just generally cheered me on. There are literally too many of you to name here, which is a very lovely problem to have. Just know your support means the world to me. Thank you.

ABOUT
THE AUTHOR

JENNA GUILLAUME is an author and journalist from Sydney, Australia. She writes about pop culture, feminism, body positivity, social media, and what you should binge on Netflix for a variety of publications. Previously she worked as editor-at-large for Buzz-Feed and as features editor for *Girlfriend* magazine. Don't miss her first novel, *What I Like About Me,* and be sure to follow her on Twitter @JennaGuillaume.